The Guardian of Oakhurst

The Guardian of Oakhurst

Book 1 of
The Children of Auberon

A Modern Faerie Tale
by J. Wolf Scott

This novel is a work of fiction. Names, characters, places, and events are either a product of the author's imagination or are used fictitiously.

Printed in the United States of America
ISBN-13:9781475039634
ISBN-10:1475039638

http://jwolfscott.com

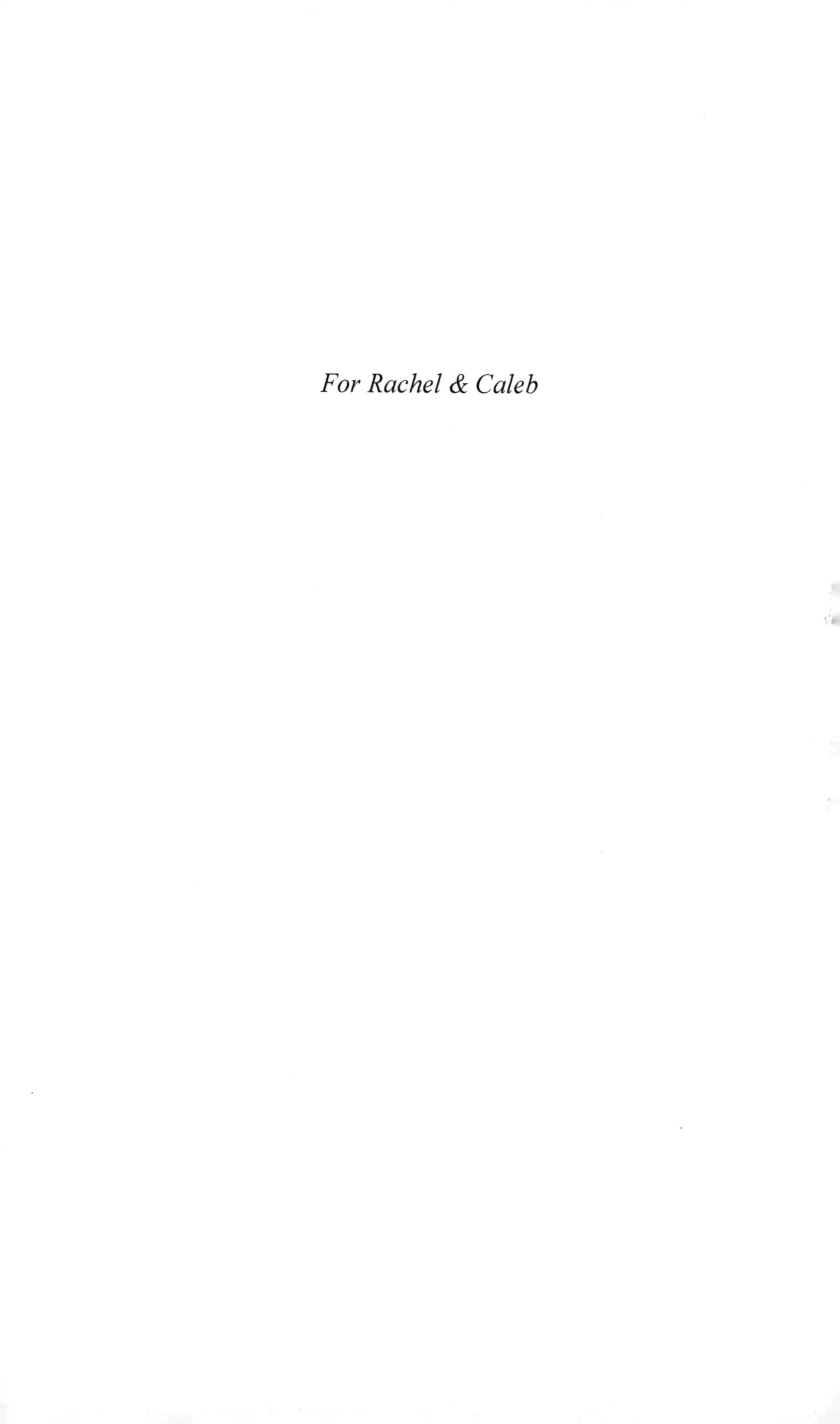

For Rachel & Caleb

A Word of Thanks

Every novel, no matter how far-fetched and fantastical it may seem, is always based on some nugget of truth. This particular novel is no different, and would not have been possible without the help of several people at Minnetrista Cultural Center in Muncie, Indiana.

I owe a debt of thanks to Karen Vincent, Director of Collections at Minnetrista, without whose knowledge of Elisabeth Ball and her family, and the granting of access to family letters and photographs, this faerie tale would never have been possible.

And to Betty Brewer and Stephanie Wiles, also of Minnetrista: Your support in this process has been greatly appreciated, and your dedication to Minnetrista has been an inspiration over the years.

To everyone else on the staff who has made our family feel welcome there, I am so thankful to have you all as friends.

To my friend, Sally Taylor, who served as my editor: I could not have done this without you. Your grammatical fine-tooth comb is amazingly effective, and I have learned tons throughout this process. If gratitude were money, you'd be richer than Midas.

And last, but not least, to my husband, Bob, thank you for introducing me to the spirit of Elisabeth Ball in the first place.

~ Julie

~ Summer, 1905

Prologue

It had been a delightful afternoon. Mother had invited Emily and her mother over for lunch, and afterward the girls played in the dollhouse while their mothers sipped iced tea and talked on the back porch of Oakhurst, the home of Mr. and Mrs. George A. Ball. It was a beautiful, stately manor, a Shingle style home in warm oak tones proudly overlooking the White River as it wound its way through Muncie, Indiana. The girls, no more than eight years of age, were best friends and had been since both of them could remember. Elisabeth Ball was an only child, and if she had imagined having a sister, she would have wanted one exactly like Emily Kimbrough.

The girls were two peas in a pod, really. Both loved to wear dresses and play at each other's houses, especially when they could be outdoors. Elisabeth's blonde hair was the yin to the yang of Emily's dark hair, and they completed each other in the way only best friends can.

After getting permission, they raided Mrs. Ball's closet from a selection of pre-approved garments that they could use to play dress-up. Feeling a little more adventurous than usual, Elisabeth decided to be bold and peruse her mother's jewelry box as well.

A lovely array of rather large button earrings lay before them, and the girls each chose a pair. Emily picked a rather smart looking pair of pearl buttons with diamonds around the edges, but Elisabeth had her eye on the most daring pair in the box. They were orange fire opals, with three diamonds on either side. She picked them up and carefully clipped them on her small earlobes.

"Won't we get in trouble?" Emily asked, sounding a little more than concerned while still clipping on the pearl buttons.

"Not if we put them back," Elisabeth answered, as she clipped on the fire opals. "How do I look?"

"Like a faerie princess."

ꙮ ꙮ

The girls played for hours serving tea in the little dollhouse behind Oakhurst that matched the mansion in both style and charm. It was a magical place, and the girls spent the afternoon chattering ever-so-politely to their collection of dolls. They would take them for walks about the gardens, playing under the arbor in the sunshine or sitting on a large stump that remained from a tree Mr. Ball had cut down. It was a perfect perch upon which to watch the river below Oakhurst.

By late afternoon their mothers found them seated atop the stump still wearing Mrs. Ball's dresses. They looked rather comical but were most serious in their play.

"Mother, we've had the most delightful journey!" Elisabeth cried, as she jumped off the stump. The dress she wore over her clothes ballooned out around her tiny legs and she landed with a thud. She ran and hugged her mother. "We visited with Queen Liliana!"

"The faerie queen, huh?" Frances said with a smile, looking at Mrs. Kimbrough.

"Is she the one who was sitting on your last bite of peas the other day, Betty?" Mrs. Kimbrough asked with a wink back at Frances.

"Oh, no, Mrs. Kimbrough," Elisabeth said in all seriousness, "that wasn't the queen – that was her daughter, Princess Verena. She's little like me and Emily!"

Mrs. Kimbrough smiled. "I would think she would have to be to fit atop a bite of peas."

ꕤ ꕤ

It was late afternoon when Emily and her mother went home. Frances cleared away the lemonade glasses and pitcher and set off to the kitchen to prepare the evening meal.

Elisabeth wandered back to the dollhouse and began to set the table for her dolls' supper. A sudden knock at the door caught her by surprise, but it was a pleasant one. Standing in the doorway was her father, George Ball.

"Hello, Father!" she squealed, as she jumped into his arms. He caught her easily and smiled wide, his eyes twinkling above his bushy mustache. He was quite a dapper fellow, dressed in his suit and tie and bowler hat straight from the office.

"Hello, Buttercup!" he greeted her. "How was lunch with Emily?"

"Oh, it was lots of fun!" Elisabeth said, as he put her back down in the door of the dollhouse. She pulled up a chair, and her father took a seat in the doorway. "We played dress-up and had lunch with Mother and Mrs. Kimbrough in the garden. And, we even took a meeting with Queen Liliana!"

"Aren't you quite the little diplomat?" Mr. Ball asked approvingly. "And how was the queen?"

Elisabeth knit her brows together in all seriousness. "She seemed a little off today."

"Oh?"

Elisabeth brightened immediately. "But I cheered her up, Father! It's those pesky wood sprites. King Rogan is not playing nice, I'm afraid."

Mr. Ball smiled proudly. "I see. Did you give him a lesson in etiquette?"

"Oh, of course not, Father! He is the king, after all, and well… that's just not done," she said in a most serious tone.

"I see," Mr. Ball responded, his manner reflecting that of his daughter. "Well, if anyone can teach him etiquette, it is definitely you, Betty." He looked down, almost forgetting why he'd come out to the garden. "I have something for you."

"What is it?" Elisabeth asked in anticipation.

Mr. Ball pulled a manila envelope the size of a half-sheet of paper from his inside breast coat pocket. "I picked these up at that little stationary shop that you're so fond of in Buffalo. I left them in my case and forgot to take them out when I arrived home."

Elisabeth opened the envelope and stuck her small, eager

hand inside pulling out several beautiful pieces of paper. Each was decorated differently with swirls of shiny gold and silver designs. Elisabeth was delighted.

"Oh, Father, they're beautiful!" she said as she hugged him around the neck. "Thank you so much!"

"You're most welcome," he smiled, holding her tight.

"I know just what I'm going to do with them!"

"More magic boxes?"

"What else?" she answered matter-of-factly.

"Mother said dinner should be ready soon," Mr. Ball told her as he offered her his hand. "Perhaps we should head that way. Etiquette and all that, you know. We wouldn't want to be late."

"No," Elisabeth replied, "that would be quite rude."

ℰ ☙

It was after dinner, and Elisabeth sat alone in the garden. A red-tailed hawk watched her from high above in the trees as she played near the little stream that babbled down through the garden to a tiny pond. She sat upon the flagstones at the water's edge, absently running her fingers along the top of the water.

"Emily can't see you, you know," she said, seemingly to no one.

"I know," Princess Verena said, lighting on Elisabeth's knee. The queen's daughter visited with Elisabeth often, and the pair had become fast friends. She appeared to be no more than fourteen human years old but, in truth, was much older than that. She stood nearly six inches tall, and she folded her willowy frame, seating herself cross-legged as she continued.

The princess's wings fluttered slightly before she tucked them in close.

"Very few humans can see us. You are special, Elisabeth. You have a gift only the rarest of humans possess. You are an old soul, able to see things most cannot, that most can scarcely even imagine."

"But it's so beautiful here. They're missing so much!"

"It's because they're in such a hurry. They get so caught up in their day to day lives that they don't see what's right in front of them."

"And what is that?"

"Happiness."

A rustle in the undergrowth caught their attention. It was Arland, the queen's personal guard. He had been thus since the loss of the king. He rarely left her side, and when he did, it was only at her bidding. He was muscular and somewhat rugged looking in a rather refined way and stood a little more than a full head taller than the princess. He was dressed in the uniform of the Royal Guard, and a sizable sword hung at his side.

"There you are, Verena," he said firmly. "Your mother's been sick with worry."

Verena tsked. "I was with Elisabeth," she answered rather huffily as adolescents will do.

"Of course, Princess," Arland replied, proper as always. "So good to see you again, Miss Elisabeth."

"Hello Arland," Elisabeth smiled back at him.

Taken aback, Arland could only stare up at the human girl with the faerie princess on her knee. Verena knew the look in an instant and immediately questioned him.

"Arland, what is it?"

Arland stared up at Elisabeth, more specifically at the earrings she wore – her mother's earrings. She'd forgotten to take them off after Emily and her mother had departed for home.

"Your ears, Miss Elisabeth," he said in all seriousness, "they are aflame."

Verena looked up at her friend and protector to discover that the fire opal earrings that she wore were now beginning to glow in the nearing twilight of the garden. Amazed, the princess could only nod in agreement.

"Is there a story behind those stones, Miss Elisabeth?" Arland inquired. "Maybe a tale you'd care to share?"

"Oh, yes," Elisabeth gushed. "Father tells the most wonderful tale of how he and mother came to have these beautiful stones they found on a trip somewhere."

"Would you care to share?" Verena echoed, excited about hearing one of Elisabeth's stories.

Arland cleared his throat.

"Perhaps an audience with the queen would be in order."

Ravensforge

It is said that relics of yore are lost for a reason. Most fall victim to greed and plunder, with the lust for power being at the root of the fall of many a kingdom. Such is the case of the Kingdom of Ravensforge, the northern-most kingdom of the faerie realm.

Chapter 1

Arn scrambled up the slope trying hard to stay just ahead of the advancing mass of darkness. Getting the royals through the portal was their main goal, but he hoped that he and their Guardian would survive the night. He looked up, watching as the Guardian helped the royals over the ridge and into the woods nearby. *Not much further now.*

"C'mon, you ruddy bastards," he muttered to himself as he quickened his pace. In an attempt to distract, he moved horizontally for a short distance trying desperately to steer them off track. If only for a short while, it might buy the Guardian just enough time to escape to the next realm.

In his haste Arn lost his balance, his foot slipping off the rock and sending a cascade of stones down onto the advancing enemy. Their beady green eyes – hundreds of them – all honed in on him and his position and trajectory, and in one coordinated move they shifted track and headed directly toward Arn.

"Not what I had in mind, but very well," Arn chided himself and headed straight up what remained of the slope. He hesitated slightly, looking over the edge. They were coming for the staff he had managed to wrest away from the Messenger. He paused for a moment knowing it would not end well.

It was sheer dumb luck that he'd laid hands on the staff in the first place, and he figured it could be used as a bargaining tool if need be. Now he began to question the wisdom of that choice.

Arn continued moving swiftly up the rocky slope of the steep hill as they fled into the night. The smoke had dissipated with distance from the palace, but remnants of it clung to the damp air around them. Ahead the two royals, still in their formal attire from the state dinner earlier in the evening, struggled to ascend the rocky terrain. Just a few steps beyond them the Guardian led the way.

"Almost there," the Guardian called, urging them onward. "Quickly!"

The royals were silent, and to their credit did not complain. At one point, the rocks beneath their feet shifted sending several large stones tumbling down the hillside. One of the royals slipped on the loose stones and fell, and the other reached down to help her up.

"Are you all right, Highness?" Arn inquired, as he steadied both of them in an effort to move them forward once more.

From what he heard in the distance behind them, he began to doubt that they would make it to the portal in time.

"Yes, thank you, Arn," she answered softly as she rubbed her knee. "I'm alright."

The threesome climbed awkwardly up the last stretch of boulders to the top of the ridge. "Not much further," the Guardian said, keeping watch. A stand of trees was all that stood between them and the portal they sought.

"This portal, will it take us there permanently?" Arn asked the Guardian, as the two young royals, barely more than teens, looked on. "Will we be able to return home?"

"Return to what?" one of the royals asked sharply. "Ravensforge is in ruin. Never before have I seen such treachery!"

A sound from the bottom of the cliff caught the Guardian's attention. Moving to the edge, one look downward confirmed they were out of time.

"Quickly! This way."

The clicking of claws on the rocks below made Arn uneasy, but his curiosity got the best of him. He shifted back slightly, peering cautiously over the cliff.

The fires from Ravensforge burned brightly now, and though still far in the distance, it provided just enough light to give him a look at what was moving up the hill – *fast!*

A horrid blackness writhed below him. Hundreds of glowing green eyes pierced the darkness, moving up the hill after them at an alarming rate of speed, snarling and growling as they came. The tangled mass of bodies held Arn's gaze longer than one would deem prudent under such dangerous circumstances, and his blood ran cold.

He raced to catch up. “We must move faster,” he urged, physically pushing them now. “They are nearly upon us.” The foursome picked up the pace through the dense forest and ran at a dead sprint by the time they reached the clearing.

They could see the portal from the opposite side of the meadow. It stood near the side of a sheer rock wall looking as if it had been intentionally placed there. It was a large boulder, the face of which had been cut and polished smooth. Much like drusy quartz, the blue center of the bolder shimmered like a thousand blue diamonds that glowed from within. The Guardian reached out to touch it, and it rippled like water in a still pond.

Hearing the approaching enemy, Arn looked back toward the trees. “We are out of time.” He took the staff in both hands and stood at the ready. “They are coming.”

The horrible clicking of claws over the stone ceased, and a new sound began: the screeching cries of a thousand dark beings who were right behind them.

“This way, Majesties,” the Guardian said. “We must go. *Now.*”

The royals looked at one another, joined hands and stepped into the shimmering portal. The event horizon enveloped them as they stepped into the boulder’s face, and as suddenly as it came, the glow at once died down after they disappeared through the portal..

Arn looked at the Guardian. “They must not know where the royals have gone.”

Moving back toward the woods to take a more defensive stance, Arn stopped just shy of the treeline. Duty and honor had been bred into him, and he would die fighting in order to ensure the royals' safety. He would probably meet the same fate as the rest of their party as they had fought the scourge off, but he was honor-bound to do so.

Keeping his distance from the trees, he stood, staff at the ready. The headstone began to glow as he held it in both hands. What came next surprised the living hell out of him.

The air around him was filled with dead silence.

Arn had a sudden feeling of coldness wash over his entire body like an electrical wave that rushed through him from his head to his heels. He turned to the Guardian, his confusion apparent by the look on his face.

They were all over him with such suddenness that he was in a state of shock. He hadn't even seen them coming! *It was as if they came up out of the ground itself.* The sheer strength of their wiry bodies was more than he expected, and he struggled with them to keep hold of the staff.

"Arn!" the Guardian cried out, moving in his direction. The blackness was all around Arn, and his cries ripped at the very soul of the Guardian. Caught in the moment between indecision and action, the Guardian froze, helpless, as the creatures attacked Arn.

Arn's efforts were wasted on the beasts as they claimed the staff and moved as one toward the Guardian's position. In the midst of them stood a hooded figure of the same stature, yet more fae than beast. It laid claim to the staff that Arn had been carrying and raised it high so that the headstone glowed to its fullest.

What happened next surprised even the Guardian. Lightning shot out of the staff toward the portal, impacting the stones just above it. They cascaded down violently, striking the Guardian, who fell onto the the portal stone. It activated, and the glittering stones turned to a watery face yet again.

The Guardian was gone.

ꟷ ꟷ

The sharp wind whipped at the royal robe of King Beltran, sixth in the line of Winslow in the House of Ravensforge, as he stood at the cliff's edge with his queen, Astra. His regal features looked grim as his dark hair whipped back toward his face. His bride of many years stood her ground with him, looking lovely as ever in spite of their predicament. The king was filled with true regret that it had come to this.

Before them stood the Royal Guardians of Ravensforge, and beyond them troops willingly created a barrier between the royals and the impending evil that clawed its way swiftly across the greensward toward them all.

Guntram, Chief of the Guard, directed the troops as they moved into position. He was taller than the king, and his muscular features attested to his strength and capable skill set of the warrior class. As Guardian to the king and queen of Ravensforge, his final role in life would be to serve as a barrier between any enemy of the state and the royals. And right now, the enemy was at hand, moving in rapidly, and there was absolutely nothing he or his men could do about it.

Six deep, they stood staunch and resolute, holding their post with honor and courage. In the twilight the coming onslaught was terrifying at best. A dark mass made its way across the meadow toward the cliff. Below the king and queen was the sea, churning and roiling on the rocks below. It was beautiful in its power, as its waves crashed and growled like a hungry beast.

Guntram had great faith in his men and knew they would fight to the bitter end to protect the royals. He could only hope that the Guardian who protected their daughters would complete the mission to lead them to safety. It had been his honor to train the Guardian himself, knowing that it was the most sacred duty he could have.

"Beltran!" came a voice from the darkened advancing mass. *"I see you have run out of meadow."*

Beltran looked up, not quite sure what to say. Silently he reached out and took Astra's hand. She looked up at him, the fear apparent only to him as she looked into his eyes. But in his heart he knew that her fear was not for them but for their daughters. He could only hope that the Guardian had taken them to safety.

"So it would seem," Beltran answered rather curtly to the voice in the darkness. He looked down at the velvet pouch that hung from his belt.

"You have something I want," the voice continued, "something I need."

"Then why don't you come and get it?" Beltran challenged the voice, knowing the answer full well.

Laughter came from the midst of the dark mass that had undulated across the face of the meadow. It slowed to a stop, and a thousand green, glowing eyes looked directly through the troops between them to the king and his queen.

As if in a trance, Beltran reached down and took the pouch from his belt. He opened the velvet sack slowly and reached into it. He stared as his hands disobediently drew the relic from the pouch. It fit easily in his hand, and he held it up in front of his face, looking directly into the relic's empty eyes.

A beautifully crafted piece, it was older than any faerie scholar could even imagine. An egg formed from a translucent stone that seemed to burn from within was guarded jealously by a young dragon that wrapped completely around it, its tail within eyesight of its nose.

Its eyes were the most haunting feature of the piece. They were missing, and the sockets stared back blankly at him, telling him nothing.

King Beltran held the relic up right in front of his face, staring directly into the blackened eye sockets of the dragon and for a moment had forgotten what he was doing. He looked down at his queen, who placed her hand on his arm, reassuring him that he had to do what was right and good.

Certain that the key to the Triad was safely out of reach, Beltran no longer feared this Messenger of Erebos. "I do not believe you can take it," he challenged the voice, "and I know that you will never have this piece. Not while I am alive."

The dark mass moved forward as one again, stopping just thirty paces short of the soldiers' position. Swords drawn and at the ready the king's men waited, anticipating the worst.

"So let it be," the voice said in a low growl. Raising his staff above his head the Messenger summoned together the creatures at his command. They roiled and snarled, gnashing their teeth, their claws clicking as they moved in unison along the increasingly rough terrain beneath them.

"Stop!" Beltran bellowed as he raised the relic above his head, matching the stance of the Messenger. "I will throw it into the sea... *I swear it!*"

The Messenger froze, but only for a second, then threw back his head and laughed heartily.

"Oh, truly, Beltran," the Messenger laughed. "Do you really think you can keep it from me?" His tone changed in an instant to one that was deadly serious.

"I will take the relic from you," he snarled. "Then I will take your queen from you. And then," the Messenger growled in a tone most foul, "I will take your life from you."

"You may take my kingdom from me. And you may take my guard, and you might even take my queen," he paused, looking down at Astra who squeezed his hand tightly. "You may even take my life. But you will never have the Keeper of Time."

All eyes watched as King Beltran of Ravensforge cupped the relic in both hands, reared back and heaved the piece soundly off the cliff. All eyes watched as the eyeless, bronze dragon and it's keep hurtled end for end off the cliff, tumbling through the air toward the sea.

"I'm sorry, my darling," he said, drawing Astra close as he wrapped his arms around her.

"Our daughters are safe," she responded, "that's all that matters."

With nothing to hold them at bay, the ghastly beasts advanced on the troops with a sudden fierceness beyond the guards' wildest imagination. It was not a pretty fight, and the king watched as he tried his best to shield his wife as, one by one, the creatures tore their men down, throwing them into the sea. Soon, there was but a handful left of fae guards between the royals and the enemy.

"You shouldn't have done that," the Messenger said, drawing the staff up, crossing his body with it as he prepared for battle.

Guntram charged the Messenger, staff be damned. Only a few steps in, the guard was struck down by an energy blast from the headpiece of the staff. His body added to the mass of corpses that lay on the ground, leaving only the King and Queen of Ravensforge.

The Messenger crossed the remaining distance between them, stepping over the fallen body of the Chief of the Guard as he brought himself face to face with the royals.

"I've been waiting for this for a very long time," he said quietly, looking at the king. "I can guarantee you this won't end the way either of us imagined."

~ Muncie, IN, Present Day

Chapter 2

The cold rain beat down hard as the young woman walked along the bridge. Uncertain of where she was going or why she was headed in this particular direction, she knew only that she was hungry. Her stomach gnawed mercilessly against her backbone, and all she could think about was how long it had been since she'd last eaten.

Problem was, she couldn't remember.

Her tunic clung to her slight frame, and her long brown hair was stuck to the sides of her face as the water dripped down into her eyes. Her nose ran, but she didn't seem to notice or care as she made her way toward the urban area ahead of her. The water in her shoes squished under the weight of her feet as they repeatedly hit the pavement, moving her forward to who knew where.

A glance over her shoulder told her they were still back there. They'd been following her for awhile now since she'd made her way up the ravine from the riverbank, and she wasn't quite certain the reason. All she knew is they made her uncomfortable. *Very uncomfortable.*

She picked up the pace, quickening her steps as she reached the other side of the bridge. She followed the street around a bend, past a statue of a man playing a flute of some sort, and into the heart of the city. The buildings weren't tall by any means, but they were more than she was used to. Though unsure of how she knew that, she sensed that this place was not her home.

Even through the rain the smell of food cooking wafted on the breeze until it reached her nose, drawing her ever forward to the source. People following her or not, she glanced back once more before changing course. Through a terminal, she crossed the street to an empty lot behind a group of buildings that huddled together to form the edge of the downtown area.

Wavering on where to go next, she leaned against the building to rest, breathing in the warm, comforting exhaust from the kitchen. She closed her eyes hoping that someone here would know her – that someone would at the very least be able to tell her who she was.

The rain chilled her to the bone, and her shirt clung to her. She reached down and pulled the amulet that hung from a chain around her neck out of her tunic. Turning the amulet over in her hand, she ran her thumb across the large, tear-shaped stone set in the middle of a simple, yet elegant, setting. It was decoratively framed in a patinaed bronze wire that appeared artfully sophisticated, and the stone's rainbow translucence seemed to change to different shades of red, orange, and yellow as she shifted it from side to side. Down the center was a rift filled with crystals that sparkled like diamonds. She admired it for a moment until a shadow passed over it.

"We'll take that, if you please," a gruff voice told her. Large and muscular, the first man held his hand out toward her, waiting for a response.

Startled, she dropped the amulet. The chain prevented its fall any further than mid chest, and she reached up and tucked it back in her shirt.

"Why?" she asked. "Who are you?"

"Let's just say we're here on official business," the second one said. He was tall and slender, but the muscles were still evident in his physique.

"I don't think so," she began quietly, shaking her head. "I don't think you're supposed to have this."

Perplexed, the big one looked to his partner.

"Why not?"

"Because it's obviously not yours. I'm supposed to... protect it."

The smaller one laughed, and the bigger one joined in.

"You? Protect that?" the bigger one chided her. "Looks like you can't even take care of yourself."

The smaller one grabbed her forearm and that was all it took. With lightning reflexes, instinct took over as she snaked her arm around his and grabbed his upper arm with her small hand while taking advantage of the element of surprise. Pulling him toward her, she thrust the heel of her hand upward, delivering a solid blow to his nose that sent him reeling backward.

Still in shock, the smaller one let go just as the larger one grabbed her from behind. She let her body go slack, lowering her center of gravity and pushed backward, hard, using the strength of her thighs to shove the larger one into the dumpster that stood near the kitchen door. It made a horribly loud noise, and she hoped it would bring someone. Feeling his grip loosen slightly, she took advantage of the maneuvering room it afforded her and delivered a swift blow to his abdomen with her elbow. Somewhat stunned, he had no recourse other than to let loose of her.

Meanwhile, the noise brought the desired response.

"Hey! What the hell's goin' on here?!"

She stood at the ready, a defensive posture, never for a moment taking her eyes off her assailants. The two said nothing.

"I *said*, what's goin' *on* here?" the voice in the doorway repeated.

Out of the corner of her eye she could see a woman on the stoop.

"Charlie, Henry, c'mere," the woman called loudly over her shoulder. *"We got a problem out here!"*

Immediately the assailants turned and ran down the alley.

The young woman sighed heavily as she slumped against the brick wall, breathing in the warm exhaust from the kitchen.

"Thank you," she said, turning to the woman.

The woman had dark, smooth skin, and her hair was in braids all over her head pulled up away from her face. Her white clothes were stained by the remains of the early shift, and her hands were covered with flour.

"You okay?" the woman asked as she surveyed the back lot. "Who were those guys?"

"I don't know," she answered.

The woman's tone softened as she stepped through the doorway into the pouring rain.

"What's your name child?"

The young woman looked puzzled for a moment, her brows knit in thought as she searched the recesses of her mind for any clue as to who she was or why she was here. Unsettled, she paused as the answer seemed to bubble up through her muddled consciousness.

"Sshhhea," she answered slowly. "My name is Shea."

ꟃ ꟃ

Seated at the stainless steel prep table in the kitchen, Shea gobbled down the plate of breakfast foods the woman set in front of her mere moments before.

"Lordy, girl," the woman said, "looks like you ain't eat in weeks!"

Shea just smiled as she continued to chew the mouthful of food.

"I'm Jackie," the woman said as she watched Shea. "Jackie Robinson. And *yes*, I was named after the baseball player," Jackie offered for clarification as her head bobbed back and forth for emphasis, as she explained for what was to her at least the hundredth time, "and, *no*, I don't much like baseball."

Not fully understanding the reference, with a bite of toast

hanging half out of her mouth, Shea stared at her host looking rather perplexed.

"My grandfather was a big fan of Jackie Robinson," Jackie answered the look with a wave of her hand. Seeing that it meant nothing to her guest, she merely shook her head.

"Thank you," Shea said quietly as she finished the last of the toast.

"What were those guys up to?" Jackie asked. "Do you know them?"

"I don't know," Shea replied. "I don't think so."

"Well, what *do* you know?" Jackie inquired, beginning to get a little flustered. To channel that, she went back to cleaning up the prep area.

Shea stared back at Jackie, unsure what to say. At this point she wasn't even sure how she felt. The morning's events had confused and unsettled her just a little, but she was none the worse for wear. At this point, finding purpose would be difficult.

"Do you know your last name?" Jackie asked as she wiped the last of the tabletop. "Surely you got a last name, don't you?"

"Rrr…." Shea began. "Shea….Rrre…." Frustrated she turned away.

"Rumsfeld? Reese?" Jackie guessed. "Remington?"

Shea just shrugged. "Wish I knew."

"Well, 'til you remember, we'll just hafta pick you a last name. How 'bout Remington?" Jackie suggested. "I like Remington. 'Cause you got *guns*." She put her arms up and flexed them showing off the muscles in her well-toned arms.

"Remington," Shea echoed back. "I need a last name?"

"Sure do," Jackie told her. "This'll have to do for now, I guess."

"Shea Remington," Shea repeated before taking a swig of orange juice. It was tart, and the jolt to her taste buds was apparent on her face.

"Where are Charlie and Henry?" she asked, looking around the kitchen.

"Who?" Jackie asked pointedly, somewhat confused.

"Charlie and Henry. You called for them," Shea told her. "Are they nice?"

Jackie chuckled, realizing her ruse had been discovered. "No, there's no Charlie and Henry. That's just what I do when I'm back here by myself. To make folks think I've got company. They're my bodyguards, so to speak."

"I don't understand," Shea said matter-of-factly.

"Never mind," Jackie said. "I just keep 'em in my little bag of tricks. It works for some reason. Don't you worry none 'bout it."

Jackie noticed the amulet hanging around Shea's neck. "Boy, that's some bling ya got there," she noted with a whistle.

"Bling?"

"Your necklace," Jackie told her. "Maybe that's what they were after."

"Maybe," Shea agreed, though she wasn't certain of much at this point.

Her clothes were starting to dry out, and she found the warmth of the kitchen comforting. Feeling unsettled and hesitant, she wasn't sure where she would go from here.

"You got a place to stay?" Jackie asked her as she leaned over the prep table.

"Stay?" Shea repeated.

"You know, where do you sleep?"

"I…don't know."

"Well, we'll just have to fix that now, won't we?" Jackie said with a smile. "I know just the place."

ꙮ ꙮ

The little apartment above the diner was cozy, and Jackie laid out some sweats and a blanket for Shea while she took a hot shower. Shea emerged from the bathroom feeling better already but was weary from the events of the morning. Apparently it showed on her face.

"I gotta go back downstairs for the lunch rush," she told Shea as she laid the blanket and pillow on the couch. "I'll be back up to check on you later. You look like you could use some sleep."

"Thank you," Shea told her.

Jackie nodded and let herself out of the door, making sure it locked behind her.

Exhausted, Shea closed her eyes and fell into a dreamless sleep.

Chapter 3

The diner was bustling with the morning business crowd, and the wait staff hustled through the tables serving hot coffee and steaming plates of breakfast fare to the nearly packed house of customers. In her daily uniform of faded jeans, white t-shirt and a well-worn apron tied up at the neck and waist, Jackie kept the delicious food flowing through the pass-thru window. The diner had always done a decent business, but since Jackie had come along, Paul, the owner, had to admit that his crowd of regulars had grown substantially.

"Hey, Jack, I need another plate of biscuits," he called out to her. "Table twelve is almost out."

"In a jiffy," Jackie hollered over her shoulder.

On cue, the timer on the oven went off, and Jackie slid her hand into the oven mitt, opened the door and pulled out a fresh pan of homestyle biscuits. She quickly piled four on a plate and put them onto the ledge of the pass-thru.

"Biscuits!" she called out to no one in particular as she went back to doling out the rest of the batch.

A glance through the window told her that she didn't have much time. Most of the crowd from table twelve rose to leave. She scooped up the plate of biscuits from the window and headed across the diner.

A well-dressed, middle-aged man with glasses, Sam Cooke was finishing his hash browns and headed into the biscuits and gravy piled on his plate. He was the Vice President of Philanthropy at Minnetrista Cultural Center, just a few blocks from the downtown area of Muncie, charged with membership and fundraising.

"Hey, Sam," Jackie greeted him sweetly, "how you doin'?"

"Hey, Jackie! Great gravy!" Sam responded. "How's it going?"

"Not bad. Not bad at all," Jackie grinned as she sat the plate of hot biscuits on the table. "Paul seems to think we don't need another espresso machine but, *we do*," she said being ever-so-obvious as Paul walked past her on his way to the kitchen.

"Yeah, yeah," he muttered. "Hi, Sam!"

"Hey, Paul," Sam waved.

"So, what's this I hear about some break-in over at Minnetrista?" Jackie asked, as she began to clear away some of the dishes from the rest of Sam's breakfast party.

"Apparently somebody broke into Oakhurst a couple of weeks ago," Sam answered between bites of gravy. "Jimmied the lock."

"Isn't that one of those big ol' Ball family houses?"

"Yeah," Sam answered. "Strangest thing, really. We'd just cleared out an exhibit from the upstairs galleries. As far as we can tell nothing was stolen. No vandalism either. I'd imagine they'll do an inventory of the property sooner or later just to be sure."

"Well, isn't that strange." Jackie sat down at the table across from him leaving the stack of plates at the empty seat next to her. "Why would anybody wanna do that?"

"I dunno. Police think it was probably just bored teenagers."

"That's too bad. What this world ain't comin' to."

"Evangeline's talking about hiring a caretaker over there. Maybe it'll help. You know, somebody to make sure the property looks lived in and that sort of thing." Sam shrugged as he scraped up the last bite of biscuits and gravy and finished it off.

"That's probably not a bad idea. When are they looking to hire?" she asked, taken with a sudden idea.

"Soon," Sam answered, as he reached for his orange juice. "Probably in the next week or so if we find the right person. Why? You know somebody?"

"Matter of fact, I think I do," Jackie smiled as she glanced across the dining room to where Shea Remington was clearing off the remains of table two's breakfast.

"I just met this girl not too long ago, but I tell you what, you wouldn't have to worry 'bout her none."

"Oh?"

"I found her out by the dumpster in a fight with a couple of guys. And they weren't no scrawny teenagers neither." Jackie chuckled raising her eyebrows for emphasis. "She cleaned their clocks pretty good!"

"Well, I don't know if we –"

"Oh, no, no," Jackie corrected herself when she realized she'd given him the wrong impression. "What I mean to say is, this girl can definitely take care of herself. These two guys were trying to steal her necklace, and she wasn't hearin' none of that. She was managing quite nicely when I found them. She been staying with me since then, and she ain't been no trouble at all. Very polite and helps out around the house, too, without bein' asked."

"Well, maybe I'll have to talk with her."

"There is one problem, though."

"Oh?" Sam said as he reached for the last of his orange juice, finishing it in two gulps.

"She kinda can't remember anything past a couple of weeks ago. When I found her, she had no idea who she was or where she came from."

"Really?" Sam asked, seeming somewhat surprised.

"Really," Jackie echoed back. "Probably a bump to the noggin or something. She's real nice, though. Wanna meet her? You got the time?"

"Sure," Sam said, wiping his mouth with the napkin.

Jackie scanned the room and found Shea headed back to the kitchen with a pan of dirty dishes. She was wearing black jeans and a t-shirt, and the apron around her front showed she'd been busy this morning.

"Hey, Shea! You got a minute?" Jackie called to her.

Shea smiled and sat the pan on the chair next to the kitchen door. Looking around, she wiped her hands on the apron and headed over to where Sam and Jackie sat.

"Shea, I'd like you to meet Sam Cooke. He works at Minnetrista just down the way," Jackie smiled warmly. "Sam, this is my friend, Shea Remington."

Sam rose from the table and held out his hand. When she didn't reach up to shake it, he somewhat awkwardly put it in his pocket. "Nice to meet you," Sam smilcd. "How are you?"

"I am well," Shea answered, not sure of what she'd just stepped into.

"How are you liking Muncie?" Sam asked her as he took his seat again at the table.

"Its fine," Shea answered, looking from Sam to Jackie, "although I really don't have anything to compare it to at the moment."

Sam chuckled nervously, then turned to his half-empty cup of coffee and took a drink. He swallowed hard as the cool, bitter drink hit his taste buds, wincing as he did. "Bleah," he said, sticking out his tongue for emphasis.

Jackie laughed as she scolded him. "Why you order that? You know you don't like it!" she tsked and shook her head.

"I'm a social drinker," he joked back with her. "Hate to be left out, you know."

"Well, with as much cream an' sugar you put in there, it may as well be a milk shake."

"Sure would taste better!"

CHAPTER 4

The gentle spring breeze rippled through the treetops high above the gardens. From such a vantage point, the city of Muncie, Indiana, could be seen in all directions. And from such a lofty perch, one might also see all that happened in the gardens beneath the canopy, although the leaves were coming in nicely and had almost completed their spring ritual of providing lush shade over the grounds.

Not that it mattered, for it was shielded from humankind even before the leaves had fully come in, the Palace of the Kingdom of Oakhurst was unseen by all from below by way of faerie magic as it swayed amongst the tree branches. It was beautiful. With golden tones and opalescent qualities that made it glisten in the sunlight, it was a shame that human eyes couldn't see it, for surely they would be dazzled by its splendor.

It was good to be back at Oakhurst. Queen Liliana loved traveling once in awhile, and though it had been a happy occasion, she was glad to be home. A fae of what humans might consider near "middle-aged," the queen was fair of face and had a quiet beauty about her. She took her duties as ruler of Oakhurst seriously, something that she hoped she had passed along to her children. Raising the next generation of royals on her own was a big responsibility, and though she was certain she had made some mistakes along the way, she was confident that her son would one day rule as his father, King Marco, once had. Proper political unions would ensure peace throughout the realm for generations to come if handled correctly.

She was troubled, however, at certain revelations King Beltran had made to her during their stay at the Palace of Ravensforge. When her son took one of his daughters for his bride, that single act would forever tie Oakhurst to Ravensforge. And while Beltran possessed certain positive attributes, Queen Liliana was not sure that his was the direction she wished her son to take. And then there was the matter of the amulet.

Liliana certainly did not begrudge him the reputation he had earned lo these many years, but she could not deny that he was playing with fire.

The amulet he had shown her in confidence troubled her. It had been known only through legend to her throughout the ages, a faerie tale at best. And yet, there it was, safely resting in a vault deep beneath the halls of Ravensforge. What he intended to do with it was unclear, and though his purported goal seemed benevolent, Liliana remained instinctively skeptical at best.

She settled in gazing over her beloved gardens. She adored them and the kingdom she ruled over, but missed her king. He had been gone since her children were very small, and the burden of rule fell to her. Truth be told, she would walk away from it all if she could, but duty was something she took very seriously. Besides, she loved her people too much to think otherwise. And then there was Elisabeth.

As a child, she had been able to see the faeries in the garden, a trait which is most rare in humans. Children are often able to see them but tend to grow out of it after being told by their parents that there are “no such things” as faeries. Elisabeth believed, nonetheless, and grew to be a trusted friend and protector of the Kingdoms of Oakhurst and Nebosham. Even after Elisabeth had grown, she remained at Oakhurst and lived out her days to a ripe old age as far as humans go, watching over both fae and wood sprites while caring for the gardens around them.

Death is a strange and mystical thing in both the human and faerie realm, and Elisabeth’s passing was no less sad for those who knew her in either realm. Though unseen by nearly all there, the royals of both Oakhurst and Nebosham celebrated Elisabeth’s life and her passing in their own way and knew that they would see her again on a different plane of existence.

The gardens were peaceful, and the queen enjoyed just being still and watching. But a sudden quickening of footsteps down the corridor told her the day was about to change.

It was Arland, her trusted Guardian and confidant. A muscular fellow, he looked quite imposing. In the time since

King Marco's passing, he had become more protective of her, and she found comfort in that.

"Your Majesty," Arland addressed her formally, bowing before her, "we have word that there has been an attack on Ravensforge."

The queen looked deadly serious. "What? How could this be?"

"We have received word from those few who managed to escape. They are seeking assistance and refuge."

"We will grant it, of course," she said quietly. "What of Beltran and his family?"

"Their whereabouts are unknown."

"Then we must return there at once."

ꙮ ꙮ

Across the compound that used to be Ravensforge the sentinels stood at the ready. Among them was Connor, who was shocked at the complete devastation around him. *Who could have done this?* he wondered. The delegation from Oakhurst had been there only days before, and there had not been even a hint of impending danger.

On this day the delegation from Oakhurst was larger, but considering the circumstances surrounding their journey back to Ravensforge, it was necessary. Queen Liliana and Arland led the way, and though the journey was somewhat daunting, they arrived safely. What met them was horrifying.

The devastation of the palace was nearly complete. All that remained was one corner in the interior of what used to be the royals living quarters. The rest was nothing more than a still-smoldering heap of rubble. Liliana made her way through the rubbish to the area which had been the family's home and surveyed the damage. There was literally nothing left.

"My Queen, it is not safe to be here," Arland advised her, ever watchful of their surroundings. "We must not linger."

"There is something I must know," she told him, "something that I must be certain of. Then we can depart. But not until then."

ꙮ ꙮ

The Oakhurst delegation searched desperately for any sign of hope. Everything was gone. Everyone was gone, and Connor's heart sank into the pit of his stomach.

The smell of smoke lingered as hot spots smoldered among the ruins of the palace. Reaching the place that had once been the Great Hall, Connor was hoping for any sign that might tell him where to find the royals, especially the king's daughters and their Guardian.

But that was not the only thing that troubled him.

From the time the delegation entered Ravensforge only days before, Connor was aware of his place, but had been utterly taken by one so fair that he dared not even utter her name. Never before had he felt like this, and though his purpose for the journey had one intention, it took a sudden turn that he had most certainly not expected.

No matter how hard he tried, Connor couldn't get her out of his head. Her beauty had beguiled him in a way that was unexpected yet exhilarating.

And totally wrong.

The state dinner had gone well according to the queen. Though the betrothal process would take a good amount of time, she was satisfied that it was under way and would be happy moving forward. From childhood she had drilled into her son's head and heart that duty and honor and legacy are what count most. This was a code she lived by, and she had raised her children in this manner. The prince, too, would be expected to raise his family the same way. Only problem was, things might not play out exactly the way the queen intended. And therein lay the crux of the problem.

It was bad enough that the prince was expected to choose between two princesses – sisters, no less! There were bound to be fireworks, of that Connor was certain. And though honor bound to choose the future Queen of Oakhurst, because there was great pressure to choose wisely, the Prince of Oakhurst had discovered he could not.

While his head came to the table prepared to do his duty, his heart, it seemed, had other ideas. For standing mere steps behind the princesses was the most beautiful woman he had ever seen. Though seemingly serious and all business, she had captured his attention when it should have been anywhere but on her.

Maybe it was the color of her eyes or her chestnut hair that fell gently about her shoulders. Perhaps it was the way she kept her eyes trained on him the whole time, though he suspected that came with the job rather than any remote chance that she was drawn to him.

More likely than not, it was the sword that hung at her side that her hand never left.

Fired in the flames of Ravensforge and blessed by King Beltran himself, the swords of the Guardians of Ravensforge were legendary. Their craftsmen were legendary for their perfectly balanced blades; their workmanship was exquisite and unmatched in all the realm.

For that one reason alone, Connor was determined to find her.

The royals had escaped, or so the evidence indicated. Connor's hope was that they had made it to safety at Hawksgate but knew the chances of that were slim at best. Serving as advisor on this journey, he leaned in to the young man in the royal traveling cloak and spoke quietly.

"I am certain King Beltran would have gotten the family out. The Guardians would have seen to their safety. Where do you think they might have gone?"

Caeden turned, clearly troubled by the devastation before them. His brown eyes scanned the remains of the castle as if he were the only one standing in the midst of the ruins. Athletic in build, he moved easily amongst the stones and debris. "Perhaps to the portal," he replied, "though it would have been somewhat arduous. Still, the Guardian might have gotten the princesses there."

"Perhaps," Connor replied.

The further they went into what had been the Castle Ravensforge only days before, the worse the carnage got. Connor glanced over at Caeden, noting his increasing unease, but saying nothing.

"We must be prepared to leave shortly. The queen wishes to move out before nightfall."

"What?" Caeden asked in a state of shock. "I – yes, yes, all right." He glanced about him again warily. "Who could have done such things?"

"I do not know," Connor answered, "but we must be on

guard from this moment on. We can leave nothing to the fates."

"Connor, I –"

Connor raised a hand to silence the young man. "We will speak later," he said quietly. "Right now we must find out what has happened here and, more importantly, where the royals of Ravensforge have gone."

Making his way through the rubble, Connor moved gingerly taking care not to step on the fae bodies scattered about. It was horrible, really, and his stomach turned with each step. Though the destruction had occurred a relatively short time before their arrival, the stench of death was thick in the air.

"Stay close," Connor told Caeden, who was only a few feet away. Caeden responded quickly, moving a little faster to catch up.

Connor could tell from the look on Caeden's face that he wouldn't last long. He nodded to one of the other guards who moved in to escort Caeden out of the palace ruins. Caeden started to protest, but Connor raised his eyebrows, looking around in a silent admonishment that read plain as day, *Are you kidding me? Go.*

"Over here!" came a cry, gaining the two men's attention. Making their way through what remained of the palace, they crossed grounds swiftly.

Connor ran to where the guard stood while the sentinels kept watch around the perimeter. Upon reaching him, he discovered that the guard had found someone trapped beneath the rubble. Quickly, Connor reached down and helped to clear the debris from the person, an older man, who looked rather worse for wear.

"You're a sight for sore eyes, young one," his voice gravelly as Connor helped the man up. He was tattered and weak, and Connor motioned for someone to bring him water. He helped him sit down, and trying not to push, yet ever mindful of their surroundings and the possible danger that still remained, he began to question what appeared to be the last survivor of Ravensforge.

"What happened here, old man?" he asked, taking the water from the guard and handing it to him.

Grateful, his feeble hand shook as he took the cup and gulped the water before speaking. He was breathing hard and covered in dirt and blood. He looked around at the delegation before speaking as if trying to decide if they could be trusted or not.

Queen Liliana made her way into the group, the guards parting to allow her access. Gently she knelt before the man.

"Minister Foley?" she asked in surprise as she recognized him as King Beltran's Minister of Defense.

"Your Majesty," the old man said as he tried to kneel before her. Liliana put a hand on his shoulder reassuring him that it was not necessary. She leaned in so he would not have to speak loudly.

"What happened here?" she asked softly.

"It was terrible," he said, his voice quavering. "It was not long after your departure that the darkness overran the palace – horrible, screeching darkness. They poured into the palace from everywhere, smashing everything. There was chaos, running and screaming. The Guard tried to protect the royals." His eyes were vacant as he recounted the horror of it all.

"King Beltran and Queen Astra sent the princesses and their Guardian to the portal. A full battalion accompanied them. He and the queen and the rest of the Guard saw to the evacuation of the palace and then set out in the opposite direction to try and throw them off."

"Who was it?" Liliana asked, some sense of urgency coming to her otherwise calm voice.

"It was him," the old man said, shaking visibly as he remembered it all.

"Who?" Liliana asked again.

"The Dark Warrior of Erebos."

The guards exchanged glances, looking about nervously. It was Connor who spoke up.

"The Dark Warrior of Erebos? I thought he was just a myth, a bedtime story to frighten little children."

Queen Liliana turned and shot him a look of scorn and silenced Connor at once.

"If this is true, by what dark magic did he manage all of this?" she asked, her focus solely on the old man.

"It was not the dark magic you have to fear, Highness. It is his army of minions. Stronger than the strongest fae and twice as fierce as any warrior I have ever seen in battle. They are more vicious than your worst nightmare and can easily and swiftly wreak havoc on their surroundings in short order." He took a deep breath and shuddered as he let it out.

"They are horrible, nasty creatures, the likes of which I have never seen."

Liliana rose and turned to Arland, who was never farther

than two steps from her. "We must find it and quickly," she said in a voice barely above a whisper. "If the Dark Warrior has found what Beltran had locked away, ours is not the only realm that will suffer."

Liliana surveyed the ruins as if searching for something in particular. She left the minister and moved with purpose to where the family's quarters had been when last she'd seen Beltran and his family.

"Your Highness," Arland implored, ever watchful of their surroundings as he stayed close to her side, "it is not safe here."

The queen shot him a look that would have cut a normal man in half, but Arland had grown used to it by now, and it was the trust between them that worked so well all these years.

Liliana led Arland through the ruins of Ravensforge to the only portion of wall that remained. It was a corner, and from the looks of things, there was nothing abnormal about it. The queen stood for a moment lost in thought, trying desperately to remember how Beltran had managed to open the doorway. Pausing only slightly, she bowed her head, opened her right hand, then her left. The wall shimmered, then revealed a doorway through which a darkened stairwell lay beyond.

Arland took a step back amazed at the sight before them. He stepped around Liliana, looked at the doorway, then peered around the jagged ruin of the wall. Beyond the remains was the greensward that led to the sea. The sun shown brilliantly on the tall grass as it waved in the breeze. Befuddled, Arland returned to the queen.

"Onward?" he asked her.

"Where else?" she answered.

Her traveling cloak billowed behind her as she descended into the stairwell. Though hooded, her beauty still shone through in the darkness as they moved into the catacombs.

"Highness, I must protest," Arland warned again.

"If what I fear is true, you won't have to worry," Liliana told him as she moved swiftly through the corridor of stone. "Then it will only be a matter of time."

At the bottom of the stairs was a torch, still burning though its wick was not for long. Arland went around Liliana and took the torch from the wall. Looking back at her with some trepidation, he turned and led the way.

Arland's sword was at the ready as they explored the bowels of what was once the Castle Ravensforge. Winding through the cavern in silence, they reached the vault where the Amulet of Fire had rested only days before. The guards who had been posted there were nowhere to be found, and the door to the vault stood ajar. Arland raised his hand, cautioning the queen, and silently entered the room. Finding it empty, he motioned her inside.

Liliana saw what she had feared. The one piece that Beltran had held above the others, had feared the most, was missing.

"Let us pray it has not fallen into the wrong hands."

ꟃ ꟃ

From the woods edge they could see the portal or rather what was left of it. Arland led Queen Liliana and the full guard across the meadow to the rocky face of the hill.

Liliana looked the portal over. Its charred remains showed battle had occurred there, and its glow was no more. Her hand hovered over its smooth, blackened surface. Nothing happened. A helmet lay at the side of the portal next to it.

Liliana picked it up, inspecting the damage to the rough hammered metal. "The king's Guard," she said solemnly. "They were here. But where have they gone?"

"This goes to the human realm, does it not?" Arland asked.

"Yes," she sighed, "or rather, it did."

"We must make camp," he urged her as he surveyed the skies. He motioned to the guards on the edge of the group and at once, they moved to their task.

As the rest of the entourage made preparations for the night, Connor and Caeden moved in on the portal unnoticed. Connor leaned closer and examined the remains as he ran his fingers across its blackened surface.

Though he had heard of the device, one of several, he had never encountered one before. He could only imagine how impressive it must have been when in action.

"Your thoughts?" Caeden inquired.

Connor paused as his hand came to rest on a chunk of jagged rock near the center of the stone. He again ran his thumb across the face of it, revealing some color beneath the charred surface.

"They may have gone through here," Connor said as he looked about, "but they certainly cannot come back through here. Nor can we follow this way."

"Follow?"

Conner's face strained a bit as he gripped the jagged piece of rock and pulled toward them. It protested somewhat, then gave way as it broke off in his hand. The stone was not quite as big as his fist, and he quickly shoved it in his pocket.

Connor smiled.

"Yes, follow."

ꝏ ꝏ

"We must find the princesses of Ravensforge," Connor said, careful to keep his voice down. In the darkness the firelight danced across their faces. They had made encampment for the night, and the queen had long since retired. All that was left was a handful of the Guard who were on watch. Caeden warmed himself at the fire and could tell Connor was serious.

"The queen would not be happy," he said rubbing his hands together.

"The queen doesn't have to know," Connor replied his eyes locked on the fire. He avoided looking up to mask the fear in his own eyes. Yet his compulsion to find the princessees overrode any fears he might have for his own safety. It was the one in his charge that he feared for.

"I cannot ask you to go," Connor told the young man.

Caeden chuckled. "Where else would I go?" he inquired somewhat sarcastically. "It's not like I have much choice."

Connor looked up at him. "There is always a choice," he replied, his voice deadly serious. "You are not bound to pursue this as I am."

"Yet, you forget," the young man said solemnly, "I am. By duty, by station, I am honor bound to find them, just as you are."

"Then it's settled," Connor said. "We leave at first light."

Chapter 5

Shea followed Sam through the front gate and to the side door of Oakhurst. He unlocked the door and keyed in the alarm code, making sure she saw as he did it.

"It's pretty easy, just don't get too distracted or you'll have Delaware County's finest on the doorstep in no time," Sam joked as he headed for the back stairs. "C'mon up and I'll show you the apartment."

Shea trailed behind him as he went up the winding staircase to the second floor landing where he was already unlocking another door.

"This apartment was an addition late in Elisabeth Ball's life," Sam told her as he swung the door open and flipped on the light. "Her caregiver lived here, and later one of Minnetrista's Presidents stayed here."

Sam gave Shea the grand tour of the tiny apartment, which took no more than a few minutes. The bathroom was on the left by the door, bedroom on the right, followed by a tiny kitchen next to the bedroom. At the end of the hallway was the living room.

Shea stepped over and looked through the window on the west side of the apartment to the courtyard below. A small stream ran through it, and she felt strangely at ease.

"It's a pretty big house, and it creaks a lot, so it may take some getting used to," Sam said handing her the keys and a slip of paper with the lock combination written on it.

"I'll be fine," Shea smiled. "Thank you."

"Just let us know if you need anything," Sam told her as he went into the kitchen, sliding open the pass-thru to the living room and raising the blinds that covered the window above the sink. "The kitchen's been stocked to get you started, and Jackie sent a few goodies from her place."

Shea smiled and watched as Sam let himself out. Though she couldn't remember what home felt like, she knew this felt comfortable. Secure. Peaceful.

Not one to sit around, Shea set out to explore the rest of the house. She started on the second floor and immediately fell in love with the light coming through the windows in the adjoining rooms on the front of the house. A smaller room across the hall featured a substantial display case that contained a beautiful diorama of the Ball brothers' homes. The case itself was a work of art made of glass and skillfully carved wood that took up most of the center of the room.

Minnetrista, which means "gathering place by the water," sat where the Cultural Center is today. It was the home of

Frank and Bessie Ball and burned down after their passing. The columns still sit on the grounds today to welcome guests.

Nebosham, which means "by the bend in the river," was home to Edmund and Bertha Ball. The beautiful English Tudor home's red tile roof was striking even in miniature.

Maplewood, a stunning Georgian Revival home, belonged to William C. and Emma Ball, and was so named for the maple trees around it. It later became a guest house for executives of Ball Corporation.

Next to it sat a tiny version of Oakhurst, Shea's new home, a Shingle style house so named for the grove of oak trees it was built in. It had been home to George A. and Frances Ball and their daughter, Elisabeth.

Shea paused enjoying the view of her new neighborhood in miniature. It was a wondrous sight to see all the detail in the tiny homes. They looked just like the real thing!

Moving further down the hall she discovered a stained glass door portraying a human silhouette which led to a bathroom. It had been converted for public use and was actually bigger than it looked from the doorway.

Heading down the front staircase, Shea paused on the landing. Before her was a door with a glass window that afforded her a view out into an amazing room. With the keys Sam had left with her, she tried each of them in turn until she found the one that opened the door before her. It led out onto a screened-in sleeping porch that overlooked the courtyard. She smiled and closed her eyes as the cool breeze came through the screens. From her perch she could see a small oak shingle dollhouse that mimicked the style of Oakhurst itself, and the pathway that wound through the garden to the Discovery

Cabin. Sam had told her that Elisabeth Ball had played in the little house as a child, and the one on the grounds was a replica of the original.

Movement in the dollhouse caught her eye, and for a moment she thought she'd imagined it. She stepped further out onto the porch and looked again. Shea paused for the longest time, and seeing nothing, decided it had been the light off the windows.

Shea closed and locked the door behind her, noting which key unlocked the door as she placed the key ring back into her pocket. She moved on down the stairs to the landing in the center of the house. It was a grand space, and Shea just took it in for a moment.

The main floor of the house was sparsely furnished as the space was usually reserved for seasonal exhibits and holiday décor. The dining room was set properly as though awaiting dinner guests, but the rest of the rooms were virtually empty.

Making her way around the corner to her right, Shea found herself in the library. The walls were lined with glass display cases, and a fireplace sat on the wall opposite the front window. Moving toward the fireplace, she paused at the brush of fresh air on her cheek a mere few feet from the hearth. Stepping back, Shea put out her hand as she moved along the cases until she found the source of the incoming air.

Carefully running her fingers along the source, she let them slip into the gap and pulled. Nothing at first, then slowly the display case gave way and swung open to reveal a hidden passageway. Looking over her shoulder, Shea stepped into the space behind the case and opened the small door behind it.

The door swung out into another screened-in porch on the

backside of Oakhurst. Thrilled at her discovery, Shea stepped out and let the fresh spring air blow full in her face. At garden level, she delighted in the view.

Shea Remington felt at peace, at least for today.

CHAPTER 6

Remembering Sam's directions on how to reach the Collections Room, Shea headed downstairs to the library in the basement of the Center. Taking a left turn at the bottom of the rather long stairwell, she went into the office at the end of the hall on the left. Standing in the adjoining room was a woman hovering over a group of boxes looking for something. Her shoulder length blonde hair hung down about her face, and she absently reached up to tuck it behind her ear as she dug through the box closest to her. Hearing the approaching footsteps, she looked up to see Shea standing in the doorway.

"Oh, good, you've arrived just in time," the woman said in a friendly tone as Shea wandered into the library. She stood amidst a good number of boxes and assorted files piled upon the tables in front of her and the floor around her. "You must be Shea."

Shea smiled and nodded as she entered the room. The organized chaos was somewhat overwhelming to her untrained eye as she looked around.

"Hi, I'm Lucy Abernathy," the woman said, reaching to shake Shea's hand.

Not quite sure what to do with herself and remembering how Sam had done likewise, Shea stuck out her hand and Lucy shook it heartily. "Sam sent me to help."

"I'm glad to have the help. Looks like we've got lots to do today!"

Shea glanced around at the assortment of boxes scattered about the room.

"Yeah, I know, it's a bit of a mess," Lucy apologized, "but I was looking for some things for the Faeries, Sprites and Lights event for GiGi before I left. There are several pieces from when the G.A. family lived in Oakhurst that will be good for folks getting an idea of how they lived, but I haven't been able to find..."

She replaced the lid on one box and opened the one next to it, her face lighting up. "There they are!" she exclaimed.

Curious, Shea moved closer to peer into the box.

Lying in the bottom of a larger box were five small white archival boxes. Lucy eagerly unloaded the contents of the box onto the table, opening them one by one. Inside each was a small, handmade box that had been crafted out of various high-quality papers. One was a matte gold background gilt with shiny golden swirls. Another was made of silver paper with the same pattern. Two more were a soft blue with flowers, and the fifth box was most exquisite of all – a page from a children's faerie tale book with faeries on it.

"What are those?" Shea asked, suddenly fascinated with the boxes on the table before her.

"Magic boxes," Lucy said matter-of-factly. "Elisabeth Ball made them when she was a child. She used them to summon faeries in the gardens around her home."

Lucy held the box with the faeries on it up to examine it more closely.

Not quite sure what to say, Shea just looked at Lucy.

"Well, she had quite an imagination," Lucy said with a grin. She gently placed the magic box back into the small archival box, nestling it in with the others in the bigger box.

"Sam told me you're leaving?" Shea inquired hesitantly.

"Yes," Lucy smiled wide as she repacked the last of the contents of the box in front of her. "I'll be on an exchange program of sorts. I am going to the British Museum to study with their director of collections. They're sending a guy here...what was his name? Darius something-or-other. Anyway, I guess he's a European expert on faerie lore of Ireland and the British Isles. Wish I was going to be here to pick his brain a little."

"Faeries?"

Lucy finished repacking the box and closed the lid. "Yeah, isn't it great? He's bringing a collection of artifacts and relics that have been associated with the faerie legends since medieval times. Should be a lot of fun."

She set aside the box holding the collection of magic boxes for later. Looking around the room she sighed.

"Ok, we're going to need to get the rest of this back into the collection room across the hall. I've left a few of the files for Susan to put back into this room, and we're good. I need to get this all done by the end of the day. My flight leaves first thing in the morning."

"Looks like you keep very busy."

"Oh, I don't think I'll ever run out of things to do," Lucy quipped happily as she loaded Shea's arms up with boxes. "Be careful with these, please. There's a few with breakables inside. They're packed well, but a tumble wouldn't be good for them."

"Right," Shea said, as she backed up to clear the door. Lucy stacked several boxes on the table, picked them up and headed out of the library. Shea followed her down the hall and through a service door into another room and toward the back where a table sat. Lucy placed her boxes on the table and unlocked the heavy steel doors. Still carrying her boxes, Shea followed Lucy into the dark room.

"The architect kind of had a funny sense of humor," Lucy said with a laugh as she disappeared into the darkness. "For some odd reason, he placed the light switches toward the back of the room." There was silence for a moment as Shea's eyes quickly adjusted to the darkness of the room.

"There you are," Lucy said, her voice sounding distant from the far end of the room as she flipped the switch. Light flooded the room, and Shea blinked as the brightness of it shocked her eyes.

"Ok, I'll show you where these need to go," Lucy said, rounding the row of shelves and moving on over to the next section. Shea followed her across the room below the mezzanine and past the art collection to a section toward the back.

"Go ahead and set them on the floor," Lucy said. "Then, if you'll go bring the rest of them starting with the table closest to the door and working your way back, I'll go ahead and start putting them away."

"Okay," Shea said, disappearing around the end of the shelves.

Lucy retrieved her boxes from the outer room and refiled them, then moved upstairs to the mezzanine. In a few moments, Shea returned with several more boxes. She went to the spot where they had been and found Lucy gone.

"Lucy?" Shea called out hesitantly.

"I'm up here." Lucy's small voice came from above her. "C'mon up."

Shea placed the boxes on the floor and moved back down the aisle to the staircase that led upstairs. She arrived at the top to find half of the lights on and a plethora of family heirlooms and historical artifacts from the region's past. A beautiful saddle that belonged to Ed Ball embossed with the image of a Ball jar on the sides greeted her at the top of the stairs. Across from it sat an antique Wooten desk, and row after row of tall shelving units behind it housed a plethora of pieces.

"Wow," Shea exclaimed, as she moved toward where Lucy's voice had come from.

"Amazing, isn't it?" Lucy said. "There is so much history up here. What's fascinating is that while most of it is from the Ball family, there is a good deal of it that pertains to Delaware County and the surrounding area."

"That's a lot of stuff."

"Yes," Lucy chuckled, "that is a lot of stuff."

ꝏ ꝏ

The afternoon flew by, and Lucy and Shea had one more task to complete before Lucy headed home to finish packing her bags. They took a few boxes, loaded them onto the golf cart and headed down to Oakhurst.

Shea helped carry the boxes up the stairs to the gallery across the hall from her apartment.

"You can just put that down over there, Shea," Lucy told her as Shea came through the door. Lucy began to open the boxes and place the pieces in a small display case.

"Would you like some help?" Shea asked.

"Sure," Lucy said, "that'd be great!"

Shea sat the boxes down just inside the door and walked over to the display case where Lucy was carefully placing the items from the box at her feet. They were the tiny little handmade boxes from earlier in the day, gently made with care, yet quite fancy in nature.

"They're beautiful," she noted quietly. "You said they are magical?"

Lucy smiled. "The little girl who grew up here believed they were. She said she used them to summon the faeries in the garden."

"Faeries?" Shea inquired, not quite sure what Lucy meant.

"Yes, you know – the little winged folks, about this big?" Lucy gestured with her hands a space no more than six inches high. "Elisabeth believed in faeries with all her heart. Said they lived here in the gardens. She spoke and wrote of them often, even after she had grown."

Lucy's phone rattled around in her pocket, and she answered it. She stepped out into the hallway, talking as she went.

Shea moved across the room to the open display case. The boxes Lucy had shown her earlier were arranged beautifully in the open glass box. She reached in and pulled out one of the tiny, shiny boxes, holding it in the palm of her hand. It was made of a beautiful gold-patterned paper, thicker than most, folded and tucked in a rather intricate manner. There was no glue on it anywhere, and the hundred year old box was sturdy in spite of its age. It was tied with a beautiful gold cloth ribbon which held the lid securely in place.

She studied the box closer admiring the handiwork, curious about what it held inside. Looking around and seeing no one, she reached up with her other hand to untie the ribbon.

"Stop!" Lucy said, louder than she was accustomed to speaking. She was standing in the doorway to the gallery and nearly dropped the box in her arms out of shock. "Uh, I mean, we *don't* open the magic boxes."

"Really? Why not?" Shea asked. "Don't you want to see what's inside?"

Lucy marveled at her naiveté. "Well, sure I want to see what's inside." She came in and put the box on the table by the window. "But we can't open them. They're a hundred years old, for heaven's sake."

"Does that mean the magic's a hundred years old, too?"

"Sure!" Lucy agreed with a laugh. "I don't think it gets stale."

Lucy came over and picked through the remaining half dozen boxes on the table. "This one is my favorite magic box," she said. "Elisabeth used to take them out into the garden and leave them for the faeries. She said she used them to request an audience with Liliana, the Queen of Oakhurst herself."

Shea raised her eyebrows. "Hundred year old magic, huh?"

"Hundred year old magic."

CHAPTER 7

The last of the staff straggled into the conference room as Evangeline Monteague moved to the front of the group.

"I'd like to welcome the latest additions to our Minnetrista family," Evangeline said cheerily as she gestured to Shea, who had taken a seat at the back of the room. "Shea Remington has joined us and will be the caretaker of G.A. House. Please make her feel welcome. She is available to help out in most areas so make good use of her."

Shea smiled weakly, uncomfortable at the attention, but knew it be over soon and she could get back to Oakhurst.

The staff greeted her with brief applause then turned their attention back to Evangeline.

"We also have a guest with us for the summer. As most of you know, Lucy Abernathy, our Director of Collections, is on loan to the British Museum in London. They, in turn, have graciously loaned us their Assistant Director of Collections, Mr. Darius Pendragon, Esquire."

Evangeline led the applause as Darius Pendragon, Esquire moved to the front of the room. She greeted him warmly, leaning in and saying something to him as she shook his hand. He turned and smiled at the group waiting until the applause subsided before he spoke.

Looking more like one suited for professional wrestling than scholarly pursuits, Darius Pendragon stood half a head taller than most of the men in the room. He was charismatic and charming, drawing in those around him instantly with his wit and gentle tone in spite of his impressive stature. His shoulder length black hair was pulled back into a short ponytail, and his goatee and freshly pressed suit projected a manner both intellectual and professional.

"Good afternoon," he greeted the staff of Minnetrista as they took their seats. "I cannot tell you what a pleasure it is to be here. I am so grateful for the opportunity to be able to share my culture's history and lore with fellow historians, and I look forward to learning more about this region as well. This summer promises to be one that I won't soon forget."

"Thank you, Darius, and welcome," Evangeline said warmly. As President of the Cultural Center, she always enjoyed working with other museums and institutions, and this was definitely a feather in the cap of Minnetrista. Though considerably shorter than Darius, Evangeline's enthusiasm more than made up for her stature, and her long red hair fell in waves about her shoulders. She absently pushed her glasses back up to the bridge of her nose as she spoke.

"We are fortunate that Mr. Pendragon has brought along an amazing collection of relics and artifacts from Europe to share with us this summer while Lucy is on sabbatical. She is participating in an exchange program and will be sharing what she learns with us upon her return in the fall. In the meantime, please make him feel at home."

"Well, as I said, I am looking forward to spending the summer months with you," Darius Pendragon began as he unloaded his laptop from his attaché case and connected it to the already waiting projector that had been set up for him, "although I am sure they will be gone in the blink of an eye." He looked up for a moment, smiled briefly and nodded.

"When I was first approached about this particular exchange program, I wasn't sure I wanted to play along, to be honest with you. But after doing a little research on Minnetrista I found that it is a veritable treasure trove for regional culture and arts, and quite frankly, I was impressed. And with the family Ball and their esteemed history, I was intrigued as well. So here I am." He got the last file opened and was ready to begin his presentation.

The slideshow began with a variety of photos of the Irish countryside. "I have to admit, I was most captured by your storied history at Oakhurst of Miss Elisabeth Ball and her faeries in her gardens. As you may well know, the Irish lore is full of tales of the fae folk and their mischief."

Darius flipped through a few more slides showing various pieces of artwork of faeries. Many were from the Victorian era, and some from the medieval period with a few more modern pieces sprinkled in.

"The Victorian flower faeries became popular due to Queen Mary's interest in the faerie artwork. Other styles of work, such as those by Victorian painter Richard Dadd, portray fae folk as vile, vindictive little creatures prone to mischief and mayhem. As I understand it, Miss Ball's faeries were not of the malevolent sort?"

Georgina "GiGi" Franklin, a young woman with dark shoulder length hair and sparkling hazel eyes, spoke up first. "Uh, no. No, they're not" she smiled, seemingly quite charmed by Mr. Pendragon. "They're friendly fae folk."

"Very good," Darius said. "We wouldn't want those nasty faeries around. How's your wood sprites?"

"Oh," GiGi said, caught a bit off guard. "Well, we've never – had…any problems. Have we?" she asked, looking around the room at the other staff members somewhat uncertain of why they were even having this conversation.

"Well," he continued in all seriousness, "I hear they can cause problems, that they don't, shall we say, 'play nice' with the faeries. Real trouble makers, really."

"Right, right," GiGi nodded, as she tried her best to look serious.

"Onward then," Darius nodded back, as he went through the slides, going over the historical high points of Irish faerie lore.

"This particular piece is one of my favorites," he said finally, gesturing to the slide behind him as he began to wind down his presentation. "The *Choimeádaí Iarsma*, known as the Keeper of the Past, or more commonly the Dragon's Keep, is said to have been a sacred relic handed down through royal generations of the faerie realm. Legend has it that it gave the king who held it untold powers, and when possessed with the remaining relics of the Dragon Triad could make a ruler invincible. In times of unrest, it assured that one kingdom would oversee the others, and in the hands of a peaceful monarchy, it allegedly worked."

"It is a simple relic, really. A crystal egg of sorts, with a cast bronze dragon wrapped around it, guarding its keep. The mineral qualities of the egg are said to react when the egg is in proximity of the other pieces of the Triad. The dragon's eyes, believed to have been fire opals, are said to have glowed as though the dragon were alive."

"As you can well see, the dragon's eyes are missing. It is likely they were stolen by looters who didn't know the true value of the piece. Legend has it that one of the kings threw it into the sea to keep it from its rightful owner."

Pendragon went on to the next slide. It was a picture of a staff, looking to be six feet tall with a headpiece, and a detail photo of the headpiece beside it. It, too, was a bronze dragon, swirled around a circular stone that looked to be approximately three and a half inches in diameter. It was polished to a smooth, perfectly rounded piece that was contained by the bronze dragon.

"Popular opinion among scholars is that there is, or rather had been at one time, an amulet that completes the Dragon's Triad. Though no one knows for certain what it looks like, it is believed to have been a substantial piece. Known as the Dragon's Heart, it is said to have shone like the sun from within and is bound by lightning." Darius looked up at his rapt audience. "However, the amulet is probably no more than a myth, as there is no physical evidence other than a mere mention in medieval folklore to support its existence."

Pendragon reached across the table and disconnected his laptop from the projector. "Are there any questions?"

"Well, then," he said after a moment's pause, "I guess you'll be able to see it for yourselves when the collection arrives."

ᘓ ᘐ

The remainder of the staff meeting consisted of scheduling and a quick recap of preparations for upcoming events, most prominent being Faeries, Sprites and Lights, which was only six weeks away. GiGi stepped forward, laptop at the ready, to bring the staff up to speed.

"It's so nice to have a new addition to our staff," she said, smiling at Shea, "so for your benefit and Mr. Pendragon's, of course –" She paused and nodded to the most prominent newcomer who was seated just to her right.

"Please," he protested humbly, "call me Darius."

GiGi smiled back at him. "And for Darius's benefit, I'll just quickly go over what "Faeries, Sprites and Lights," otherwise known as FSL, is. Here at Minnetrista we are fortunate to have a rich family history where the Ball family is concerned." She flipped through several photographs of FSL's past, filled with adorable little girls dressed as faeries and the staff in character. "One of our most treasured traditions is that of sharing the story of Elisabeth Ball who grew up in the house known as Oakhurst. As an only child she spent countless hours playing in the gardens of Oakhurst, as well as those of Nebosham, Maplewood and Minnetrista, the homes of her uncles."

"Elisabeth believed faeries lived amongst the flowers and trees on the grounds, and we even have photos of the faerie parties that occurred here." GiGi continued on through the photos from the Heritage Collection, stopping on an old black and white photo of children in costume. "As you can see here, there were close to fifty children all dressed in faerie outfits in front of Maplewood. It is Elisabeth's love of faeries that we celebrate."

"There are two preview events, Queen Liliana's High Tea, held the morning before each evening event. It's a rather formal tea, and mothers and daughters are encouraged to come in dresses and hats, much as they would have in turn of the century Muncie."

"The evening events, which run from six to nine pm, will include faeries all about the garden grounds, dancing and silently interacting with guests, many of whom are also in fae dress. You'd be amazed at how many mothers dress in wings along with their daughters, most in full fae dress. The little boys, eehhhh…not so much," she said, wincing. "We end up with a few wood sprites each year, a pirate or two, and an occasional wizard from the realm of Rowling."

"The local Civic Theatre presents a faerie tale-type play, and wandering minstrels entertain the guests with folk music. Our cast of actors portray a variety of characters, and they interact with guests making the event both exciting and more real for guests. They are trained to stay in character no matter what, and even the support staff has fun with that."

"This year we are adding a dance on the final evening. It will run from seven to ten, which is a little later than usual, and the Muncie Symphony Orchestra will provide a string quartet to play the music. Dress will be turn of the twentieth century, optional of course but encouraged, to honor the traditions celebrated here at the Ball family homes. They entertained often and always did it up right. Our hope is to attract a broader range of guests. Currently the average demographic is families with small children. We would like to be able to expand on that."

"Sounds delightful," Darius said with a smile.

"Oh, I almost forgot!" GiGi added quickly. "The collection of relics Darius spoke of earlier should arrive any day now. The pieces are rife with faerie lore and legends and will make a great addition to FSL. We will open a new gallery in the top of the Carriage House."

Darius smiled and nodded as the rest of the staff *oohed* and *aahed* in approval.

"Thank you, GiGi," Evangeline said, as GiGi took her seat. "As you can see, Darius, we have much going on around here for you to absorb during your stay with us. Make yourself at home, and I'm sure if you have any questions, folks will be more than happy to answer them for you."

"Thank you," he said.

"There will be a reception with the Board of Trustees tomorrow evening to welcome Darius, and you're all invited," Sam added.

The meeting broke up after a few more housekeeping items, and Evangeline asked Shea and Darius to stick around afterward.

"Please let me know if there is anything you need," Evangeline said with a smile. Shea and Darius both thanked her and Darius began to pack up his things.

"Where are you from, Miss Remington?" he asked from behind a rather charming smile that made Shea feel somewhat uneasy.

"Not far from here," Shea replied. It was only half true, as the first thing she remembered was climbing up the steep slope from a cave near the riverbank. Uncertain of why, she felt the less people knew of her circumstances, the better. At least until she knew more about herself.

"I see," he replied with a nod. "Well, I look forward to getting to know you."

Shea nodded in return and left the room. She could feel his eyes on the back of her neck and found it unsettling. She noted to herself that she would have to keep her guard up awhile, at least until she had settled in at Oakhurst and knew its rhythms and sounds.

ꙮ ꙮ

Nebosham sat proudly at the head of the boulevard, its red tile roof standing stark against the bright blue sky. The damp spring morning was cool on Shea's face as the breeze blew spray off the canopy above the sidewalk. She enjoyed the view above the river and counted herself lucky to have fallen into such an opportunity. She hoped that her memory would return soon and felt safe in her current set up.

Clearing the trees between Maplewood and the front yard of Oakhurst, movement caught her eye near the back courtyard, making her stop short of the gate.

She couldn't tell but thought it might be a child. Probably someone out enjoying the sunshine or a school group. Sam had told her there would be lots of those. Curious, she made her way down the brick path toward the small garden behind Oakhurst.

The breeze rustled through the leaves as she rounded the corner into the courtyard. Sunlight shimmered through the wet leaves, and a decent sized patch of sunshine warmed Shea as she came through the gate and crossed the tiny bridge in the back yard.

Seeing no one, she turned back the way she came. Suddenly, a large bird flew up out of the groundcover, the flap of its wings beating against the still morning air. Shea jumped, startled at the bird's presence, and watched as it perched in a tree overhead – a red-tailed hawk. It sat on a branch well out of reach and eyed her as she stared back at it.

She surveyed the area once more. "I guess this is your home more than it is mine," she admitted to the bird, hoping that would change. "At least for today."

CHAPTER 8

Shea spent time with several different staff members over the next few days as she became acclimated to her new surroundings. Though she couldn't be certain, she felt as though she had never lived in a more beautiful place. The house and surrounding gardens were more than she could have ever hoped for, and she took great pains to be a good steward of her felicitous fortune.

Because her main task at hand was to be the caretaker of Oakhurst, she began with the maintenance department, learning the ins and outs of the structure itself and the systems that it housed. She took it all in, determined to care for it as if it were her own.

The gardening staff gave her the guided tour of the campus, sharing their knowledge of the perennials on the grounds and history of some of them that were original to the Ball family homestead.

She made friends easily and enjoyed spending time with Carolyn and Chef and the kitchen staff. On the occasions she helped with evening events in the set-up and tear-down of tables and chairs, Carolyn always made sure her pockets were stuffed with cookies or other treats afterward.

On one such evening Shea was headed back toward the house, a parcel of goodies in hand for later. She made the rounds, closing down the gardens and locking the gates when something caught her eye along "Aunt Emma's path," the walkway between Oakhurst and Maplewood. She couldn't be certain, but it looked like a child.

She locked down the service gate and headed up Aunt Emma's path to Oakhurst. She noticed the small figure dart across the pathway and into the garden behind the house.

Picking up her pace, Shea moved swiftly toward the garden, clearing the gate to find…nothing.

"Hello?" she called out. "Anybody here?"

Her eyes scanned the woods directly behind the house. She gazed up into the trees, hoping to at least catch a glimpse of the hawk she'd seen on her first night in the house. Again, nothing.

In the growing twilight Shea decided she'd had enough for one day and had probably imagined it all. Tired from the day's work, she sighed and headed to the front yard where she locked the gates. Her task complete, she retired to the house for the evening.

She made her way to the back door and let herself in. The door swung shut behind her, and in her tired state she missed the little girl peeking around the corner of Oakhurst after her.

ജ ഗ

“Today we’ll have you down in the Collections Room with Darius,” Sam told Shea, as he looked at her from the other side of his desk. “He’s unpacking the crates he brought with him from London. Seems they got hung up in customs. You should find that pretty interesting.”

Shea smiled, not sure what to say. Life these days was good, and she was building a new chapter for herself. She just wasn’t sure what the previous chapters had held for her. In other words, she had no idea if she would find the collection interesting or not.

She thanked him and went downstairs to the library. Through the glass she could see that the table and countertops around the room were all covered with boxes and crates. Seeing no one inside, she let herself into the office and went through to the library.

Several of the crates were open but had yet to be unpacked. Shea made her way around the room, peering into those that already had the lids removed. The contents were mostly covered in packing material, and she walked along the countertop to the two large windows that looked out into the shelter of the bushes at ground level. Beyond the foliage was the loading dock and parking lot.

Shea looked down into the box in front of her. An aged bronze piece stuck half-way out of the packing material. She reached down and grasped it with her left hand, moving the packing away with her right. She lifted it up to eye level to examine it. It was beautiful.

It was a substantial piece, and the weight of the crystal egg and patinaed bronze dragon sat heavily in the palm of her hand. She reached up and turned it with her right hand, admiring the craftsmanship and beauty of the piece. Wrapped around the egg as if to guard it from would-be thieves was the small, yet fierce looking, dragon she'd seen the day before in Darius Pendragon's presentation. Her gaze followed it from its tail all the way around to its face, punctuated by two large, empty eye sockets.

"Exquisite, isn't it?" came a voice from behind her.

Shea jumped, nearly dropping the egg. She bobbled it for a moment, recovering just in time to keep from sending it through the plate glass window a mere foot or so in front of her. Seeing the man's reflection in the window before her, Shea wheeled about to find herself face to face with Darius Pendragon himself.

"Oh, hello," she said, smiling weakly as she placed the egg carefully back in the box. "I'm sorry, I – I didn't…."

Shea stopped and took a deep breath.

"I'm sorry," she said again gathering her thoughts. "Sam sent me down here to help."

"Oh, yes, I see," Pendragon nodded as he raised his eyebrows, never taking his gaze from her. "Well, we'll just have to put you to work then, won't we? There are more of these crates out on the loading dock. Their contents will need cataloging, of course."

Shea gave him a half smile. "Whatever you need."

Chapter 9

At the end of her shift down in Collections, Shea was mentally exhausted. She wasn't used to keeping her guard up all day long. There was just something about Pendragon that made her uneasy, but she couldn't quite put her finger on it. All she knew was he wasn't like the other people she'd met at Minnetrista. Perhaps it was because he was from Europe or some other such quirk. Then again, who was she to judge what was normal and what wasn't?

The walk through the garden was relaxing, and as she closed the gates up one by one, she felt her tension ease. She felt at home in Oakhurst already, and though she hadn't been there long, she decided she would stay as long as they would let her.

Coming around to the Discovery Cabin she stopped dead in her tracks. There on the porch sat a little girl playing. She was dressed very much like the child Shea thought she had seen the day before, wearing a light-colored dress with dark tights and patent leather Mary Janes. Not wanting to startle her, Shea moved slowly down the walk toward her.

The little girl continued to play with her doll and paid no attention to Shea.

"Hello," Shea said softly, as she came up to the porch.

The little girl looked up, her short blonde Buster Brown haircut framing her sweet face nicely. "Hello," the girl replied with an easy smile before going back to her doll.

"Do you live around here?" Shea asked her.

"Yes," the girl answered without looking up.

"Oh," Shea said, looking around the garden. "Do your parents know where you are? Are they here?"

The little girl laughed. "Yes, Father and Mother know where I am." She scooped up her doll and ran up the path toward the dollhouse. "Do your parents know where you are?" she called over her shoulder.

"Strange," Shea said, shaking her head as she headed toward the back gate to close it.

ᘓ ᘐ

Shea loved to sleep on the sleeping porch on the second floor. It was amazing to be able to wake in the morning to the sound of the birds in the trees and be at the same level they were. She was almost certain there must be nothing like it, nothing so wonderful as awakening amongst the treetops, and she unlocked the door carrying her pillow and blanket with her. Some contemporary wicker pieces furnished the room, and in the glow of the security light from the Carriage House just beyond the trees, she could see the light sparkle through the leaves making it a magical place.

It was unseasonably cool and had been for several days. Shea had been trying to wrap her head around all that had occurred over the past few weeks, all that she couldn't remember. How difficult it was to not know where she came from, who she was, or even what she liked. She didn't even know what the choices were which made it all the more difficult.

Jackie's words came ringing back to her from a couple of weeks ago. "Some folk would give their right arm to be able to start over," she'd said. "You've been given a wonderful chance – a blessing. Don't waste it, girl.'"

It would have been easier to stay at Jackie's. It might have been safer. But to have taken the chance and been able to live here was worth it. Shea smiled and made her makeshift bed on the couch. She laid down and pulled the blanket up to her chin, glad for how life had treated her, if only for the few weeks she could remember.

Each night she would try to let her mind go to where it knew itself best, to where it knew the truth about her past. She would relax and breathe deeply as she closed her eyes, letting herself merely float away. Most nights she would fall asleep straight away. But other nights, in that place somewhere between asleep and awake, she would see things that gave her hope.

It wasn't much really, just faces or occasional, yet brief, moments from her life. It was much like – what was it Sam called it? A *movie* where the story unfolds and you see it all played out before your eyes in front of that little box in Shea's apartment. She didn't care much for it and couldn't figure out why the people inside the box wouldn't respond to her questions or warnings. Frustrated, she had simply shut it off and pushed it back into the corner.

Shea closed her eyes and exhaled, giving herself the opportunity to relax and just be. She was content, really, and though she felt somewhat empty, if her life here at Oakhurst continued as it was, she wouldn't mind. But that got her to wondering: Was what she had left behind really so terrible? Did she have family? Friends? Someone who cared about her? Was there someone who depended on her? These were the questions that gnawed at her soul.

Her hand rose to her chest, and she placed it over the amulet that rested beneath her sweatshirt. No one knew about it but Jackie, and she'd just as soon leave it that way. But where it came from and why she possessed it was a bigger mystery than the things she didn't know about herself.

She sighed and rolled over on her side adjusting the blanket as she went. The crickets and night birds serenaded her, and she smiled to herself. It was glorious to be up amongst the treetops, and she decided she would stay there forever. It felt like home, really, but she had no reason why.

Slowly she began to drift off to sleep. There would be no recollections tonight, no breakthroughs or insights into who Shea Remington really was – only peaceful, restful sleep.

A gentle breeze carried the scents of the night through the screens singing a quiet song that whispered the secrets of the garden below. Shea dozed off, unaware as dozens of faeries made their way in to enjoy the peace of the sleeping porch as well. They had slipped easily under the gap at the bottom of the walls that let the air flow through when humans slept on the floor. It somehow managed to keep things nice and cool even on the hottest of summer nights.

To them this night was like any other.

Unbeknownst to Shea, it was the beginning of something magical.

ꕤ ꕤ

Shea spent most of the next morning helping set up for a wedding in the Formal Garden. It was to be a large affair, and the crew was occupied with setting up tables and chairs. Volunteers had been called in as well to help with the preparations, and they all worked busily together.

"Say," she said to GiGi who was offloading chairs from the truck, "do you know anything about a little girl that plays in the garden?"

"Little girl?" GiGi asked, not missing a beat with the chairs.

"Yeah, there's been a little girl playing in the gardens in the evening. I've seen her a few times."

"I don't know," GiGi said, pausing for a moment to take a drink from her water bottle. "Maybe she lives nearby?"

"Could be. She seems to spend a lot of time here."

"Probably one of the neighbors."

ꕤ ꕤ

The late afternoon wedding in the garden was gorgeous. The happy couple celebrated with family and friends in the tent afterward, and a formal dinner and dancing ensued.

Shea stayed on the fringes watching the festivities and the people enjoying themselves. She decided to take a walk to kill time until she had to help tear down.

She hadn't gone very far when she saw the little girl again. She was dressed in a rather fancy dress this time and was without her doll. Shea decided to be a little bolder.

"Well, hello again," she greeted the child cheerily. "How are you?"

"Fine," the girl smiled, looking down at the flowers next to her.

"Are you here for the wedding?"

"Sort of," the girl answered.

"What's your name?"

"Elisabeth."

"Elizabeth – that's a very nice name."

"No, not Elizabeth," the girl corrected her, "*Elisabeth*."

"Oh, begging your pardon," Shea replied, though not sure why.

"I don't like the shape of the Z," Elisabeth explained, with a smile. "It's rather harsh."

"Very well, Elisabeth it is. Are your parents here? At the wedding?"

"Not exactly," Elisabeth said.

"Do you live nearby?"

"I live here."

"Here?" Shea asked, looking around at the garden. "In the garden?"

There was no answer. "How can you –"

She looked back down to find Elisabeth gone.

ꟃ ꟃ

It was a long evening after that. The crew had to tear down and put away everything but the tent. They had finished by eleven pm, and Shea made one last trip around the garden to make sure the gates had been locked. Exhausted, she entered the mudroom of Oakhurst from the courtyard door just beneath her apartment.

She flipped the light switch and took off her shoes, setting them next to the door. She walked through the room to the doorway by the stairs and turned off the light. Two counts later the light was back on, and Shea Remington was once again in the mudroom.

Gazing up at the photos hanging there, Shea's brows knit together in disbelief and amazement. The walls were covered with enlarged photos of the Ball family that had lived in Oakhurst a century before. Looking ever dapper was George A. Ball and his wife, Mrs. Frances Woodworth Ball, and their only child, a little girl. She was dressed in a light-colored dress with dark tights and patent leather Mary Janes, and there was no mistaking the sweet, round face and the Buster Brown haircut of Elisabeth Ball. *The same Elisabeth that Shea had met in the garden!*

Wide-eyed, Shea could only stare at the photos. One after another they all showed the same face, some at different ages, but the same face nonetheless. The girl in the garden looked to be maybe eight or nine years old in Shea's estimation, though she was by no means an expert on children. And yet, there was no mistaking that the girl in the garden was the same girl in the photos.

Chapter 10

Shea could scarcely sleep. Her discovery earlier in the evening, that the little girl frequenting the garden bore such an uncanny resemblance to Elisabeth Ball – the same Elisabeth Ball who had lived in this house a hundred years ago – was just a little disquieting. She didn't have this kind of problem when she was living with Jackie! The worst she had to expect there was maybe a late night drunk stumbling about in the lot below their window at night. Nobody told her the gardens were haunted!

She decided she'd have to have a word with Sam about that one.

Admitting defeat in the sleep department, she got out of bed. A gentle summer breeze came in through the window as she headed out into the hall. Not wanting to do much of anything, she left the apartment heading over into the room across the hall. Pictures of Elisabeth Ball later in life hung on the walls. There was even one of her as an old woman standing with her gardener. *Why would she appear as a child?*

Shea was not fearful, merely unsettled that such a thing was going on, although she couldn't be exactly sure why. This was small potatoes compared to not knowing where she came from or who she was. That gnawed at her soul daily, and she wished desperately she knew how to fix it.

What did she enjoy before? Who was her family? Did she have a family? Where did she come from? All this and more pestered her, nearly to the point where it was difficult to function. She had no clues whatsoever, save the amulet that hung from her neck.

She lifted it out from under the t-shirt she was wearing and ran her thumb across the face of the stone. It was beautiful shades of orange and red with glittering shades of the same that hinted at the secrets it held. It was so radiant it looked as if it bore flames within. Surely this amulet must hold the key to her past. But the question of how to learn more about it seemed daunting at best.

"You have many questions," a small, soft voice said from behind her.

Unlike her encounter with Darius Pendragon in the Collections Library, Shea didn't flinch. At this point, she had almost expected this. She straightened as she tucked the amulet back in her shirt. She wasn't frightened, and really wasn't too surprised.

"Yes," Shea answered, not yet ready to turn around.

Silence hung in the air, and for a moment Shea wondered

if it wasn't simply her imagination running wild. She held her breath, then slowly let it out.

"Are you Elisabeth Ball?" she asked.

"Yes," Elisabeth giggled, at the seemingly obvious question. "I am Elisabeth."

"Why arc you here?"

"Well, this is my home," Elisabeth said plainly. "Where else would I be?"

A fair question, Shea thought, though she had no idea where she expected her to be.

Shea turned around and stood face to face with the version of Elisabeth Ball that was no more than a child of eight or nine years of age. Her face was sweet, though somewhat longer than the photos downstairs, and the Buster Brown haircut had some length to it as well. She wore a light-colored cotton dress with sleeves that poufed out at the tops. Her dark stockings covered her legs and matched her dark shoes.

"Why do you look like that?" Shea asked, unsure of why else than out of utter curiosity.

Elisabeth looked perplexed and tilted her head to the side. "Why do I look like what?"

"Well, like that?" Shea reiterated as she swept her hand up and down the length of the girl before her.

Elisabeth's brows knit together in child-like confusion, somewhat baffled by the question.

"Like a child," Shea finished, gesturing to the photos on the walls. "These pictures here all around, Elisabeth Ball is a grown woman, and here Elisabeth Ball is an old woman. Down the hall and downstairs in the photographs, Elisabeth Ball is a young child, but you did grow up, did you not?"

"Yes, that is me. I did grow up here," Elisabeth reflected fondly as she looked at the photographs around them. "I had a wonderful life here."

"Are you trapped here?" Shea asked her. "What are you? A ghost? An apparition?"

Elisabeth laughed and a smile warmed her face.

"A friend."

ꝏ ꝏ

Shea and Elisabeth sat in the windows of the upstairs room on the front of the house that had been Elisabeth's bedroom. They talked for hours, as Elisabeth told Shea of her life at Oakhurst, her family, and the wonderful, amazing life they all had shared there.

She spoke of her best friend, Emily, whom she had grown up with and had remained lifelong friends to the end. They had played in the gardens of Oakhurst as children and shared many adventures together. And such imaginations! Elisabeth began to speak of the faeries in the garden but stopped herself as if she had a task at hand to finish.

"Oakhurst was such an amazing place to grow up," Elisabeth sighed. "Mother and Father, my aunts and uncles and my cousins were all here along the boulevard, and we had such wonderful times together. We travelled a lot, and even when I went to boarding school it was as if I never really left. Mother and Father always made certain I knew what was going on at home through letters and postcards. Father was such fun!" Elisabeth looked over at the picture on the wall of herself at four years old smiling happily as she hung over her father's back. It was obvious the love shared between father and daughter.

Shea smiled at her, but it faded quickly as she remembered she had no memory of her family. "I wish I could remember my family," Shea sighed. "I'm not even sure I have one."

Elisabeth smiled knowingly. "In due time you will remember."

"Is that why you're here? To help me remember?" For the first time since her arrival, Shea was hopeful.

"In time, you will remember everything," Elisabeth reassured her. "In time you will know your purpose, why you're here. In time, Shea Remington, you will know the truth."

Shea looked out the front window of Oakhurst. The sun was glimmering through the trees as it rose over the high school across the river. It was beautiful, and she felt a sense of peace wash over her, as if, in some sense, she were already home. "I hope you're right," she said.

Shea sat for a moment pondering Elisabeth's words. Perhaps this little girl was the key to her past. She began to ask another question and pulled her eyes from the beautiful sunrise to find that Elisabeth had disappeared.

CHAPTER 11

It had been a long day. Running on hardly any sleep was not high on Shea's list of favorite things to do, but she had made the best of it, doing odd jobs around the Center most of the day. It was well past five o'clock when she headed back down to Oakhurst. A shortcut through the grounds at Maplewood to check the service gate found it locked as it should be, and she let herself in with her key, locking the gate behind her. It would be a couple of hours before the rest of the gates needed to be closed, so she decided to wait it out at the house.

Though relatively short, Aunt Emma's path between Oakhurst and Maplewood was Shea's favorite. If only for a moment, one could imagine being far out in a forest somewhere, miles from the city in which this little botanical gem had been plunked. Oakhurst must have been a truly magical place when Elisabeth was a child and Muncie was much smaller and more rural in nature.

As the path spilled out just short of Oakhurst, something in her peripheral vision caught Shea's attention. Crouching down over by the Carriage House was Elisabeth. She was studying something intently and seemed unaware of Shea's presence. Quietly Shea made her way down the path toward her as she tried to see what had so captured the girl's attention. She was petting something and speaking to it in low tones. It looked to be a hawk, and Shea moved ever closer for a better look.

Suddenly spying her, the hawk startled, its wings spread wide to make it look even bigger than it truly was. From ten feet away Shea couldn't be certain, but it looked as if something was riding on the bird's back. Elisabeth leaned back to give the hawk clearance, reaching out with her hands behind her to keep from landing fully in the grass. The hawk backed up several steps, then took off, flying just over Elisabeth's reclined body. The girl sprang to her feet and turned to watch the bird fly off into the trees. She waved to it, then turned to Shea.

"Hello," she greeted her cheerily. "How was your day?"

"Uh, fine," Shea answered. "What was that?"

"A hawk," Elisabeth answered matter-of-factly.

"Well, I could see that," Shea chided her. "I mean, what was that on its back?"

"A faerie."

Shea stood there just looking at her wondering if Elisabeth was simply pulling her leg. But she knew what she saw, and *something* was riding on that hawk's back.

"Look, I know these folks around here are all into that faerie thing. We've got that festival coming up in a couple of weeks. You know, I've heard the story of how you got out of eating – what was it? Peas at Emily's house for lunch?"

Elisabeth giggled. "Yes, Emily was a little perturbed with me at first, I'm afraid. She said her mother would have never let *her* gotten away with that sort of nonsense." It was apparent the memory was a fond one for Elisabeth. "But there truly was a faerie sitting upon that last bite of peas, and I simply couldn't take her seat away!"

Shea smiled figuring it wouldn't hurt to humor her.

"Emily couldn't see them," Elisabeth said wistfully. "She wanted to, with all her heart she wanted to, but I don't know if she ever did. No matter. We sure played like she could see them!"

"So not everyone can see them?"

"No, not really. Children, mostly, can see them and some adults, but not very many. Those are few and far between."

"But I saw –" Shea was a little flummoxed and a whole lot of confused by this point. Clearly no longer a child, Shea knew what she saw.

Elisabeth began to explain. "Sometimes faeries are reborn in human form," she said. "They are old souls who tend to seek out one another. It is imprinted on their very souls where they came from, and this is why most of them can see faeries. They are creative at heart and never fully lose the child inside of them."

"Like you?"

"Yes, like me," Elisabeth agreed with a smile. "The world is so much more enjoyable to behold when one looks at it through the eyes of a child. Even the tiniest of wonders of everyday life become a small miracle. The flowers in the garden, a nest of baby bunnies secreted away in the tall grass by their mother – even the sunset through the trees – all are miraculous in their own, small way. But when you put them all together, one must wonder how it all works in such harmony."

"Look at you, tiny philosopher!" Shea teased.

"Yes, well, let's just say my soul is much older than my hundred-plus years. I've been around the block a few times."

"How does that work? That whole crossing over thing?" Shea asked.

"There are different ways. Most who cross over are simply born into human form. Some come here through other ways, ways of magic."

"Magic?"

"Some ways are allowed. Other ways – dark methods, really – are there, but they are not spoken of in polite company."

"I see," Shea nodded, somewhat on the skeptical side. She decided to move on to more practical matters. "So how old are you, really?"

Elisabeth looked pensive. "That's rather difficult to say. Time in the human realm is not the same as time in the fae realm. To humans a hundred years is a very long time. To the faeries a hundred human years is a much shorter span of time."

"So they've been around a long time."

"Yes," Elisabeth agreed, "and they age very slowly. Queen Liliana, for example, looks to be what the humans call middle-aged, probably equal to a woman in her early forties. She has a daughter, Verena, who appears to be about your age. But in reality, or what passes as such, they are much older than that. Honestly, the math is staggering."

Shea laughed. "I've discovered that math is not my strong suit either. That's why Molly won't let me work in the gift shop anymore!"

The pair laughed as the sun began to sink through the trees. Shea was feeling at home here, and for the first time since she'd arrived, the past no longer seemed to matter.

"Why are you here, Elisabeth?" she asked.

"Don't you see?" Elisabeth replied as she stood and dusted off her hands. "I've come here because of you."

"Why? What makes me so special?" Shea asked quietly.

Elisabeth smiled. "In time, you will know."

CHAPTER 12

Shea came out of her tiny apartment and locked the door behind her. She had much to do today and was ready to get at it. She felt a sudden wave of unease wash over her and unsure why, she turned around to find Darius watching her from behind an open display case in the gallery across the hall. He held in his hand one of the magic boxes Elisabeth had made decades before. She opened her mouth to caution him about the delicacy of the box, then decided perhaps it was not her place to tell him so.

"Hello," she said instead.

"My apologies," Darius responded, with a smile as he placed the magic box back into the display case and locked it closed again. "I hope I didn't startle you."

"Oh no, not at all," Shea attempted to lie. It wasn't working. "I...was just heading up to the Center."

"Of course, don't let me keep you. I have heard so much about the collection on display here in the house, I wanted to see it for myself."

"Helps to have keys," Shea said, keeping herself between the doorway and the top of the stairs. She would have to keep that in mind.

"GiGi let me in, actually, although I do have keys to the display cases." He paused, sensing her unease. "It must be strange living alone in such a large old house."

Shea shrugged. "It's not so bad," she said, as she slid her keys into her pocket. "I've actually gotten used to it pretty quickly."

"I see," he responded with a nod. "You're not afraid to live here alone?"

Shea stiffened visibly, startled by her own reaction. "I don't scare easily," was her reply.

"No," Darius said, "I'd imagine you don't."

Somewhat unsettled Shea turned and headed down the stairs, checking her door handle again to see that it was properly locked. She was already out in the sunshine before she realized Darius had followed her. His steps quickened, and he caught up to her in no time.

"I must say I have thoroughly enjoyed your parterres around the grounds. They are simply exquisite," he said with a smile, trying yet again to be cordial.

Shea gave him a quizzical look, unsure of what exactly a parterre was. Seeming to sense her question, Darius continued.

"Whoever cares for the flower gardens must be quite knowledgeable of Victorian gardens and such." He smiled at Shea in an attempt to put her at ease. "They are to be commended."

"I'll pass along the good word," she told him. "I'm headed that way anyway. Clair and the others will appreciate it."

"Lovely. I'll walk with you," Darius invited himself along, "if you don't mind."

"Not at all," Shea lied.

The morning sun was warm as she lifted her face and closed her eyes, soaking in its rays.

"How long have you been here?" he asked as they walked along Aunt Emma's path.

"Just a few weeks," she responded.

"I would think that living in a large house such as Oakhurst would be unnerving for a young woman such as yourself."

Shea stopped walking and looked at him, trying to get a sense of exactly what he was getting at. A few paces past her, Darius stopped.

"Oh?"

Darius did not turn around. Instead he inspected the flowers before him.

"I merely meant that, well, someone told me that you have no family nearby. They said you suffered some memory loss?"

Someone said too much, Shea said to herself.

"Some," she countered, "but I am beginning to remember a few things. Flashes, really. Nothing more."

"Pity," he said turning toward her. "I would very much like to know your story."

Shea shifted uncomfortably. "I'm not sure there's much to tell. My guess is, it is a rather short and boring tale."

"Oh, I very much doubt that," Darius said, as he began

walking again. "Often it is the ones who believe they have the least to tell often have the most intriguing stories of all."

Chapter 13

The garden was tranquil and still as the early morning light glistened in the dew on the leaves. Verena loved this time of day best, and took her walks daily amongst the groundcover and flowers meticulously kept by the humans at Oakhurst. Her mother and brother and the rather large group of soldiers accompanying them wouldn't be back for days, so Verena had some time to herself. She hoped she would spend some of it with Royce.

Her mother would never approve; it was evident each time Liliana spoke of Royce's father, King Rogan of Nebosham. There had been a rather small misunderstanding generations ago that had continued through to Liliana and Marco's reign, but it was his disappearance that had cinched it for the queen. To this day she still blamed Rogan for what happened to her beloved king.

Verena had learned a most important lesson the day her father had disappeared: to always trust her instincts. She had felt uneasy that day, and knew something was not right, that something was going to happen – *something bad.* But instead of listening to her inner voice that her father told her to always heed, she dismissed it. The simple act of saying nothing weighed on her still. She had been very young at the time, and the lesson of that single day stuck with her into adulthood.

She trusted those instincts where Royce was concerned and sensed there was no more malice or deceit in his heart than there was in that of his father. However, the queen would hear none of this. If there was one thing that was difficult to do, it was to change the mind of Liliana, Queen of Oakhurst.

Verena decided to take flight and stretched her wings flitting up above the groundcover to get a better view. Landing on a relatively low branch, she was able to see halfway to Nebosham and sat lightly on the leaf, her weight bowing it just slightly.

She could see him in the distance. *Funny prince*, she thought, as she watched him headed toward their usual meeting place. From her perch it was more than obvious – almost comical – that he was searching for her amongst the flowers. She watched him for awhile, and when she could contain it no longer, a giggle bubbled up out of her. Royce stopped and looked around, knowing she was watching him.

"Verena?" he said tentatively.

She giggled again letting him look about a moment longer before putting him out of his misery. She lifted gracefully off of the leaf, flitted along just above the groundcover and lit silently behind Royce.

"Looking for someone?" she asked, startling him.

"Uh, maybe?" Royce teased, pretending to be miffed. "I mean, I thought I was, but now I'm not so sure."

"Oh, well, fine," Verena retorted, acting rather put out. "Guess I'll be on my way." She turned and began to walk away.

"Wait," Royce said, hand up reaching after her.

The warmth in his voice brought her to an abrupt halt and a smile to her face. "Yes?" she said without turning around.

"Okay, I was."

"Well, in that case," she said, turning around and smiling, "I guess I'm glad to see you."

She reached for his hand and greeted him with a kiss as the couple headed toward the Colonnade Garden on the southwest corner of the grounds. It was her favorite place to go, away from Oakhurst and Nebosham, set aside in a special place all its own.

"Mother has returned to Ravensforge," Verena told him as they walked along holding hands.

"Weren't they just there?"

"Yes, Mother took my brother there for a betrothal introduction," Verena said.

"So much for free choice," Royce grumbled.

"It will not be that way with me," Verena vowed. "I will choose whom I marry, or I will not marry at all. The last thing I want is to be part of a political union."

"Well, I can 'bout guarantee your mother would not approve of the kingdoms of Nebosham and Oakhurst being forever bound together by marriage of you to, oh, say.....me."

Verena laughed heartily. “No,” she said, shaking her head and pursing her lips, “no, she definitely would not.”

“Well, that’s too bad,” Royce said. “I suppose I’ll just have to find another.”

Verena smacked him hard on the shoulder. “That’s not even funny.”

“I know. Not funny, but oh so true.”

Verena paused just past the dollhouse armed with her own witty retort when she noticed something unusual. In the distance behind Royce, she saw a glint amongst the greenery along the flagstone edging of the stream. “What is that?” she asked.

“What is what?” Royce echoed, turning to look in the same direction.

“That gleam along the stream. Do you see it?” she asked, as she moved in that direction. Royce started after her trying to keep up. He watched as her wings fluttered anxiously. She reached the flagstones ahead of him and seemed to float across the tiny pond. Shaking his head, Royce made his way around the water feature.

“Sorry,” she said sheepishly, “I keep forgetting.”

“That’s okay,” he said, slightly out of breath. “I’m getting used to it.” He grinned at her as he looked toward the object. Just beyond her sat a beautiful gold box. It was handmade out of golden paper with golden matte swirls winding their way around the box. It was tied up neatly with a beautiful golden bow that sparkled in the sunlight.

Verena walked out from beneath the leaves and looked around making certain she was not being watched. The beautiful golden box stood before her, nearly half as tall as she, and she circled around it holding her hand just above it while closing her eyes, feeling the magic within. It was always a good thing to find one of Miss Elisabeth's magic boxes in the garden, and she relished it each time.

But this one was different. It had an odd feel to it, an energy that was somewhat out of balance. True, it was one of Elisabeth's boxes. Verena could tell by the folds near the base.

"What is that?" Royce asked.

"A magical box," Verena informed him, as she walked around it examining it. "Mother used to tell us stories about how Miss Elisabeth would leave them in the gardens. She would use them to request an audience with my mother and father."

"Miss Elisabeth?"

"A human who lived here long ago."

"But I thought humans couldn't see us," Royce said as he looked the box over.

"Usually they can't, but some can. Mostly old souls or fae who have chosen to become humans or are reborn in human form. All in all they are rare, and she became a guardian of sorts to our kingdom." Verena reached up to untie the bow. A short distance away, her hand stopped.

Royce looked at her face. Her expression was mixed with confusion and uncertainty, something he'd rarely seen in her. "Something wrong?" he asked.

"I'm...not sure," she said, withdrawing her hand for a moment. "Something is...off, maybe?"

"Off?"

"Yes," she replied, as she continued to study the box. "There is magic in there...I can sense that. But it's different."

"How so?"

"It's hard to explain," she said, as she turned to him. "There's light magic, and then there's dark magic. This feels somewhere in-between. Not totally light, but not quite completely dark either."

"Well, maybe we should take it back to the palace?" Royce offered.

"What if it's a trap of sorts?"

"Then that would be bad."

The decision to open it was not taken lightly, and Verena held her breath as she pulled the ribbon slowly untying the ribbon on top of the magic box. First one loop, then the other until it was just the ribbon around the box that held the lid on. She slipped it off the box letting the ends drop to the ground. She looked at Royce for reassurance then lifted the lid off the box.

Nothing happened.

Royce shrugged, and Verena leaned closer to peer inside the box. The box appeared empty but only for a moment. A black vapor rose slowly toward her. Startled she backed off, not sure what she was getting into. She quickly retreated and lit behind Royce, the pair watching as the vapor wafted up from the box.

Verena felt a shiver run through to her very core as she watched it appear to climb over the top edge of the box and drift down along the outer wall of the box to the ground. It coasted to the nearest tree then went vertical, rising swiftly up the side of the trunk, moving more like an animal than mist.

"What was that?" Royce asked, concern etched on his face.

"I do not know," Verena whispered, "but I have a bad feeling about this."

"Should we tell your mother, perhaps? Or my father?" Royce was running out of ideas. "Or at the very least, Arland when they return. He will surely offer you words of counsel."

"Or *he* will tell my mother," Verena sighed.

The Portal of the Realm

Chapter 14

It was just before sun up when Connor and Caeden left the camp. They crept along in silence until they were well out of earshot of Arland and the guards.

"I do not see why we did not bring along a detachment," Caeden said matter-of-factly. "It would have been wise to do so."

"To *do* so would have made the queen unhappy," Connor reminded him. "Besides, if we are successful, we won't need a detachment."

"How far is it?' Caeden asked.

"Tired already?" Connor teased him.

"Merely curious. I'm just wondering how long I have left before the queen lops off my head."

Connor laughed. "I think we may have more to fear if Arland gets ahold of us before the queen does."

He thought back to his childhood. Though Arland had not taken the place of his father, Connor often regarded him as such.

He had taken Connor under his wing at an early age teaching him everything he knew about defending himself. From stealthy pursuit to hand-to-hand combat to full on battle tactics, Arland made sure he got a well-rounded education in the art of war. They sparred often, and Connor was grateful to have his counsel.

"One day you will do great things," Arland told him, as they battled back and forth in the garden recently, sword blades clanking as they talked. Arland said it would build his strength and stamina to be able to converse while fighting, and some of their most insightful conversations came from these matches.

"Do you think that tying Oakhurst to Ravensforge is wise?" Connor asked him, advancing his position.

"It is not my decision to question," Arland responded, pushing back at the younger man while moving forward. His blade flashed more quickly, and Connor had to work to defend his position. Unable to do so, he retreated behind a sapling to catch his breath. Arland chuckled and stood down. "The queen has her reasons, and mine is not to question them."

"Yes," Connor said, leaning against the sapling, "but if it were yours to question, what would your response be?"

Arland, never one to let his guard down with anyone, waited. "But it is not; therefore, to do so is merely a waste of time."

With that he came at the young man with his sword again. Connor dodged him rather awkwardly and nearly took a tumble trying to escape. Sword at the ready, he came at Arland, and the sparring began again.

"What do you think, Connor?"

"I am not sure," he said between breaths. They had been at it for a while now, and he was quite certain he'd learned enough for one day. "There is much responsibility involved, is there not?"

"In joining the two kingdoms? Most assuredly," Arland replied, advancing on Connor again, "although there are benefits to it. Power and security are the two that come to mind."

"With you, of course," Connor laughed, as he jumped up onto a stone trying to get an advantage on his mentor. He shored up his stance and waited, but not for long.

What happened next caught Connor completely off guard. In one fluid motion the teacher reached down, grabbed a stick and spun fluidly around, striking the young man behind the knees. By the time Connor hit the ground, Arland's sword was back in its sheath and he was standing over Connor trying hard not to laugh. He was failing miserably.

"Power and security are my life," Arland laughed, as he offered Connor a hand. "There are no other options."

Connor accepted the proffered hand and rose quickly off the ground. Dusting himself off, he placed his sword in its sheath and looked at Arland in awe of all that he knew.

He owed much to his mentor and knew that his disobedience to the queen would not be taken lightly by Arland. He would be disappointed, of that Connor was quite certain. The last thing he wanted to do was disappoint him.

But what choice was there? Arland had also taught him

critical thinking, and that sometimes the answers were farther outside the box than most were willing to go. Connor knew one thing was true: he and Caeden were almost as far outside of the box as they could get.

ꟷ

The prince and his guardian made their way along the tree line as night fell. They had journeyed the entire day, and though it had been a rather arduous excursion, Connor felt it would pay off. Young Caeden had kept up well over the course of the day, but Connor sensed he was tired. "Not much longer," he tried to reassure him.

"Connor," Caeden said as he walked along behind, "I think there's someone following us."

"There is," Connor answered back. "Been there most of the day."

"Really?" Caeden asked, sounding somewhat concerned, just short of panicked.

"Guard," Connor reassured him. "Been there nearly all day."

"Our Guard? *Really?"* Caeden looked behind them quickening his pace a bit. "Why would they follow us?"

"The queen does not approve," Connor reminded him. "There'll be hell to pay."

"True," Caeden admitted with a nod.

"But they will prove useful here shortly."

"Why?"

"Because," Connor told him, "where I am going – if I am successful – you cannot follow."

"But, my –"

"Aht!" Connor stopped him putting his hand up. "There'll be no arguing."

"But –"

"*Shhh….*" Connor placed a finger to his lips. Before them was the mouth of a cavern. Firelight flickered against the walls providing just enough light that the two young men could see one another better. "You must follow my lead. Do not speak unless I address you. Do you understand?"

Caeden nodded silently. Connor gave one last look over his shoulder then stepped into the mouth of the cave.

CHAPTER 15

Slowly Connor and Caeden made their way into the cave. The firelight danced on the walls in the distance, and they crept along the passageway in silence until they reached the room where the fire burned brightly. Sitting with his back to them was the troll Connor was seeking.

"Come in, fae prince," the troll said, in a voice most gravelly. "I have been expecting you."

Connor looked at Caeden. "Let me handle this," he whispered. Hand on his sword, he approached the troll. "I have come –"

"I know why you are here," he interrupted Connor, raising his hand to silence the young man. The troll glanced his way looking him up and down. He was a hideous creature and wore a patch over one eye. His face was scarred and his hair wild, and he looked and smelled as though he'd been used as a dog's toy.

"Sit," he invited them.

"We don't plan on staying that long," Connor answered for them.

"Suit yourself," the troll said, minding the fire before him. "What is it you want?"

Connor laughed. "I thought you knew."

"Well, that just takes all the fun out of the *game* now, doesn't it, *Connor?*" The troll looked up at him again staring at him with the one eye. "What is it you seek? Your heart's desire, perhaps?"

"That is no concern of yours, troll. I seek those who went through the portal last – before it was destroyed."

"Friends of yours?"

"Not necessarily," Connor replied, trying not to give away too much of what he had planned.

"It is complicated," the troll said, going back to tending his fire.

"How so?"

The troll chuckled, his shoulders shaking a bit beneath his scraggly, furry coat. "The intent was to arrive in one place. The outcome, however, did not go as planned."

"Oh?" Connor inquired, trying to act nonchalant.

"The *Nasties* followed them," the troll said, his voice dripping with contempt.

"The Nasties?" Connor wasn't sure he wanted to know.

"Minions of the Dark Warrior of Erebos."

"Apparently he didn't want to get his hands dirty."

"Apparently not," the troll agreed.

"Can you tell me where they went?"

"I will need to touch the portal."

"Will this do?" Connor asked, as he retrieved the broken off piece of the portal from his pack. "We're kind of in a hurry."

In the distance he could hear voiccs just beyond the mouth of the cave. He nodded to Caeden who went back down the corridor.

"I don't have much time," Connor urged the troll. "If you please..." He handed him the stone that had broken off the portal. It was charred but still glistened like diamonds beneath the carbon coating.

The troll took the stone, rolling it over in his hands. With the tail of his ratty shirt he polished the black off the top of it until it shone. Wrapping his hands around it he closed his eye.

"There were three of them," the troll said.

"Yes," Connor said.

"Those you seek were split up. Two made it where they intended, the third did not."

"Which two? Where did they go?"

"I cannot be certain," the troll replied, sounding a little put out.

"Can you send me there?"

"I cannot guarantee where you will end up."

Caeden came sprinting back down the cavern pulling up short at the mouth of the chamber. "The Guard is near," he told Connor, still out of breath.

Connor turned back to the troll. "I'm, uh, kind of in a hurry,"

"Of course, of course," the troll said, not moving any

faster than before. "I'll need something in return," he croaked, looking Connor up and down again. "Something of – value." His one decent eye came to rest on the sword on Connor's hip.

Connor's hand instinctively went to the weapon. Knowing the true worth of the sword, his stomach turned. It was a rare item, a gift. Forged in the fires of Ravensforge and blessed by the king himself, it was a truly remarkable piece, not just for its craftsmanship but what it represented. Perfectly balanced yet light to the touch, its blade was unmatched, and its artistic presentation breathtaking.

"But –" Caeden protested.

"That is my price," the troll stated, as he tossed the stone back at Connor. "Take it or leave it."

Connor reached up with one hand and snatched the stone out of the air. Voices came from just outside the cavern and he knew he'd run out of time.

"The Guard," Caeden said quietly, as the panic rose in his voice.

Connor looked back down the passageway, the footfalls drawing nearer.

"Your answer?"

Connor turned to the troll.

"Done."

ഌ ര

Arland led the guard into the cavern. He could hear voices, and there would be hell to pay, of that he was certain. But if he did not return with his objective, the queen would have his head for sure. With ten fae warriors behind him, they pressed onward. He knew they would hear them coming but hoped that might make it sound like there were more of them than there really were. He had not been able to spare any more men than this, and the queen was insistent that he lead this detachment personally. She was not worried about her own safety – never was, really. That was his job. Her main concern was that her son was returned safely to her side. She would deal with this lark of his later.

Rounding the final bend he could see firelight in a room ahead. He raised his hand and the troops slowed, their steps more measured and quiet. In his final steps to the doorway he could see the fire clearly, and a hooded figure in a plain traveling cloak warming himself by the fire. He recognized the prince's cloak instantly and was relieved that they had found him relatively unharmed.

"Your Majesty," Arland said with a sigh of relief. "Your mother was worried."

The cloaked figure reached up to remove the hood. Arland's look of relief turned to one of disgust and plain old pissed off in half a heartbeat.

"Well, that tears it. She'll have both our heads."

ꝏ ꝏ

Out under the stars Connor followed the troll into the glade. It was beautiful here, and a small waterfall came out of the stone outcropping just twenty feet above them, the water tumbling into the waiting pool below. Connor hoped they had lost Arland and the Guard, because they wouldn't be able to hear them coming even if they wanted to.

"Give me the stone," croaked the troll, holding out his hand.

Connor obliged him, saying nothing. The troll placed the newly polished stone, no bigger than his fist, on the boulder before them and held out his hand. "The sword, if you please."

Connor sighed heavily, and the trade weighed on him. He knew he had to do this, but he was also painfully aware of the full cost of what he was about to do. The long and short of it was that, if he went through this way, chances were good he would never be able to return to his homeland. Dark magic was nothing to be trifled with, and one often paid a heavy price for making use of it, even with the best of intentions.

Silently, he unsheathed the sword and handed it over to the troll.

"Now," said the troll, "step into the pool."

The troll had caught him off guard. "What?"

"Step into the pool," the troll repeated, a little impatiently this time.

"But I –"

The troll cocked his head and stared at Connor with his one good eye. Frustrated, he rolled it back into his head and groaned. "Really, I don't have all night."

Uncertain of whether it was a good idea or not, Connor followed his instructions. The water was cold, and Connor took in a sharp breath as he waded out to his waist. He looked back at the troll.

"A little further," the troll instructed him. "Just a few more steps."

The cold water was beginning to take its toll, and Connor was starting to feel as though he'd been had. He shivered and took two more steps out. He could feel the cool spray of the falls as it hit the surface of the pond sending ripples his way.

"And...*stop.*"

Connor turned just in time to see the troll raise the Sword of Nobility above his head. With a horrific scream the troll brought the flat side of the blade down soundly atop the shard from the portal. Sparks flew and light filled the night sky as a burst of energy filled the air. The water around him began to swirl, and the light found its way up from the growing whirlpool twisting its way through the water toward Connor.

He could feel the current tug at his legs, and the water, now up near his armpits, drew him forward. He tried to fight it, but the pull was too strong. He turned in an attempt to make it back to the shore, but the stones beneath his feet were slick, and he couldn't get any traction.

The last thing Connor saw was the troll waving to him, sword in hand. He managed to suck in a deep breath, hoping it wouldn't be his last.

In a flash, Connor was gone.

Chapter 16

"My parents traveled frequently," Elisabeth began as she continued to poke at the rocks in the tiny stream with a stick. Shea settled in next to her on the ground, as this promised to be another lengthy tale, which she didn't mind. At least Elisabeth knew where *she* came from.

"During one trip to Europe Father found the most beautiful earrings and bought them for Mother. They were fire opals and very rare for the region in which they were traveling: Great Britain, Ireland, the British Isles."

"They were beautiful earrings, but it was the story that went with them that so captured Mother's imagination and secured their purchase. The jeweler told them that the stones had been found in the shallows of the river by a shepherd who took them into town to the local pub owner and traded them for a week's worth of ale."

Shea raised her eyebrows but said nothing.

"The shepherd didn't know their true worth, and the pub keeper, in turn, sold them to the jeweler for a rather handsome sum."

Elisabeth stopped, a smile crossing her face as she remembered. "Father used to love to tell that story every time Mother wore them."

"One day my friend Emily and I were playing dress up and we borrowed the earrings from Mother's jewel box. I had forgotten to take them off that day. Later, after Emily had gone home, I went into the gardens to play and the princess was there. She seemed most interested in the earrings, especially the story of where the stones had come from. Her guard suggested that I share the tale with Queen Liliana, and I did. King Rogan of Nebosham was with her at the time, so I gave each of them one of the earrings, mostly so they wouldn't fight."

"Do they do that often?" Shea asked, as she pulled her knees up to her chest.

"Yes, but most of the time they don't really mean it."

"So where are the earrings now?" Shea asked.

"The stones are revered as sacred relics in the Kingdoms of Oakhurst and Nebosham. I couldn't just hand them over, so I made little magic boxes, one for each of the kingdoms, and placed an earring in each box." Elisabeth was beaming as she remembered that day. "I left the boxes where Queen Liliana and King Rogan would find them. They were most pleased."

"What did they do with the stones?" Shea asked.

"Each ruler placed them in a temple of sorts in their palaces. They are revered and apparently have some deeper purpose than just decoration." Elisabeth seemed pleased. "The fae have a penchant for found *objects d'arte* and these, it appears, are the cream of the crop."

ꟹ ꟹ

Exhaustion and a growing sense of grief weighed on Queen Liliana as she sat upon a rock watching the sun set through the trees just beyond the cabin. The trip from Ravensforge had been arduous, and the fact that her son was missing only added to her worries.

Arland was with her keeping watch as always. He was most protective, and Liliana appreciated his efforts though she longed for the days when she was free to go about the gardens as she saw fit. But things were different now and had been for quite some time. A darkness had come to the garden, and though she could not see it, Liliana could sense it. And worse, her daughter, Verena, could see it when no one else could.

Verena was gifted with discernment and had the ability to sense good and evil in everyone. This was quite valuable when dealing with other kingdoms, but somewhat bothersome when trying to lead a normal life.

It was one thing to avoid birds, cats, and other predatory creatures in the garden. But what was coming was something far worse than any creature the fae realm had ever seen.

She hoped to find some sense of peace once her son returned home. Until then, she would not rest well.

"Your Highness," Arland said quietly from just behind her. "We really should be going."

Queen Liliana sighed. "Just a moment longer."

Chapter 17

Just a few weeks into her stay at Oakhurst, Shea felt comfortable in the big, old house. Almost at home, really. Though it was a bit much for just one person and didn't serve as a home so much as a museum in its own right, it provided her with a quiet haven to retreat to after a long day's work. For that, she was grateful.

It was early evening, and she sat on the back screened-in porch of Oakhurst. Although the Indiana air was thick, the breeze through the trees was just enough to make it bearable without air conditioning. Shea enjoyed spending time in the "secret room," and she often sat and read books she'd borrowed from the library several blocks away. It was a good escape, and she found it entertaining.

She felt as if she was being watched for a good while now and tried to shake the feeling but found she could no longer ignore it. Without moving a muscle her eyes peeked over the top of the book scanning the woods in the growing twilight just beyond the screened-in porch. After a few moments of watching that went unrewarded, she returned to the book.

There it was again.

She just couldn't shake the feeling, and yet, though she saw nothing, she *knew* someone was there.

Slowly, she put the book down and walked to the back door of the porch, letting herself out into the garden. Around her the birds sang their final song of the evening and for a moment, Shea felt silly. She knew Elisabeth frequented the gardens at this hour but wasn't exclusive to them or predictable.

"Hello?" she said quietly. "Elisabeth? Are you there?"

Nothing.

"Hello?" she called again, a little louder.

She crossed the footbridge over the tiny stream behind the house and walked along the flagstone edge of the water feature as she moved off the path. The humid twilight was rife with mosquitoes, and Shea smacked one on her arm as it bit her.

Heading toward the dollhouse, she went around the fence and for a moment thought about heading back to the house.

"This is silly," she muttered.

Suddenly a red-tailed hawk came up out of the weeds just two steps ahead of her and flew straight up into Shea's face. Startled, she screamed and flung herself backward to avoid the bird as it veered sharply and headed skyward. She lay on the ground for a moment getting her bearings.

Again, she felt as if she was being watched. Though she couldn't remember her past, she knew one thing for sure: this made her very uneasy, and her instincts told her to pursue it. Shea was ready to get up when she heard something off to her right – *breathing*. It was shallow and quick, trying desperately to hide from her, and she knew it.

Shea turned her head and found herself face to face with a faerie hidden away in the underbrush. She was a tiny little thing and incredibly beautiful. Her dress was a pale blue and her translucent wings shimmered as they fluttered nervously.

"Hello," Shea said softly, in an attempt not to scare her away.

"Hello," the little fae replied.

The ground was hard under Shea's back, and she rolled over on her side, putting her hand under head. "A friend of Elisabeth's, I presume?" she inquired.

"Yes," the fae answered, taken somewhat aback. "How do you know of her?"

"We visit frequently in the gardens. Actually, we've become friends."

"Humans don't see us often," the fae said.

"I'd imagine not. Unless they spend a lot of time on the ground," Shea said. There was a sense of wonder about her as she realized she was speaking to a real, live faerie. It was one thing to have a little girl talking about them and telling you they're real, but to actually *see* one...well, it was really something.

"Should you really be out here this time of night?" Shea

asked a little concerned. “That hawk would have made quick work of you. About two bites and you’d be gone.”

The faerie winced a bit, then chuckled. “Oh, I don’t have to worry about him. Besides –”

A sudden snap of a twig nearby silenced the faerie, grabbing her attention. Turning back to the human she said, “I don’t have to worry about him.”

“I’m Shea,” the human introduced herself.

“I am Verena,” the small faerie responded in kind, “Princess of Oakhurst.”

“A princess? Out here? *Alone?*” Shea wasn’t sure why but that bothered her. On some level she instinctively knew it was inappropriate and very wrong. “It is dangerous out here for one so small, is it not?”

“I am not alone,” Princess Verena replied. “Besides, I am on business by order of Queen Liliana of Oakhurst.”

“I’ve heard of her,” Shea said. “Elisabeth speaks fondly of her.”

Verena nodded knowingly as she stepped out from under the leaves. “Then perhaps you are to be trusted.”

Still lying on her side, Shea shrugged. “I wouldn’t see why not.”

“Then you may have my trust until you prove otherwise.”

“I do not think that advisable Your Highness,” came a male voice from further behind the leaves where Verena had been secreted away.

Seeming somewhat annoyed, Verena looked to where the voice had originated. Apparently her ruse of being alone was no more.

“Begging your pardon,” the guard apologized, stepping

back away from the princess.

"You are not alone," Shea observed, raising an eyebrow. "Probably a good thing. I've seen a cat skulking around here on several occasions."

"Flight is always an option," Verena indicated.

"Of course. But still, two of you alone against the world…and a hawk?" Shea pointed out, glancing around in the twilight. I think I'd rather take my chances with a busload full of school children instead of a hawk or a cat if I were you. At least they wouldn't eat me."

"The hawk is of no concern," Verena said pointedly. "And it is certainly no concern of yours."

"Suit yourself," Shea said, as she finally rose from the ground. She brushed the dry leaves off her shorts then squatted back down to nearly Verena's level. "Still, I'd not linger long."

Verena watched her in silence as the human headed back toward the house.

"Highness, I –" the guard began.

Verena put her hand up to silence him. "She is no concern at this point."

"Yes, but –"

A harsh glance from Verena put him in his place and at last the guard was silent. "What have we to fear?" she asked, not expecting an answer as she looked up into the trees above. There, hundreds of fae warriors stood at the ready to protect Verena should the need arise.

She had never for a moment been alone.

Chapter 18

Elisabeth was silent for a moment. Shea watched her as the child knelt and placed the magic box on the ground before her, tucking it gently beneath a small stand of Lily of the Valley. It was still rather early on a Saturday morning, and the cool breeze felt good. Shea had yet to open the gates and was really in no hurry to do so.

"What's inside?" Shea whispered.

"A request for an audience," Elisabeth answered matter-of-factly. "One does not simply drop in on the queen of Oakhurst unannounced."

"Oh?"

Elisabeth *tsked* and rolled her eyes as if Shea should already know the answer. "It's rude."

"Oh, right," Shea responded with a mischievous grin.

"Formal little folk, aren't they?"

"Don't call them little. They don't take kindly to that." Elisabeth stood and scanned the garden. The stream gurgled softly as it flowed through the back yard of the house.

"Lucy calls it 'hundred year old magic,'" Shea told her.

Elisabeth smiled. "Actually, it's much older than that."

She took a step back, turned around three times and whispered something as she stopped. She smiled and opened her eyes.

"Now what?" Shea asked.

"We wait."

ꕤ ꕤ

"To what do I owe the pleasure, Miss Elisabeth?" the queen asked as she welcomed her audience of two. She sat upon a beautiful throne made of found human objects that was nearly twice her size. She was surrounded by several other fae, most notable being Princess Verena to her right and an armed guard to her left. The guard stood at the ready, his hand on his sword, his eyes never once moving from Shea.

"Your Highness, I thank you for the opportunity to speak with you. It is, as always," Elisabeth said with a curtsy and a nudge to the ribs prompting Shea to do the same, "a great honor."

Shea glanced over at Elisabeth trying to ignore the not-so-subtle jab and followed suit, curtsying and lowering her head while still keeping her eyes on the guard watching her.

"I see you have brought a guest," Queen Liliana said.

"Yes, Your Highness. This is Shea Remington. She is new in Oakhurst. She now lives in my home as its caretaker."

"A very noble cause, caring for the home of our dear friend, Elisabeth," Queen Liliana nodded in approval. "My daughter tells me you frequent the gardens daily, and that your soul appears to be of good character."

"My soul?" Shea repeated, not sure where the queen was headed with this.

"Verena has the gift of discernment. She can tell when people are good and just, and she can tell when they are lying and deceitful."

"I have nothing to hide, Highness," Shea offered. "I know nothing of my past beyond my arrival in this place. I have been fortunate enough to be taken in by kind people who saw my need and gave me a station, a purpose." She sighed, wistful that she remembered nothing.

"It troubles you, not knowing where you came from?"

"Yes," Shea replied.

Queen Liliana studied the young woman's face for a long moment saying nothing. Finally, she spoke. "You are welcome in the Kingdom of Oakhurst, Shea of Remington, for as long as you choose to stay."

"Thank you, Your Majesty," Shea replied.

"Highness," Elisabeth spoke up, "there is a matter that needs your attention."

"And that would be…."

"I spoke yesterday with Fraelin of Hawksgate. He told of the devastation of the kingdom to the north." Elisabeth looked at Shea again before she spoke. "Those missing are still unaccounted for. All that remain are a few stragglers who managed to escape. The rest are feared dead."

"I am aware of the situation," the queen replied calmly.

"We returned from there only a few days ago. It was devastating." Liliana looked away, regaining her composure as if wanting to say more. After a moment's pause, Elisabeth spoke up.

"I am so sorry, Highness," she said quietly.

"I fear this is only the beginning of worse things to come. Sources from other kingdoms tell me that there is a growing threat, one that has lay silent for generations." The queen sighed heavily, looking up at Elisabeth.

Elisabeth looked to Shea as she gave her reply.

"I fear you are right."

ഋ ଓ

Dark magic had been forbidden in the fae realm for eons. It could blacken even the purest of hearts. It turned brother against brother. And worst of all, it was what made the kingdom of Erebos so dangerous.

Castle Nebosham was dark, and though the guards made their usual rounds, the intruder was not intimidated, nor fearful of capture for the simple fact that he had been indoctrinated in the practice of dark magic. It was simple, really, this elemental mind trick of *tromp l'oeil* which allowed him to simply walk past those who sought to keep those like him out. This would be easier than he thought!

Staying close to the gilded walls, the intruder silently made his way along, heading toward the Altar of Flame. All it would take was the capture of this one holy relic to send the King of Nebosham on a downward spiral taking his precious kingdom with him. And soon after, the Kingdom of Oakhurst would fall as well.

It was only a matter of time.

And then they would find the hidden Kingdom of Hawksgate soon enough.

But that would have to wait for now. Concentrating on the task at hand, the thief looked around. Finding himself alone in the corridor, he slowly opened the heavy double wooden doors to the reliquary and let himself in. Guards standing on either side of the sacred relic looked at one another, obviously perplexed that the doors had opened yet no one was there.

"Who is there?" one of them called out, reaching for his sword.

The second guard followed his lead pulling his sword from its sheath. Both stood at the ready, seemingly prepared to defend their charge.

It was too easy, really. The thief nearly laughed as he stepped well clear of the guards and moved in close behind the altar placed in the center of the room. The relic, a brilliant orange-red stone that glowed as though a fire burned within, was his for the taking. It was framed by three large diamonds going up the right side of it and nearly the size of a full grown faerie's head. The stones sparkled brilliantly in the firelight of the temple.

Slowly, carefully – way too easily – the thief removed his cloak and covered the relic with it. The fire inside it immediately went out. The guards were preoccupied with trying to figure out how the doors had opened moments ago, and he almost laughed at their stupidity.

Maintaining his concentration the thief gathered up the relic and moved over to the wall and waited. Silently he eased along the wall moving ever closer to the doors. The guards, looking out into the corridor and seeing no one, returned to the temple chamber to find the relic missing.

Not one to waste an opportunity, the thief slipped out the doorway as the guards called for help. There would be hell to pay, of that there was no doubt, as the thief ran out of the palace into the night.

Sprites are such simple creatures, the thief thought – *easily fooled and easily riled, the theft of the relic was only the beginning.* The more difficult task lay ahead: obtaining its mate. The Sacred Relic of Oakhurst was a mirror twin of the Sacred Relic of Nebosham. The three diamonds climbed up the left side of it, sparkling no less brilliantly than that of Nebosham. Elisabeth had said that each was a complement of the other, a perfect match that bonded the two kingdoms together so that there would peace and harmony throughout the eons.

However, the thief had one thing to his advantage at Oakhurst – easy access to the temple itself. Dark magic would not be necessary there, nor would it be possible with Princess Verena's gift of discernment. Not only could she spot a liar a mile away, she could sense darkened souls, and it was all the thief could do to keep up the façade of goodness and light.

But not for long.

Little more than a fortnight and it would all be over. Little more than a fortnight was all it would take to bring the royals of Oakhurst and Nebosham to their knees. Little more than a fortnight was all the humans had left before their own realm would be thrown into chaos.

And that, the thief reasoned, *would be worth the wait.*

Chapter 19

In the quiet of early morning Queen Liliana sat cross-legged on Elisabeth's knee in the backyard garden of Oakhurst. The girl had made herself comfortable on the ground near the tiny stream as was their custom. They were old friends, really, and Elisabeth cherished times like this with her. But today was different. Liliana was troubled beyond anything Elisabeth had ever seen before, and she hoped they would be able to figure it all out.

"Truly, I could scarcely believe my eyes," Queen Liliana began softly. She shook her head trying to make sense of it all "There was destruction like I have never witnessed nor ever wish to again. King Beltran and his family are missing," she sighed heavily, "and so is my son."

"I'm sure he will be all right," Elisabeth tried to reassure her. "He does have a bit of an adventurous heart, as you well know."

"I'm afraid I do not have the luxury of worry today," the queen told her. "Whoever destroyed the palace at Ravensforge is after bigger things than the fae realm."

"Oh?"

"There is a portal through which faeries and other such woodland folk can cross over to the human realm. The mortal portal allows fae to pass back and forth between realms. Some become human and choose to stay. Most travel over, accomplish what they need to do, and then return. Their lives are longer and richer in the fae realm, but some are drawn to the human life and stay. For them, their lives play out as it would in our realm, and they are none the wiser. But the fact of the matter is time is different on the other side of the portal. While years pass by quickly, it is merely days and months to the fae."

"But why would anyone want to give that up?" Elisabeth asked. "I mean, I've lived life as a human and know that they do not want to die. They try to prolong life as long as possible. But I also know that it is possible to live a full and rewarding life as a human." She smiled at the thought, remembering many great times with her parents and extended family on the grounds of what was now Minnetrista.

"The Council of Royals decided long ago that the Portals of the Realm must be hidden so as to prevent what I fear may be about to happen. Four generations ago they decided that it posed a grave danger to have the portals open to just anyone, so they hid them. This would prevent travel to the human realm, where one might wreak havoc and destruction on a fae kingdom with the intention to return to pick up the pieces."

"That would tip the balance of power greatly," Elisabeth agreed with a sigh.

"And would be disastrous for all."

"Who knows their whereabouts?"

"Only the royals, and that knowledge is entrusted to a select few of the elite Guard, who are sworn protectors of the royals. It is passed down from generation to generation as a safeguard for both the fae and human realms. Most fae know it only as a human tale, a bedtime story for children, full of wild and fantastical stories of the magical world of human life."

Elisabeth laughed. "Humans would say the same of faeries."

"Those in the outer kingdoms have never seen a human, and one would be hard pressed to convince them of their existence. The fae of Oakhurst and the sprites of Nebosham have lived with the presence of humans for generations as you well know," Liliana said. "But the common fae of Ravensforge, and to a greater extent those of Hawksgate, know little or nothing about humans, much less harbor any belief in them."

"When we last met, King Beltran told me of rumblings throughout the region that the Dark Palace of Erebos was rising to power again."

"Erebos?" Elisabeth asked, unfamiliar with the name.

"Long ago there was a great and mighty king who ruled with compassion for all. His was a peaceable kingdom, one any ruler would envy. Their resources were plentiful, their people loving and open to all. But a rising evil began to creep in, and it was the king's closest advisor himself who led the final assault on the kingdom, throwing it into darkness and all manner of chaos."

"How awful!" Elisabeth exclaimed. "What happened?"

Liliana continued. "Legend has it that a wizard enticed the advisor, a warrior in the king's guard, promising him great power, even greater than that of the king if he would join forces with him. The wizard taught him dark magic that would make him immortal and give him control over dragons and other creatures of chaos."

"That sounds bad."

Liliana chuckled at the understatement. "In our world, it is bad. In the human world, it is worse than bad."

"Why?'

The queen paused for a moment gathering her thoughts. "Each realm is separate yet connected. The fae realm is contained within the human realm much like the gardens of Oakhurst are contained within the city around it. There is a big iron fence with gates than can be opened and closed to contain it, keep it separate. If damage is done to the gardens, the city remains. But if the city is destroyed, so the garden will be also."

"That would be dreadful," Elisabeth said somberly as she considered the analogy.

"Truly it is," Liliana agreed. "Those creatures of chaos are allowed into the human realm from time to time in order to stir the pot, so to speak, testing the waters to see if the time is right for the Dark Warrior to strike. He has been biding his time, lo these many generations, and I fear the time is right for him to unleash his power on the human realm."

"How do we recognize him?"

"No one knows for certain what he looks like, only that he is scarred from battle with the dragon in which he broke its will. He controls it and all others like it."

Elisabeth shifted slightly, and Liliana rose and flitted gracefully to a stone nearby. Her tiara shone brilliantly in the sunlight as she again settled in. Elisabeth leaned in, speaking softly. "And what of the wizard?"

"No one knows for certain. Some say he was betrayed by the Dark Warrior, whose hunger for power caused him to destroy the wizard. Others say he is biding his time, waiting for the opportunity to reappear and join forces with the Dark Warrior. One can only hope it is not the latter."

"What has kept the Dark Warrior from coming through the mortal portal and destroying the kingdoms? Surely he knows the whereabouts of the portals by now?"

"Legend has it that the king withstood great torture at the hands of the Dark Warrior and took the location of the portals to his grave."

Speechless, Elisabeth sighed.

"Though there are many sacred relics in the fae realm, three are key to gaining the power necessary to control the human realm. The wizard is said to have had one, the Dragon's Staff, one with an ornate headpiece that is believed to have power over the dragons and minions of the realm. Those minions are as dangerous as any dragon and can overrun a kingdom in no time." Liliana looked out across the tiny, peaceful woodland behind them. "I fear that is what was unleashed upon Ravensforge."

"King Beltran shared with me that he held one of the pieces the Dark Warrior seeks. I believe that is what led to the destruction of Ravensforge."

Queen Liliana sighed heavily. "It is said that the Dark Warrior, when he possesses all of the Relics of the Dragon's Triad, will have the power to become a dragon himself. Instead of being a beast who serves, he will become powerful beyond measure. He will still retain all the knowledge and power he has now."

She paused, looking across the gardens. "If that happens, nothing can stop him."

ଃ ଂ

In the pre-dawn light, the human knelt, accepting a small package from the fae thief. Though they exchanged few words, the human seemed pleased at his acquisition and paid the fae handsomely. Trinkets, really, nothing more. But the value of what he had acquired was far more valuable than anything he'd had to pay.

Not much longer and they'd all pay.

He'd see to that.

CHAPTER 20

Queen Liliana paced on her perch. She was not fond of being in the trees at this time of day, and if Arland discovered she'd gone without a security detail, she would never hear the end of it. Though a genteel disposition and the full decorum of her station dictated her manner, she'd just as soon be free to come and go as she pleased.

She crouched on the branch at the sound of footsteps coming down the pathway. Big footsteps. *Human* footsteps. Liliana covered herself with a leaf, becoming nearly invisible from below as she waited to see who it was.

The heavy footfalls drew nearer, and Liliana held her breath as the human came around the bend. She recognized him in an instant, and he looked much as he had a generation ago, only…*bigger*. He was searching for something, and her hope was that it wasn't her.

Liliana nervously fluttered her wings, and though nearly ten feet away, he stopped. Scanning the branches overhead his eyes narrowed as he searched for the source of the small sound. She crouched further and closed her eyes tight.

After what seemed like a lifetime Liliana heard the footsteps moving away. She opened her eyes to see the faerie-turned-human go through the gate and head for the back door of Oakhurst. When she heard the door close behind him, she allowed herself to breathe again.

ꝏ ꝏ

It was nearly noon, and Shea headed back to the house for lunch. She had been busy most of the morning helping Steve in the woodshop and had a great time. They'd been building pieces for a new exhibit, and Shea still had sawdust on her shoulders from hefting the freshly-cut boards around.

She took the scenic route letting herself in through the service gate and heading up Aunt Emma's path. Hearing something, she stopped short.

"Pssssst!" came the urgent little sound.

Shea cocked her head and listened again. She wasn't even sure she'd heard anything but the wind and was ready to take another step when she heard it again.

"Pssssst! Over here!"

Shea looked around suddenly discovering Elisabeth about ten feet off the well-worn brick path.

"Elisabeth! So good to –"

Elisabeth quickly put her hand up to quiet Shea's rather exuberant greeting, placing her finger at her lips to silence her.

A little confused, Shea looked around her and, seeing no one, waded her way into the thicket.

"What's up?" she said much more quietly when she was closer.

"I need your help."

"Well, sure, anything," Shea replied.

"Actually, Queen Liliana needs your help," Elisabeth clarified, "only she doesn't know she needs your help. Yet."

"Oh?" Shea was intrigued.

"She is not exactly trusting of humans and what she saw this morning disturbed her greatly." Elisabeth sighed.

"She trusts you, doesn't she?" Shea reasoned.

"Well, yes, but I'm…..different."

"True," Shea agreed, "but what about when you were a little girl? A hundred years ago?"

"Again, different." Elisabeth was beginning to lose her patience, and it was becoming apparent to Shea that perhaps she should just let it go.

"My apologies," Shea submitted, with a slight nod. "Continue, please."

Elisabeth looked around. Though she saw no one, she lowered her tone even further. "The queen was in the garden early this morning. Alone. She –"

"Isn't that against the rules or something?"

Elisabeth looked up at her with something bordering on exasperation and disdain. She shook her head and sighed.

"You still have much to learn, Shea, but you are correct. The queen usually does not travel anywhere unless escorted. Usually."

"And this morning was unusual how?"

"Queen Liliana heard through a messenger from Nebosham that there had been a theft in the wood sprites' palace. She believes she saw the thief this morning."

"Who is it?" Shea asked. "Another wood sprite? Or a faerie?"

"Worse," Elisabeth said. "A human."

"Well, maybe it was an accident. Maybe this person thought it was a child's plaything or some such."

"No," Elisabeth responded. "It was a deliberate act, and it was someone the queen believes she knows."

༄ ༄

Holding court in the garden behind Oakhurst, Queen Liliana awaited the arrival of King Rogan of Nebosham. Her daughter, Verena, sat at her right side while her counselors surrounded her conversing in hushed tones.

Elisabeth and Shea sat on the ground amidst the thicket, safely out of sight should anyone be wandering through the gardens.

"Who is that?" Shea wondered aloud as she watched the fae huddled together on the flagstones along the tiny brook that wound through the garden. "The one doing all the talking."

"That is Sullivan," Elisabeth whispered, leaning in toward Shea. "He is the Minister of Defense in the Kingdom of Oakhurst."

"Defense?" Shea asked. "Are they preparing for war?"

Elisabeth sighed. "No, not yet. There are rumors that something has happened, but that is all it is thus far. The queen prefers to be prepared in any eventuality."

Elisabeth stopped as if listening for something. Shea watched her as the child cocked her head. "They are coming."

Ten yards or so into the wood the underbrush rustled ever so slightly as the party from Nebosham approached. As they came near, Shea could just make out the guard leading the way surrounding their king. Several other wood sprites walked with him keeping him safe from any possible treachery, real or imagined, on the part of the Kingdom of Oakhurst.

Queen Liliana bristled visibly at their approach. "Are you so distrustful, Rogan," she called to him, "that you would bring armed guards to my court?"

The guard parted, and Rogan stepped forward boldly flanked by his son, Prince Royce. "I could ask the same of you, Liliana," he shot back at her. "Your Minister of Defense? Really?" He shook his head somewhat dismayed at her chiding. "My scouts brought word of a cat on the prowl in the gardens. One cannot be too....*careful*."

Liliana rose from her seat and approached him. "Welcome to Oakhurst," she greeted him with a slight nod, her voice absent of ill will.

"My thanks," Rogan replied, as he let his guard down somewhat. "My son, Royce," he indicated with a slight sweep of his hand. Royce responded with a low bow.

"Your Majesty," Royce said.

Queen Liliana nodded to him. "My daughter, Verena," Liliana indicated with a sweep likewise. Verena remained seated merely nodding to the visiting royals.

"You bring news?" Liliana asked, preferring to stick to the business at hand. She had no patience for wood sprites holding them just a step and a half above full-on contempt. It had not always been so, but the centuries had not been kind in the relations between the two kingdoms.

"Have they always gotten along so well?" Shea asked Elisabeth sarcastically.

Elisabeth shot her a look that made Shea shut her mouth.

"Why are they here?" Rogan asked rather loudly so that all were certain he was displeased. "They are interlopers. Humans are not to be a part of these proceedings."

"Rogan," Liliana chided, "you remember Elisabeth. She is friend and Guardian to the Kingdom of Oakhurst."

"Miss Elisabeth, begging your pardon," Rogan nodded in Elisabeth's direction. "So good to see you again."

"Likewise, Your Highness," Elisabeth said with a smile. "I am here to serve both kingdoms."

"Thank you," he said, then to Liliana, "I meant the *other* one."

Taken somewhat aback, Shea could only sit and listen.

"Begging your pardon, Your Majesty," Elisabeth interjected, diverting all eyes back to her. "I brought her. She is here for reasons which I cannot divulge at this point in time. You do realize, do you not, that simply because she can see you makes her special?"

Rogan nodded to her. "As usual, I will defer to your judgement."

"Thank you," Elisabeth nodded. She looked at Shea who understood the look meant she should mind her place. Shea nodded to Elisabeth once Rogan turned back to Liliana.

"Very well."

Liliana sighed, resigned to the fact that she would have to tolerate Rogan's outbursts in order to achieve her goals. She took a great pause, gathering her thoughts before she spoke and choosing her words with care.

"I have recently returned from the Kingdom of Ravensforge....or what was left of it, which was not much. Intel reports that it was under attack shortly after our return from a royal dinner celebrating the impending betrothal of my son to one of King Beltran's daughters."

"Yes," Rogan interrupted, "where is the young prince?"

"He and his guard detachment remained to investigate in order to find the whereabouts of the king and his family." The half-truth came out easily, and Liliana kept her eyes locked on Rogan so as not to reveal everything. "When we find them, we shall have our answers."

She glanced around at the wood sprite delegation gauging their commitment to the crisis. "There is much more at stake here than anyone realizes. I am not at liberty to disclose what it was, but a sacred relic was missing when I arrived at the palace ruins. King Beltran had shown it to me and said nothing more than that it had to be kept in secret so that it would not fall into the wrong hands. Word has it that the Palace of Erebos is on the rise."

The Nebosham delegation exchanged glances as they understood the ramifications of what was said.

Rogan spoke first. "Erebos has been silent for eons. How can this be? Do they possess any of the Triad Relics?"

Liliana shot him a warning look before she continued. "The Triad Relics have been lost for many generations," she said flatly. "I am under the impression that Beltran knew something of them. That was why he had secreted away this particular object. It was no secret that he possessed the Keeper of Time, but to my knowledge, no one knew of this other piece."

"Why did he share this with you?" Rogan asked, a little on the testy side.

"Again, my son was to marry one of his daughters. This would have cemented the two kingdoms together ushering in a secure peace, which is more than I can say for Oakhurst and Nebosham," the queen shot back.

"Now, see here," Rogan protested. He opened his mouth to speak, but the queen raised her hand to silence him.

Verena and Royce exchanged long glances which Shea noted almost immediately. Seemingly no one else noticed that the pair's eyes remained locked for some time before looking back to their parents. Continuing to watch them a moment longer, Shea finally turned to Elisabeth. The girl was concentrating on the proceedings, paying no attention to Shea.

"Rogan," she began quietly, "we must guard our relics. You know as well as I that should the Sacred pieces our kingdoms possess fall into the wrong hands and be used in legion with the Triad Relics, irreparable damage will result, both in our realm and theirs." She nodded to the humans as if they were children to be cared for and protected.

Elisabeth understood immediately the damage that could be done, and Shea watched as the tensions rose. Rogan stood rather suddenly seeming anxious and a little more than put out.

"Then I believe we have a problem," the king said tersely.

"Oh?" Liliana replied, raising her eyebrows slightly.

"We must speak in private," Rogan said suddenly, aware of the breach in protocol he was proposing.

"Is that truly necessary?"

Hands open, he approached the throne out of growing desperation. "Our circumstances are such that we are…desperate."

"That you would seek help from us?" the queen retorted.

"Just what are you implying, Liliana?" he growled, forgetting all formality.

"Merely that there are forces at work – forces that are dark in nature – that we must guard against at all costs. I want to leave no stone unturned, no possibility unexplored. We must be on guard at all times or the situation will quickly get out of hand." She turned and looked up at the humans. "If that happens, no one will be safe on either side of the divide."

"Then I am afraid," Rogan sighed, "that we have a *serious* problem."

CHAPTER 21

Shea returned to her apartment shortly past eight thirty in the evening. She had just finished locking down the grounds and decided to lie down on the sofa and rest her eyes for a few moments.

Her mind wandered to the place it knows her best, and she began to dream of faeries and palaces and places far from the House of Oakhurst. It was a lovely dream, really, and Shea felt at peace there. At home.

Through the fog of her consciousness, she realized she had fallen asleep. Though she had laid down on the couch in her tiny apartment for what seemed like a moment, she was suddenly awakened by the strangest sensation – like someone was watching her. Thinking it part of her dream, she opened her eyes to find Elisabeth kneeling before her, her face mere inches from Shea's. Startled, Shea jumped and sat upright.

"Elisabeth!" she hissed in annoyance, as she rubbed her eyes. "What are you doing here?"

"We must go," Elisabeth urged her quietly. "They are coming."

"Wha—Who?" Shea asked, a little louder, a little more annoyed. "Who is com—"

"Shhhhh!" Elisabeth scolded. "Quickly. Follow me."

Still dressed from her day's work and unsure wether she was dreaming or not, Shea padded barefoot across the tiny living room and down the hall to the door.

"They're out there," Elisabeth whispered, her tone deadly serious.

"Who –"

Elisabeth raised a hand to shush her again, and Shea quieted her tone. "Who are you talking about?"

"The Dark Warrior's minions. They've come searching for Queen Liliana's Flame Relic."

The look on Shea's face told Elisabeth she still wasn't quite awake. Annoyed, Elisabeth *tsked* at her. "Mother's *earring!*" she whispered rather harshly.

"Oh, right. Right." Shea replied softly, as she rubbed her eyes. "How many of them are there? Two? Three?"

"Hundred," Elisabeth responded.

"Two or three *hundred*?" Shea asked, her eyes widening. "How are they all gonna fit? I mean, this house is big, but it's not that big."

"They're not that big."

Shea opened her mouth to say something trite but nothing came out as the sound of scuttling claws hurried past the closed door. Shea's eyes opened nearly as wide as her mouth.

"What was that?" she asked Elisabeth.

"Gutiku."

ꝏ ꝏ

Slowly, cautiously, Shea opened the door slightly and peeked out into the darkened hallway. The staircase was only a few feet away, and if they had all come upstairs, Shea reasoned she and Elisabeth could make it down the stairs and out the door, although she wasn't sure they were any safer outside than in. Screeches and a crash of glass and wood in the map room told her the uninvited guests were otherwise occupied, so she motioned to Elisabeth to follow her.

Silently she crept to the stairs carefully making her way down to the first landing. She turned and was within a few steps of the main floor when the step she put her full weight on betrayed her with a creak so loud it was as if she had dropped a ton of bricks on the staircase. For a moment, the house stood in complete and utter silence.

Then, sudden screeching and clawing and the skitter of sharp, hooked toenails on every surface imaginable came from all over the main floor, and it sounded like a thousand boiling crabs climbing up the walls, across the floor and along the ceiling – *all coming toward Shea!*

"Run!" she called to Elisabeth, who was still at the top of the stairs. Shea turned and scrambled up the second flight, tripping and falling hard before picking herself up and hurtling headlong back down the hall. Remembering the racket in the

map room, she grabbed ahold of the doorframe and flung herself into the first gallery on the left.

She tumbled headlong into the unassembled exhibit the crew had brought in that afternoon, knocking it over with a horrible crash, pieces flying everywhere. Shea fled through that gallery into the next and out into the hall just above the main staircase. By now the minions in the map room had abandoned what was left of the diorama, taken to the ceiling and came along after them, joining the horde that had flowed toward the front staircase.

Shea let out a screech herself, wheeled about as she passed the restroom and flung open the beautiful door, placing the stained glass man between herself and the Gutiku. He did his solemn duty to protect her and took out several of the little buggers in one swing of the door before shattering in vain. Through the empty, jagged frame she saw dozens more scrambling along the walls and across the ceiling toward her!

Seeing the futility of the fight, Shea barreled down the stairs. Her bare feet smacked firmly on the floor, and in the incandescence from the security light outside she could see the front door, but something looked wrong. Mere steps from the front door, she froze in her tracks, terrified.

The front door was covered with them, and they all swung their wobbly noggins about on scrawny necks to look directly at her. At least a hundred green, glowing, beady little eyes stared back at her. They were nearly four times the size of any faerie Shea had seen and black as pitch. What passed for their skin was stretched taut against their bony arms and legs. The room began to reek with a stench so foul Shea gagged. They looked like a cross between a bat and a wood sprite, *and there were more of them right behind her!*

Not a moment to spare, Shea sprinted toward the back door. Barreling through the formal dining room, she whipped around the corner in time to see the back door swarming with the nasty little beasts. Things were not looking good at this point, and Shea knew she had few options left.

She bolted back to the butler's pantry and closed the door behind her, locking it to buy herself a little time. The security light just outside the back door brought a soft glow into the butler's pantry. Finding the windows too high to climb out and no other doors, the small room offered little in the way of escape. Shea found herself surrounded by a few display cases, cupboards and the dumbwaiter.

Clawing and horrible screeching at the door told her she had precious little time. She opened the dumbwaiter, crawled up onto the counter and carefully backed into it. It was a snug fit, but she was convinced it might work.

The doorknob rattled and twisted back and forth until at last it burst into the room with such force it hit the wall adjacent to where Shea had crammed herself into the dumbwaiter. Lightning fast, she reached up to close the door and—

It stuck! She tugged and tugged, but it wouldn't budge!

One of the nasty little buggers stuck his head in through the hole where the doorknob used to be. Beady little eyes scanned the room, and Shea froze, trying not to attract any attention. She pushed her folded-over body against the back of the dumbwaiter and held her breath. The shift in her weight made the side of the metal box pop, and the creature was through the hole and on the counter in front of her in record speed and headed straight for her!

It wrapped its nasty, clawed hands around Shea's arm and pulled. *Hard.* The claw tips dug into her skin, and it was all she could do to keep from crying out. She balled up her other hand into a fist and hit the creature square in the face, once, twice, three times. It responded by digging the claws deeper into her arm and screeching loudly.

Hunkered over, Shea was running out of options. She tried desperately to pry the bony fingers from her arm and, leaning forward, she did the only thing she could think to do: she gave the little bugger a head butt.

Dazed, the creature released her arm and registered his complaint rather loudly. It was about to come back at her when it noticed what it had come for and froze. Dangling about Shea's neck was an amulet with the fiery tear-shaped stone in the center of it.

Reinvigorated, the minion reached up and grabbed at the amulet grazing Shea's chest with its claws. It pulled hard and for some reason the chain held. It was almost comical as the nasty little thing leaned back and pulled. Making no headway, it looked over to the hole in the door, laid back its head and screamed. It was a horrible, grating sound that made Shea wish she could cover her ears.

Suddenly, the evil little black creatures inundated the tiny room via the hole vacated by the doorknob. They poured through like sand in a booby-trapped pyramid ready to suffocate any who dared to venture in.

In desperation, Shea punched the minion squarely between the eyes. Dazed, it released the amulet. She reached up with both hands and with two sharp tugs managed to slam the door to the dumbwaiter down with a sharp *crack!* The creature on the other side beat fiercely on the door as Shea released the lock and cautiously lowered herself to the basement. She could only hope they hadn't figured out how to get there yet.

Once she reached the bottom, she stopped and listened. Hearing nothing she eased the door of the dumbwaiter up. Taking care not to make a sound, she unfolded herself and moved out into the basement. The stairwell light gave her little to see by, but it would have to do.

She turned to find Elisabeth in the corner.

"Wondered where you got off to," Shea whispered.

"We must go," Elisabeth told her.

"We're running out of options," Shea retorted, "so I'm open to any ideas. How do we get out of here?"

"Through the tunnels."

Chapter 22

Shea opened the door to the tunnels and felt around on the wall. She found a light switch and flipped it on. Bare low wattage light bulbs lit the way at regular intervals but offered little in the way of light. The tunnel was somewhat narrow but at a height that Shea could stand fully, and she followed Elisabeth into it.

"My family used this for heating and such," Elisabeth told her. "We can reach each of the houses from here."

"Thanks for the history lesson," Shea replied smartly, as she reached back for the door.

Suddenly, one of the creatures grabbed hold of the door. Startled, Shea did the only thing she could think of: she slammed it. *Hard.* It was heavy and from the scream of the being on the other side of the door, she could tell she'd done some damage. She reached up and threw the ancient brass bolt at eye level. It slid a little rough at first but did the job.

"We gotta go," she told Elisabeth as she headed down the dimly lit tunnel amidst the banging and screeching at the door behind her. "Where did you say this comes out?"

"It leads to the other houses," Elisabeth replied, "but there is another exit."

Shea let Elisabeth in front of her, and they picked up the pace. They had gone only a short way when Shea heard the rip of metal behind them. The screeching grew louder, and she could hear the claws against the concrete floor and walls.

And then came the distinct sound of bolts popping and the crackle of electricity, as the lights flickered and the tunnel went black.

ꟃ ɞ

The White River flowed along, cutting its way through the city in the pre-dawn light. Above her the trees swayed in the gentle breeze.

As if shot from a cannon, Connor suddenly flew headlong out of the steep riverbank just below Oakhurst. In a manner most unbefitting royalty – something his mother would have definitely disapproved of – he screamed in mid-flight.

The river came up on him quickly, and before he knew it, he went in headfirst, mouth still wide open. Mere seconds later he surfaced, coughing and sputtering and flailing his arms in a pitiful attempt to impede his progress downstream.

The swift current tangled him almost instantly in the traveling cloak he was wearing, and he tumbled along through the water attempting to right himself and free his legs from the garment. His arms were caught up in the fabric as well, and several times the cloak acted like a sail of sorts beneath the surface of the water dragging him under as a result.

His feet tried to find purchase on the riverbed beneath him, but years of algae and silt made that nearly impossible as the current pushed him onward toward the downtown area. At one point he managed to stop himself, climbing onto a large rock, but that small success was short lived. The current pushed Connor's feet out from under him, and he found himself once again floundering downstream.

The waters dragged him along under a bridge, and for a moment Connor's eyes focused upward at the steel structure above him. He briefly relinquished control to the river, choosing to float along on his back momentarily. This was his biggest mistake yet.

He heard the waterfall before he saw it. He could hear the churning waters that awaited him like an angry mob as his ears bobbed along beneath the water's surface. He didn't want to but suddenly felt compelled to look toward the increasing roar ahead.

Though still mostly dark, the streetlights from the bridge gave him some sense of what was ahead without spilling the whole story. The falls weren't big, but he didn't know that. The light only showed him the top of the falls and that the river seemed to drop off to nowhere.

Desperate paddling back toward where he came from was met with greater resistance on the river's part as the current picked up. Flailing again, he could only scream as his body tumbled down the short incline, hitting rock after rock before landing in the churning waters at the bottom.

Managing to finally get a foothold, Connor clawed and sputtered his way to the riverbank. He could see the spray from his breath in the early morning air as he crawled up onto the cool, wet grass. He collapsed, sucking in oxygen as he let himself rest for a moment.

He finally managed the strength to make his way up the riverbank. He looked around, fascinated by the street lamps and sidewalks as he walked back in the direction from where the river had taken him, seemingly oblivious to his surroundings or the imminent danger the empty street posed.

He followed the street back to the bridge, turned left and was walking straight up the middle of Wheeling Avenue when he noticed lights. Two of them. They were in the distance, and at first he thought they were stationary, but upon further observation, he realized they were moving. Toward him. Fast.

He stood there spellbound, but only for a moment as the steel beast approached. The roar of the creature fascinated him as he stood in the middle of the road, his head cocked to one side to listen. The car's muffler didn't work, and it bellowed as it moved toward him. Suddenly seeing Connor in the middle of the street, the driver swerved and honked. Connor dove toward the sidewalk. The concrete pounded back at his shoulder as he hit and rolled to the curb.

Shaking himself, he was tempted to just lie there and not do anything, but he knew he must press on.

Startled, he looked up at the figure standing over him.

"Hurry," she said. "we haven't much time."

ᘐ ᘓ

Shea crawled up the access tunnel, felt around until she found the hardware and released the latch on the cover. She eased the lid open and cringed at the loud groan it gave as she gave it a good push. It was a substantial piece of steel, and she released it a little sooner than she'd anticipated. The heavy hatch hit the ground with a resounding thud.

She looked around trying to get her bearings. She was somewhere in the woods behind the house. The sun was just coming up, and she could see it filtering through the trees.

Rather awkwardly she managed to make her way out of the tunnel access and turned to help Elisabeth. The hole was dark, and Shea called down to her.

"Elisabeth," she whispered.

Nothing.

"Elisabeth, where are you?" she called in a little louder whisper, peering down into the hole.

Without warning one of the Gutiku scrambled up the wall, screeched at her and grabbed yet again for the amulet around her neck. Getting a firm grip on the chain, the creature pulled hard nearly sending Shea headfirst back into the dark tunnel. She had both hands on the steel rim of the access hatch that dug into her palms as she desperately tried to free herself from the little beastie's grasp. In the distance of the tunnel below, she could hear more claws on the floors and walls, *all coming her way.*

Shea grabbed the chain with one hand as she tried to beat at the creature with the other. This one was a little smarter because she was having a hard time connecting with it at all. It was even more aggressive than the one that had cornered her in the dumbwaiter, and for a moment she thought it might win.

She pulled backward, hoping the minion wouldn't follow her out. She couldn't believe the strength of one so small as she held onto the steel rim of the tunnel. Her eyes frantically scanned the ground around her for something – anything – to hit the thing with. Putting her back into it, she released the frame of the hatchway and felt around on the ground until her hand came across a thick part of a tree limb. She took it and swung at the creature expecting that to be the end of it.

The creature dodged her swing and held on for all it was worth, yet suddenly became a little more insistent in its efforts. The sunlight was growing through the trees, and the beastie apparently wanted nothing to do with it.

Seizing the opportunity Shea set her weight back on her heels, sending one last, hard punch directly into the Gutiku's face. It released her, and Shea fell backward on the cool, muddy ground still holding tightly to the amulet around her neck.

Sudden footsteps behind her – swift footsteps – ran to where she lay, and quickly a figure moved in to slam the hatch shut, latching it soundly. Exhausted, Shea could only lie on the ground and breathe. She closed her eyes for a moment, and when she finally opened them again, she found Elisabeth standing over her, smiling.

"You did well," Elisabeth told her approvingly.

Shea grinned and closed her eyes, chuckling a bit as she lay on the ground. "Thanks," she said, breathing hard. It was several minutes before she opened them again. This time there were two faces above her.

Startled, Shea scrambled to her feet so fast it made her dizzy, somehow managing to take a defensive stance even though gravity threatened to pull her back down to the ground.

"Who are you?" she demanded of the newcomer.

The young man standing next to Elisabeth smiled, although Shea was not sure why.

"I am Connor," he replied with a smile. "I am –"

"A friend," Elisabeth finished for him as shc smiled at Shea, then looked up at Connor with an expression that Shea couldn't quite read. Too exhausted for mental gymnastics, she let it go.

"Thank you for the help," Shea said, as she relaxed her posture slightly. "It is greatly appreciated."

"My pleasure," Connor answered.

Suddenly Shea was motionless, struck with a thought.

"Wait – he can see you?" she asked Elisabeth, her eyes still locked on the grinning Connor.

"Yes, he can see me," Elisabeth replied. "You seem surprised."

"Well, I…" her voice trailed off. This was getting more confusing by the minute. "Never mind," she sighed heavily.

The sun was up, and a cool breeze rustled through the trees as Shea looked toward the house. She was heartbroken as the thought of the damage to the interior came crashing back down upon her.

"Elisabeth," she whispered, turning back to the little girl. "Your home. I'm sorry. I couldn't stop them. I –"

"No one expected you to," Elisabeth replied. "This time."

೩ ೧

The trio made their way down the walk along the side of the house. The back door was slightly ajar, and for a moment

Shea felt panic in her gut as the thought of what awaited them inside hit her squarely.

"Here, let me," Connor said quietly, as he moved in front of Shea. Instinctively his hand went to his hip before he remembered the sword was gone.

The early morning sun barely lit the main floor of the house, and Shea braced herself for the devastation that awaited them. Connor stepped through the door first, followed by Elisabeth, then Shea. She closed her eyes, took a deep breath and stepped over the threshold. A few paces ahead of her, she could hear Connor's footsteps and opened her eyes.

Her brows knit together as she looked around. The back hallway didn't look so bad. Maybe they hadn't really done that much to this part of the house. She made her way down the hall pausing at the butler's pantry door. The antique glass knob was exactly as it had been the day before. Her gut churned as she thought of what might still be behind that door, and though the house was silent, Shea braced herself as she turned the doorknob and opened the door.

The butler's pantry, like the entryway, was as it had been before. Shea moved slowly into the room looking upward to avert any leftover surprises and walked to the corner where the dumbwaiter awaited her. The door was closed, and Shea nervously put her hand on the handle. Bracing herself for whatever might come flying out at her, she quickly slid up the door to the dumbwaiter. It hit the stop at the top rather loudly sending Connor and Elisabeth running to her.

Nothing. The dumbwaiter sat there as if nothing had happened.

"I don't understand…" Shea said quietly. "They came in

through that door," she said, pointing to the doorway where Connor and Elisabeth stood, never taking her eyes off the dumbwaiter. She reached up still finding the amulet hanging around her neck beneath her shirt.

Shea followed Connor into the dining room and through the parlor and into the library. All was as it had been the day before. There was no damage at all! Shea began to wonder if it had all been a nightmare, but the claw marks on her arms and the scratches near her neck argued otherwise.

The upstairs of Oakhurst was pretty much the same as the downstairs. The wallpaper, doors, and even the exhibit pieces in the first gallery that she could have sworn she had knocked over, were all intact. The stained glass man on the door to the bathroom stood guard as always at the end opposite the apartment, and the map room was intact as well. Nothing, it appeared, had been affected.

Shea wheeled around to Elisabeth as she stepped into the next gallery, the sunshine filling the room with warm light. "I don't understand," she cried. "They were here! They tore the house up!" She looked at Connor, adding, "I am *not* crazy."

Connor raised his eyebrows, saying nothing.

"They haven't crossed over yet."

"What?" Connor and Shea both said at the same time.

"They haven't fully crossed over to the human realm yet."

Elisabeth looked at the pair who waited expectantly for an answer.

"Well, it's complicated!" Elisabeth said, somewhat exasperated. "I wish I could explain it..."

CHAPTER 23

After a bit of time to calm her nerves, Shea excused herself and got ready for work. She left Connor to entertain himself in Oakhurst, but it was not long before he wandered out into the garden behind the house. He crossed the footbridge and let himself out the gate heading up Aunt Emma's path.

The midmorning sun bathed the Formal Garden in a beautiful light that made the greens more brilliant, the flowers more vibrant. Drawn to the arbor he walked beneath the shade of vining flowers toward the bench in the middle of the walkway where Elisabeth sat waiting for him.

"Connor, it is good to see you," Elisabeth said, though her expression didn't exactly tell him that.

"So it is with you, Miss Elisabeth," he replied. "Are you well?"

"As well as can be expected," she smiled knowingly. "It's a balancing act, really. I'm starting to feel like a circus acrobat."

Connor smiled at the reference, not fully understanding it. Miss Elisabeth was known throughout the kingdoms of Oakhurst and Nebosham as protector of all. Though there was an uneasy peace between the two palaces, it had remained all this time in no small part through Elisabeth's gentle counsel. Her patience and kindness were legendary, and she was well respected by both fae and sprite alike.

"Connor, when I came here I did so willingly with a purpose. Though it took time to re-establish myself as a human, I managed to figure it out. Yours apparently is a different story. Why have you come?"

Connor sighed. "I, too, came here willingly, with a purpose." He paused, gathering his thoughts for a moment.

"We had traveled to Ravensforge. A necessary trip, I suppose, although I wasn't quite sure I was ready for it. Nonetheless, we went. Rumor had it that there was unrest in that region, so we traveled with a very large accompaniment. "

"How many guards?"

"There were six for every royal, three per minister, and another two dozen besides." Connor looked grave as he remembered the journey.

"We arrived safely, and the dinner went well. King Beltran was most accommodating, and his daughters were beautiful, everything a prince could ask for in a wife."

"It was a betrothal then?"

"Introductions with the intent to betroth, yes," Connor said.

"And I'd imagine *that* went well," Elisabeth smiled. She loved formal events, having experienced many of them in both the fae and human realm.

"Certainly," Connor smiled back. "The Princesses of the House of Ravensforge were as engaging and charming as they were lovely, and any man would be lucky to marry one of them. Only one thing tangled that whole scenario."

"What was that?"

"Their Guardian," Connor replied.

"Oh?" Elisabeth inquired, raising her eyebrows in surprise.

Connor scowled a bit. "No," he protested, struggling to put his thoughts into words. "I mean—well, it's complicated."

"Really?" Elisabeth teased. "But as you are well aware, love and politics are *always* complicated."

Connor laughed. "Yes, I am quite aware of that," he agreed. "But I wish it didn't have to be."

"The queen is most concerned," Elisabeth said.

"I would imagine she is. But I cannot worry about that now. Does Arland still have his head?" he asked mischievously.

Elisabeth laughed. "Yes, but you will probably be on the wrong end of his wrath after Queen Liliana is through with you."

"I have no doubt that is true. But after seeing what we saw, I had no choice. Surely she has to understand that."

Elisabeth waited in silence as Connor gathered his thoughts.

"When we learned of the destruction of Ravensforge, we

immediately regrouped the troops and returned. The queen and Arland went on some sort of mission within what was left of the castle walls," Connor said, a tone of formality in his voice, "though she did not speak of it afterward. The only thing I truly know is that whatever it was, it was grave enough for her to order increased patrols around Oakhurst."

"The devastation was heart wrenching. Never could I have imagined such carnage and destruction." Connor hung his head and sighed. Finally looking back into Elisabeth's face, there were tears in his eyes. "The king and his family and their closest protectors were gone. Everyone else, with only a few exceptions, was slaughtered."

Connor stood and walked to the arbor's edge. "There were a handful of survivors. One managed to tell of the king's escape. The Guard split into two factions, one to the north and one to the south of Ravensforge. The king's faction made for the sea. His daughters headed toward the foothills and made their way to the portal, the gateway to this realm. You know of it?"

"Yes," Elisabeth replied, "I am familiar with the mortal portal."

"When we arrived, we discovered that it had been destroyed. It was no longer working properly, and there were signs of struggle there. It was unclear whether the princesses and their protectors made it through or not."

"And that is why you have come?" Elisabeth asked. "To seek out the princesses?"

"Yes," Connor replied. "It is my duty, my responsibility. I owe them that."

"And what of the queen?" Elisabeth inquired.

"She must not know I am here."

ᘓ ᘐ

Evening fell on the gardens of Oakhurst, and Queen Liliana held court in the mid-range branches out of view of the pathways through the grounds. Shea and Elisabeth settled in comfortably on adjoining branches about ten feet up.

"The threat posed by the forces of Erebos is worse than we thought," the queen remarked gravely, as she settled in to her throne woven of tiny branches and little purple flowers that filled the air with a gentle fragrance.

"Has something happened?" Minister Foley asked.

All eyes turned to Shea and Elisabeth. Elisabeth held out a hand to Shea and nodded. Slightly nervous, Shea cleared her throat.

"Last night there was an attack on the House of Oakhurst," she said. "I still bear the marks of the attackers." She raised her forearm for all to see the claw marks. A gasp rolled through the crowd of faeries.

"Attackers?" Arland inquired. "How many?"

Shea looked at Elisabeth. "Too many to count," she answered hesitantly. "They were horrible, gangly little things, and very strong for their size."

"Gutiku," Elisabeth added.

This time a murmur grew as the fae folk discussed the ramifications of a Gutiku attack in their midst.

"Arland, we must increase the guards until we are certain the danger has passed," Queen Liliana ordered.

"Yes, My Queen," he responded.

Shea looked from Elisabeth to the queen in surprise. "I don't think you understand," she said, almost pleading at this point. "These things are terrible. At least twice the size of Arland there, and *strong*."

"Thank you for your concern, Shea," the queen said as she rose from her throne. The issue was as good as closed. "We will handle the problem."

This was becoming almost more than Shea could bear. In confusion she looked around as the queen prepared to depart.

"How?" Shea demanded, a little louder than she'd anticipated.

The queen turned around slowly, and the look of growing annoyance at the human's reaction was beginning to show. "I *beg* your pardon?" she asked at the breach of protocol. This was Shea's warning.

Shea cleared her throat. "I said, how are you going to handle the situation?"

"Like we always have," the queen answered, standing her ground.

"But they're big and strong, and you're so…so –"

"Careful, Shea," Elisabeth cautioned. It was too late.

"—small," Shea blurted.

A gasp bigger than the first told Shea she'd truly stepped in it. The look on Queen Liliana's face sealed it for her. She drew herself up and walked down the branch toward Shea in the most regal manner possible.

"Shea, you are a guest in my kingdom," the queen scolded, "and I suggest you behave as such."

ꝏ ꝏ

“Well, that went well,” Connor remarked sarcastically as Shea and Elisabeth climbed down out of the oak tree.

“How long have you been down here?” Shea asked.

“Long enough to know you’re not exactly on the queen’s good side.” Connor smiled at her mischievously. “You told hcr shc is small? Rcally?”

Shea just looked at him.

“Bet she didn’t see that one coming,” he chuckled.

Unable to contain herself, Elisabeth burst out laughing. Remembering her relationship to the queen, she quickly regained her composure and took on a countenance of total seriousness.

“Most inappropriate,” she said in a somewhat dignified manner. “Inappropriate, indeed.”

Chapter 24

Shea decided to take a short walk through the woods before heading up to the main building for the day. It had been nearly a week since the Gutiku attack, and she had finally managed to get some much needed sleep only the night before. The air was warm already and promised even more heat throughout the day. She took the path down past the doll house all the way out to the Discover Cabin and around the front side of the property. She came past the main gate which was already open and kept going.

She had just reached the arbor when she saw a familiar face working amongst the flowers. Halfway down the walkway, she crouched low, her intended victim unaware of her presence behind the beautiful flowers.

"Hi there!" she called rather spiritedly, as she popped up

from her hiding place.

The gardener, startled beyond belief, let out a cry and fell backwards, hand tools and top soil flying everywhere.

Shea grinned at her deviousness. "Why, Connor! So nice to see you again. Are you well?"

"Well, I was…" he grinned, as he dusted himself off and rose to meet her. "Of course, my heart may have stopped."

"What're you doing here?"

"A man's gotta eat," Connor observed, "so apparently a man's gotta work."

"That would be true," Shea agreed.

"Seen anymore of your imaginary creatures around lately?"

Shea rubbed her arm absently. The claw marks were nearly invisible, but mentally her arm still ached.

"No, thankfully," Shea replied. "Elisabeth doesn't seem to think they'll be back."

"Good. Nothing to worry about then."

"I hope you're right."

ꕥ ꕥ

Verena had been out in the Colonnade Garden longer than she had intended to be, but her opportunities to spend time with Royce had grown fewer and farther between in recent days simply because her mother had been more protective than usual of late. Perhaps it was that her brother had still not returned from who knew where, or that the queen was merely struggling with the burden of rule in these uncertain times. All Verena knew was that she wanted to spend as much time as possible with Royce. It brought her a great sense of comfort knowing that she could count on him.

In spite of all the troubles at the palace, it was the Colonnade that brought her a sense of peace. It was her favorite place to enjoy the sun in the late afternoon, and she never missed an opportunity to spend time there.

It was Royce who finally broke the silence. "You seem preoccupied."

Verena sighed. "I was thinking of Mother, actually," she said. "You know how worried she's been lately."

"And you're not?" Royce countered, taking her hand. "I know it has weighed on you since you found out Connor was missing."

Verena walked along the flowerbed taking care not to venture too far from the easy cover the nearby underbrush provided if necessary. Finding the perfect spot on a patch of moss, she sat down. Royce sat down behind her as he often did, and situated himself so she could lean her back against his and enjoy the time they had there. He'd have preferred to sit face to face, but often this was when they had the most honest conversations.

Folding her wings in tight, Verena gladly leaned back against Royce and listened as he prattled on about something his father had done recently. She could hear him, but she could also feel his voice through her back and found that strangely comforting. She lifted her face upward, enjoying the warm sunlight on her skin.

It would be good to know what happened to Connor, she thought to herself.

"My father said he would gladly send warriors to find your brother if he thought your mother would allow it."

"Really?" Verena asked, her eyes still closed. "It would be a miracle if she allowed it." Her face grew cool, as if the sun had disappeared behind a cloud. "Honestly, Connor has probably –"

Verena opened her eyes to see where the sun had gone.

"Connor?!"

"What?" Royce asked, perplexed.

"Hello, Verena," came her brother's voice from above her.

Stunned, Verena sprang to her feet, nearly knocking poor, unsuspecting Royce over as she ran toward the kneeling human above her.

"Good to see you," Connor said, as he towered over his sister.

"I am so glad to see you!" she squealed, as she leapt into his open hand. "We all thought you were – well, that something terrible had happened!" She had tears in her eyes as he lifted her up for a closer look. "I am so glad to see you," she said breathlessly.

"You too," he answered back. "I haven't been gone that long, and it looks like you've taken up with some unsavory characters." Connor grinned knowing how it grated on Royce. He really didn't mind the guy in spite of the fact that he was a sprite, but honestly, he wasn't going to let him know that. Verena already knew the truth, so it didn't really matter.

"Bloody well 'bout time, Connor," Royce chided him playfully as he rose and dusted himself off. A sharp look from Verena brought a sincere grin to Royce's face. "Truly," he said, "we are most pleased to see you."

"Thank you," Connor told him. "Although I can't imagine Mother being too pleased that you're spending time with my sister."

"Yes, well, I –" Royce stammered.

"And I can't imagine Mother being too pleased that you are, well, a little too big for your britches!" Verena retorted. "Oh, she'll be so happy to hear you're alright! I can't wait –"

"Verena, you can't tell her you saw me," Connor cautioned her. "Not yet, anyway."

"But she is sick with worry. Surely you must let me tell her *something*."

"Then I'll just have to tell her who you've been spending your time with," Connor shot back with a side glance to Royce. "I'll keep your secret – for now – but you must swear that you won't tell her mine."

Verena winced at the thought of her mother's reaction.

"Very well," she acquiesced. "How did you get this way?"

"Never mind," Connor told her. "I have come searching for the Royals of Ravensforge."

"Any luck yet?"

Connor sighed. "I'm afraid not," he said. "It is somewhat complicated, but I believe I have found someone who can help me in my search. Problem is, she doesn't remember who she is."

"But you do…" Verena said slowly, as she began to understand what Connor was thinking. "Do you think she can help you?"

"I'm counting on it."

CHAPTER 25

Shea enjoyed the solitude of the Collections Room. It was fabulous, really, and she could spend hours exploring the boxes filled to overflowing with objects that had belonged to various members of the Ball family. From a fainting couch that had once been owned by Francis Scott Key and used in one of the Ball family homes, to Elisabeth Ball's extensive collection of mismatched china, there was a little bit of everything in there.

There were also antiques from local families of note as well, including several from one that had owned a mortuary downtown. There were pieces of beautiful furniture that had been made by the funeral home people, a rather nice collection of handmade walking sticks, and there was even a Civil War-era wicker casket that was used to retrieve and transport bodies of the deceased to the mortuary when they had passed at home.

Her favorite piece was a beautiful old stove that was black with a lot of shiny chrome on it. It had been purchased for use in an exhibit and was of no historic significance on the local level but was a striking specimen nonetheless. She made her way to the upper level and managed to distract herself looking through the various antiques.

The original purpose of her presence there was to retrieve several items for the exhibit GiGi was working on with Darius for the new Carriage House gallery. The space had been renovated specifically for FSL, and there was an added air of excitement about it with the relics and artifacts that Darius had brought from London.

Shea had been in there quite awhile when Lucy's words echoed back to her about the timer on the lights. Not thirty seconds after that thought ran through her mind, the lights went out. While it was nothing out of the ordinary (other than the fact she'd been in there longer than she probably needed to be), she had to admit it was somewhat unnerving.

Her eyes adjusted to the near complete darkness as she felt her way along the row of massive shelving toward the front of the mezzanine. The timer on the switch downstairs had performed its duty as well, shutting down twenty minutes before the lights upstairs. But being back amongst the racks, she hadn't even noticed.

She rounded the end of the row of shelves and made her way to the far corner of the upper level. After feeling around on the wall for a moment, she finally located the switch, flipped it on, and blinked at the brightness of the light. She turned and headed back down toward the front of the mezzanine and had nearly reached the end of the aisle when she heard the door open downstairs. Two pairs of heavy footsteps entered the room, but she was still a good way from the edge to see anything. She neared the end of the aisle and was about to call out when the pair began to argue.

Instinctively she froze, her eyes darting to the small triangle of light from the doorway that slowly disappeared into the semi-darkness on the main floor. Ducking down, she made her way to the end of the row, silently moving toward the front of the mezzanine. Shea crouched low and peered over the edge just as the lights on the main floor came on.

She just caught view of the second person disappearing beneath her and moving toward the aisles. Their conversation wafted up to the second floor and though she didn't recognize the voices, she definitely recognized their angry tones.

"Why have you not yet recovered the pieces I seek?" one voice asked accusingly. "I do not believe you fully understand their value."

"Well, apparently not," said the other voice with a bit of an attitude. "And *I'm* guessing *you* haven't realized the importance of prompt payment for services *rendered*."

Beneath her, Shea heard the scuffling of feet on the concrete followed by a heavy thud and the clinking and rattling of fine china in the boxes as a body was slammed against them. She strained her ears, shifting ever closer to the edge to get a better listen.

"You'll get *paid* when I get *results*, and not a moment sooner. Is that understood?"

A gurgle was the only response the other man was capable

of giving. Shea heard him being slammed against the boxes again before he fell to the floor gasping. Deciding the edge was not the best place for her, she scooched backward, straight into a trio of ornately decorated diamond willow walking sticks that were leaning against the end of the shelf directly behind her. They clattered to the floor sending out a resounding alarm.

Shea froze, unsure of what to do. She could try to play dumb, but after the gurgling sounds she thought it best to avoid discovery. Silently she crept toward the far corner of the mezzanine desperate to find a hiding place, yet fearful that she might choose poorly. Push came to shove, she could resort to a backup plan. *If she had one.*

Determined to shift the balance of power in her favor, she made her way back toward the light switch. She paused, listening for any movement from below. She had just reached the switch when she heard them – *footsteps on the stairs!* Without hesitation she did what she had set out to do. She crouched low taking a defensive stance, reached up and flipped off the lights.

Though not as dark as she'd have liked it to be, it would have to do. The light from the main floor offered little in the way of light as her eyes once again adjusted to the darkness. Shea's ears strained to hear even the slightest shuffle or breathing but heard nothing for a brief moment. *Then footsteps again.* Slowly, carefully, they too were avoiding being obvious, attempting to make good use of the element of surprise. The grit on the soles of their shoes ground against the concrete floor as they patiently and methodically made their way toward her.

A subtle movement at the far end of the aisle on the other side of the shelves made Shea hold her breath for what seemed like forever. She found little comfort in knowing where only one of them was and determined to evade them at all costs. Cat-like she climbed up the end of the heavy shelving unit, not completely confident that the sheet metal wouldn't give under her weight, and was relieved when it didn't make the horrific *pop!* it was wont to do. She crept along the top of the shelves, moving slowly as she felt her way through the furniture and assorted antiques. For lack of a better idea and because it did her little good to keep them open, she closed her eyes and imagined in her mind's eye what the room had looked like when the lights were on.

Deciding against sandwiching herself between works of art in the hanging collection, she continued on her way across the top of the aisles and was about to descend from her perch when she froze in mid-transition. Straddling the aisleway, she hung from the pipes overhead and sensed a presence just beneath her.

She could hear him breathing!

Shea felt her hands slipping but dared not adjust her grip for fear of the horrible screeching sound that would result, surely giving her away. Her palms began to sweat, as did her face, and she could feel the beads of perspiration begin to form on her forehead. *This was not gonna be pretty.*

Shea steeled herself for the inevitable and was ready to go on the offensive when a horrible clatter followed by a barrage of curse words, most of which she had never heard before, came from the other side of the room. The body beneath her issued a heavy sigh, paused a moment longer, then slowly moved off toward the noise in question. She knew she could wait no longer, and hid herself away the first opportunity that presented itself.

Again, the footsteps and slight breathing made the rounds in the darkness. Shea closed her eyes and regulated her own breathing as much as possible while trying desperately not to let her mind get the best of her.

A moment later she heard a familiar noise – the door to the room swung open again.

"Hullo?" came another man's voice from the doorway. "Anybody in here?"

The footsteps stopped, only a few feet from her hiding place, pausing briefly before moving back toward the stairs.

"Oh, thank the heavens!" said the voice descending the stairs. "I was in here doing some research and the bloody lights went out! And I couldn't find the switch!"

"Oh, that's easy," Larry said, as he made his way into the room. He ascended the stairs to the darkened mezzanine and headed toward the far corner of the level. "It's back this way."

"Yes, yes, of course," replied her pursuer. The voice sounded familiar but from this far away Shea couldn't be certain. She held her position – there was still the second man. He'd been gurgling earlier, and she bet he wasn't in any mood to be trifled with. The light once again flooded the mezzanine and from her hiding place Shea could make out the figure of the gurgling man as he stood at the railing waiting for instruction. It might be a fair fight with Larry on board, but she hoped it wouldn't come to that.

The door swung open yet again, and the rest of Larry's crew came in talking amongst themselves. The man at the railing waited until they all fully entered the room, gone to where Larry directed them – three rows in on the main floor to retrieve a rather large and heavy bronze sculpture – before he quietly descended the stairs. Shea listened until she was certain she heard the door click behind him before letting out a rather heavy sigh of relief.

Larry and the other man spoke briefly as they returned to the main floor before the other man exited the room. Larry told the crew what they needed to retrieve and where it was located, and left them to their task.

From her hiding place, Shea watched the stairs and was quite relieved to see Connor reach the mezzanine. He paused to admire Ed Ball's beautiful saddle emblazoned with a Ball jar on either side before going to retrieve his quarry – a set of steamer trunks the family had used on their many journeys. Confident this was the opportune moment, Shea opened the lid of the wicker casket and sat up.

Connor didn't see her at first as he was busy hefting the trunks about. Awkwardly he scooted them around, then thinking better of it decided to carry them out one by one. He got the larger one out first, then went back a second time. It was on his third trip, carrying a trunk fit for a child's wardrobe, that he saw someone sitting in the wicker casket on the shelving unit two-thirds of the way to the wall calmly looking back at him. Startled, he nearly dropped the trunk.

"*Shea?!* Shea, is that you?" he whispered rather harshly, looking around to be sure there was no one else up there. "What are – How did you get up here?"

Somewhat amused, she smiled back at him, mostly relieved that the others were gone. Gingerly she climbed out of the casket taking care not to make a sound. Not quite sure how to play it, she decided less was more and walked down the aisle toward the stairs.

"Hi, Connor," she greeted him, as she reached the top of the stairs. She gave him a pert little wave and quickly made her way to the main floor and out the door. She went through the outer office and past the woodshop to the loading dock. Needing fresh air she exited through the open bay door and jumped off the dock onto the pavement below. The sunshine felt warm on her face, and she was relieved to be out of the collection room, out of the darkness...*out of that casket!*

She decided she'd had enough for one afternoon and turned back toward the east lawn. She thought she caught a glimpse of someone on the loading dock, but when she turned to look she saw no one was there.

Must be my imagination, she thought to herself, as she walked toward the rose garden.

She should have followed her instincts. She should have turned around, for she would have seen Darius Pendragon watching her from the loading dock drive.

ꝏ ꝏ

The walk back to Oakhurst was somewhat disconcerting after what she had heard in the Collections Room, and Shea found herself repeatedly looking over her shoulder to be sure she wasn't being followed. On more than one occasion she startled at the breeze rustling through the underbrush and decided to take the long way back to the house down the boulevard.

"Hello, Shea," came a familiar voice from right beside her.

Shea nearly jumped out of her skin. She was relieved though slightly annoyed to find Elisabeth walking beside her.

"Can anyone else see you?" she asked her.

"No, why?"

Shea was silent for a moment before she spoke. "I had a rather unnerving experience in the Collections Room."

"What happened?" Elisabeth asked, obviously concerned.

"I was in there gathering a list of items for the faerie event that GiGi had asked for. I had apparently been in there too long because the lights went out. I was going to turn them back on when someone came in. There were two of them, and one of them was very angry. He was looking for something and sounded desperate to get it."

"Who was it?"

"I don't know. Thought I recognized the voice, at least one of them, but I don't want to make any accusations until I know for certain."

"What were they looking for?" Elisabeth asked.

"I'm not sure. But whatever it was, the angry guy wanted it pretty badly."

Elisabeth looked up at her. "How did you get away?"

Shea laughed. "Funny thing, really. I was fumbling around in the dark and decided it was better to hide after nearly falling on the guy's head. So I hid."

"Where?"

"We-ell," she started off slow, a grin spreading across her face. "You know that wicker casket upstairs? The one that came from the mortuary family?"

"Yeah," Elisabeth grinned back.

"I hid in there."

"Eeewwwwww!" Elisabeth squealed.

"I *know!"* Shea agreed, as she reached down and hugged Elisabeth around the shoulders, relieved to be out in the sunlight again.

ꙮ ꙮ

In the early evening hour Connor made his way down the boulevard toward Oakhurst. The sun was still above the houses across Wheeling but it would be dark soon. He was going on a single hunch, but needed to confirm his suspicions before he continued any further.

Just in front of Maplewood he glanced around and seeing no one in sight, he walked to the edge of the ravine. He reached for a sapling and began to make his way down the steep slope toward the river. His feet became tangled in the weeds about halfway down, and he skidded several feet before regaining his footing. Once he reached the river's edge, Connor moved west along the bank scanning the hillside for any sign of where he'd come from.

On his third pass a darker area just about a third of the way down from the top of the hill caught Connor's eye. It was covered in weeds, but the shadow underneath them was more pronounced and contained more depth. Slowly, cautiously, Connor made his way back up the hill toward the hole.

He pulled back the curtain of vines to uncover a small cave hidden directly below the House of Oakhurst. Though not very deep, it was just big enough to possibly house the portal through which he had arrived. At some point he would have to consider how to return home, and the sooner he worked on solving the problem the better.

It was a miracle in and of itself that he had been ejected through the mouth of the cave as he made his grand entrance into the White River only a short time ago without injuring himself. He was surprised at the relatively small opening and the fortuitous accuracy of his trajectory from it.

Peering inside he knew he had to make his assessment quickly. It was nearly dark, and he dared not draw any attention to himself or the cave during the daytime. Returning with one of those devices the humans called "flashlights" was always an option, but he preferred to get it over in one trip.

Crawling in over the lip of the entrance Connor rose and dusted himself off. The cave was more spacious on the inside than the outside divulged, and he was amazed that it remained relatively untouched. The room was empty except for a pile of something metallic against the far wall.

Connor's heart quickened as drew closer for a look, and he marveled at the craftsmanship. The thrill of his find was like discovering hidden treasure, but he knew the task had set out to complete had also just become more complicated.

Chapter 26

The day's events had exhausted Shea and after locking down the gates promptly at eight thirty, she changed clothes, grabbed a light blanket and her pillow and headed for the sleeping porch on the second floor. It was a calm night, and the woods were still.

Shea lay down on the wicker sofa and doubled her pillow over, affording her better support for her neck as she settled in for the night. Her long, silky hair fell loosely on the cushion and felt soft against her cheek.

It was beautiful there amongst the trees, and she was sure she'd have no trouble falling asleep on this night.

Shea closed her eyes and almost at once began to dream of three beautiful faeries who came to visit her in her treetop hideaway. Their hair was black as ebony, each with a thousand glistening stars scattered in amongst their wavy locks. Their eyes were a magnificent shade of aqua, shining as brilliant as any gem, and their olive skin was smooth and radiant. Drowsy, Shea rubbed her eyes to get a better look.

"Can I help you?" she asked, for lack of anything better to say as she sat up.

"We have come to show favor to you, Shea of Oakhurst," the faeries said in unison, as they hovered in flight just a couple of feet in front of her.

"Favor? I don't understand."

"Our King wishes to honor you for your service to the Kingdoms of Oakhurst and Nebosham. Your involvement is most…welcome."

"Your King?" Shea asked, somewhat perplexed. "Which kingdom did you say you represent?"

"Our kingdom is far beyond the gardens of Oakhurst," they said, moving slightly closer. "Your name is great within the faerie realm."

"I don't understand…" Shea was sure she was dreaming, simply because nothing made sense at this point.

"Such lovely hair," the trio noted in chorus. "We have come to make you beautiful. There is an upcoming ball, a celebration, and the eye of a certain prince will not go uncaught."

"A prince?" Shea chuckled. "Now I *know* I'm dreaming."

"May we be of service?" the faeries asked again, as they edged ever closer.

"Sure, why not?" Shea said with a wave of her hand. "I'm dreaming. What can it hurt?"

Immediately, the trio moved in close around her head,

untangling strands of her silky chestnut hair as they sectioned it off. Each, in turn, would take a section, wrap it around her waist and twirl her body toward Shea's head. After a two-count, they would release the hair, allowing it to fall about her shoulders in perfect ringlets. Two of them continued on while a third moved back in front of Shea. With a wave of her hand, a shimmering pool opened vertically in front of Shea's face, and she saw her reflection.

"See how beautiful you look," the celestial faerie told her. "Fairest in any kingdom."

Shea looked into the pool and saw her reflection. The fae was right – she was gorgeous! So much so, in fact, that she hardly recognized herself. She turned to the faerie and smiled.

"Oh, thank you," she said. "Thank you so much!"

"Only the best for Shea of Oakhurst," said the faerie.

"I just can't believe it! I – *ow!* Hey, that hurt!" Shea squealed. A sharp pull of a good amount of hair at the base of her neck caught her attention.

"Oh, a thousand pardons, milady," said the celestial faerie next to her right ear. "Your lovely locks seem to have caught in this rather cumbersome chain around your neck. Perhaps if you could take it off, I can continue?"

"Yes," Shea said, reaching up to the clasp to undo it. "Of course. I –"

She froze. Suddenly, the image of the Gutiku that fought so hard to take the amulet from her in the dumbwaiter was as clear as if it were right in front of her. Carefully, Shea's gaze shifted from side to side, looking for the faeries that still held her hair.

Shea reached up and rested her hand on the amulet that lay

just beneath her shirt. "I cannot take the chain off," she told them. "I am sorry."

"Is it cursed or something?" the faerie near her left ear asked. "Surely something so beautiful cannot be cursed."

"No, I suppose not. Still, I prefer to leave it where it is, thank you."

"That is most unfortunate," said the faerie in front of her, her tone growing cold. "I had hoped this would go smoothly." With a sweep of her hand the reflective pool vanished.

A sharp tug at the hairs on the back of her head made Shea wince. "Hey, watch it!" she cried. Her protest was followed by two more sharp tugs on the other side of her head. She began to swat around as the celestial faeries twisted and knotted and teased her hair, cackling as they orbited her head. The third faerie joined in, and the game was on.

They laughed and sang as they made chaotic mischief of what had once been Shea's beautiful, silky hair. Round and round they went, ratting sections and creating dreadlocks on the crown of her head.

Near panic, Shea jumped up and screamed, swatting at the faeries more seriously. She caught one of them with a good hit to the midsection, sending the little bugger flying across the sleeping porch. She hit the screen and went right through! Reaching up she caught another one as it made a pass back toward her ear and threw it as hard as she could. It hit the wall, stunned, and made its way under the wall to the garden. The third pulled up just short of Shea's face.

"This is not over," she said sharply. "The king will not be pleased." The celestial faerie flipped her raven hair and flew swiftly away, heading off into the night.

Shea reached up and felt her hair. It was a knotted mess! She tried and tried to run her fingers through it, but it was no use. The harder she tried, the worse it got. Finally, she decided to go inside to see the damage.

She opened the stained glass door and stepped into the bathroom. The small mirror above the sink showed her the horrible truth.

Shea's hair stood a good ten inches off of her scalp all the way around her head. The dreadlocks were wound into half-done braids and she could see the wall behind the thin layers of hair that the nasty little beasties had ratted with their hands. It was just awful!

"Wow," came a familiar voice from the door. "What happened to you?" It was Elisabeth.

Near tears, Shea wasn't sure what to say. She sighed, trying to compose herself.

"I'm guessing it wasn't a dream."

☙ ❧

Connor sighed as he raised the scissors. "Are you sure you want me to do this?" he asked hesitantly. "Maybe GiGi knows somebody who could do a better job than me…well, actually, *anybody* could do a better job than me." Right now he'd rather be giving the one-eyed troll a delousing than having to cut Shea's hair.

Elisabeth jabbed him in the ribs with her elbow, shooting him a cautionary look. Shea just shook her head.

It wasn't that he didn't want to be around her. He did. It was more that he knew from past experience with his sister that a woman's hair was her crowning glory, something that men should never mess with short of running their fingers through it once in awhile.

"I don't want anybody to see me like this," Shea sighed. "I don't know what I was thinking."

"That it was a dream," Elisabeth said. "Regrettably, that is understandable. The celestial fae are cruel tricksters. They've given most all faeries a bad name over the years."

"That's for sure," Connor lamented, warranting a sharp look from Elisabeth.

"Just cut it, Connor," Shea sighed. "Do what you can."

Of Fae and Sprites

Chapter 27

Oakhurst itself was set for Faeries, Sprites and Lights and looked stunning. Several paintings and sculptures by local artists graced the main floor of the house, and the finishing touches were being put on the rather large collection of fae homes in the library.

Shea wandered through the exhibit, nodding to the artist and smiling to herself, wondering what Queen Liliana had to say about all this. It had been a week and a half since the celestial faeries had paid her a visit, and Shea ran her hand through what was left of her hair as she remembered the mess they'd made.

Connor had actually done a decent job. He'd had to take a razor to it and cut it off in longer layers. The dreadlocks were the worst, and he'd really worked hard to thin it all out. What had once cascaded to the middle of her back now barely reached the base of her neck. There was still a good deal of it, but the layers made it seem like hardly much of anything remained. *No matter,* she thought to herself, *it'll grow back.*

When the library cleared, she stepped through the secret passage behind the bookcase and onto the screened porch in the garden concealing herself as she pulled the bookcase to behind her.

Through the trees she could see the candles on small shepherd's hooks along the pathway in the woods. Though the sun was still just above the trees across the street, in the waning daylight she could make out the tiny lights as they danced in their jars.

She sensed a presence next to her and didn't need to look to know that Elisabeth had joined her.

"Has it always been so beautiful here?" Shea asked her, eyes still scanning the garden.

"Even more so," Elisabeth replied. "There was a sense of harmony here. Balance."

"Kind of difficult to feel harmony when the King of Nebosham is ready to wage war on the Queen of Oakhurst."

"True," Elisabeth replied. "It's not the first time Rogan has been cross with the queen. I'm afraid it won't be the last, either."

"Oh?" Shea asked, looking at Elisabeth.

"It could get worse," Elisabeth said. "Much worse."

ᘓ ᘐ

The gardens of Oakhurst sprang to life just before six o'clock in the evening as the volunteers readied themselves for the arrival of the guests. An amazing event in its own right,

Faeries, Sprites and Lights offers a bright spot in the local summer festival schedule, providing guests a magical evening with historical grounding to it.

Part of the set up crew for the evening, Shea had been at it for hours helping haul various items back and forth from the main building. She had the distinct advantage of locality and had the opportunity to rest a bit in her tiny Oakhurst apartment before the festivities began.

Options of dress for the evening for staff included regular work-casual, early twentieth-century attire, or the ever popular faerie wings. Some of the women on staff went all out, choosing dresses and make-up that fit the theme nicely. Shea chose a beautiful, wispy summer dress she'd found in a shop in nearby downtown and a large set of filmy wings in beautiful pastel shades of blues and greens with a touch of lavender around the edges. The pearlescent finish on the sheer fabric made them perfect for the evening.

Shea descended the back stairs of Oakhurst so as not to draw attention to herself and headed through the parlor and into the library where a variety of handcrafted faerie homes were on display. The artist had created a variety of shops, retreats, and palaces out of found objects using her vast imagination to give new life to them. From a faerie dress shop with gowns made of butterfly wings to a winter home nestled snugly in a discarded ice skate, the tiny village delighted guests and sparked the imagination of countless children who came to visit.

"Aren't they amazing?" GiGi asked, on her way through the library to the hidden screened-in porch. She checked the door to make sure it was unlocked, then turned back to Shea.

Shea smiled. "She must've spent a lot of time creating all of these."

"Such a great imagination." GiGi headed back across the room. "Where are you stationed this evening?"

"The Visitor's Bureau tent for Faerie Town," Shea giggled. "I pass out the maps for the scavenger hunt."

"That'll keep you busy. Be sure to get in on the Unlighting Parade at the end."

"Unlighting Parade?" Shea asked.

GiGi grinned. "At the end of the evening we have a parade that runs the pathways around the grounds. Part of it is to gather the guests and usher them out, but the other part is to unlight the candles along the pathways."

"Sounds like fun," Shea said, as they headed out the front door. "Count me in."

ꝏ ꝏ

There were human-fae children everywhere. From teeny-tiny to grandmother aged and everything in between, the garden teemed with magic. Shea watched from a table near the tent as the guests arrived, one by one being welcomed by a staff faerie who admitted them through the magical doorway to Oakhurst Gardens. It was a beautifully rendered free-standing door that had a smaller door nestled into it for the "wee-folk," and though rather plain on one side, it was painted as something wonderfully magical on the other.

In the Bubble Garden nearby, a pair of faerie artists sat upon ornate stone benches painting pictures of faeries and dragons. Their works were framed and scattered amongst the foliage around them.

The occasional human-wood sprite child was even more rare, and Shea was delighted to see a brother and sister pair in full wood sprite and fae dress bolting straight toward her. She knelt and greeted them with a smile.

"Hello! Welcome to Faerie Towne," she grinned enthusiastically. "Would you like a map for the scavenger hunt?"

"Yeah!" they both chimed in unison.

"Thank you," their mother said, from just above them.

"You're welcome," Shea replied. "Have a good evening."

"If you could bottle that energy you'd be a rich woman," Sam said from behind her, as he filled the basket with giveaway pins decorated with beautiful faerie drawings.

"Don't I know it," Shea laughed, as she passed out the maps to yet another family.

Life at Oakhurst was truly good.

ᘐ ᘑ

The evening's magic wore on, and Shea finally took a break toward closing time seizing the opportunity to make the rounds on the grounds with the festivities in full swing. Larger faeries, dance students from a local studio, leaped and twirled in the Formal Garden near the arbor as guests watched, and little fae-wannabes imitated their larger counterparts. The play put on by the local civic theatre had just let out, so the girls had an even larger audience who were delighted with their performance.

On up along Aunt Emma's path Shea went veering back

toward the Carriage House, then down through the sunken garden. She could hear the wandering minstrels as they played their music near the bronze statue of a small boy playing a flute to the rabbits that surrounded him. Avoiding the crowd she turned and headed on down toward the pathway that ran along the front side of the property.

Suddenly, a strangely dressed man in dark attire nearly ran her down. He seemed rattled and in a great hurry.

"Can I….help you?" Shea inquired, as the man brushed past her in a hurry.

"No," the man responded, as he kept on his way, not even pausing in his reply.

Thinking little of it, Shea continued on down the path. Seeing trampled undergrowth, she stopped suddenly and was about to investigate when she heard someone behind her.

"Hey, thought I might find you down here," a voice called to her. Startled, Shea resisted the urge to jump and turned to find Connor standing there. He was dressed in his work casual.

"Out looking for me?" she teased.

"What? Oh, no….no," he stammered. "Just getting folks rounded up for the Unlighting Parade," Connor grinned like he had a secret. "Care to join me?"

"Why not?" Shea replied, and the pair headed down the pathway toward the cabin. "Where's your wings?"

Startled, Connor stopped. "What did you say?"

"Where are your wings?" Shea repeated, somewhat confused at his reaction. "You know, your wings?" she said, lowering her shoulder and making the fabric wings on her back flutter as best she could. "Or are you one of those wood sprites? I hear they're pretty rare around these parts."

"I am *not* a wood sprite," Connor blurted defensively.

Shea stopped and looked at him, surprised by his tone.

"Oh…right, my wings," Connor chuckled rather uneasily. "I, uh… I left them at home." Little did Shea know that was about as close to the truth as she was going to get at this point.

"Sheez, Connor, lighten up," she chided him, as they headed down the path.

The crowd started to thin out a bit, but several still remained at the craft station and the dancing area. Parents watched in delight as their children played as faeries in the growing twilight.

"Who wants to be in a parade?" Connor called out to the human-fae children dancing in the garden alcove next to the cabin.

A chorus of *"Me! Me! Oooh, I do!s"* came from the flock of faux fae as they ran toward him.

"Head right up that path, and they'll get you started," he instructed their parents, as he moved along the path up toward the dollhouse.

Shea smiled and greeted folks along the way directing them up to the front gate as well. This would make her job of closing down the gates much easier and even more enjoyable.

Coming up the pathway behind the house, Shea stopped suddenly, sending Connor nearly running into her. "What's wrong?" he asked.

Looking up toward the house in the growing darkness, Shea could see the light on in her tiny apartment.

"Funny," Shea started, "I don't remember leaving a light on upstairs."

"It's been a long day. Maybe you just forgot?"

"Maybe."

"We'll check it after we've finished up. How's that?" Connor reassured her.

"Sure," Shea answered, only halfway convinced.

ꝏ ꝏ

The Unlighting Parade was a grand event. Led by GiGi, faerie wings and all, she escorted the small legion of human-fae and -wood sprite children and their parents along the paths of Oakhurst talking about the magic of the fae folk who lived on the garden grounds. She spoke fondly of Elisabeth Ball when they came along the path near Oakhurst itself and down past the dollhouse where Elisabeth spent so many happy hours as a child.

Shea and Connor brought up the rear checking for stragglers as they went and picked up any stray trash that may have missed the cans. When the procession finally reached the front gate and the magical doorway back to the "real world," GiGi gave her final spiel, and she and several volunteers bid the humans *adieu* for the evening.

The crowd still milling about, Shea stood watching them. When she turned back to Connor, she found him watching her.

"Is something wrong?" she asked him, unsure of the look he was giving her.

"What? Uh, no," he said. "Why?"

"I just wondered. You looked like you wanted to say something."

Connor thought for a moment, Elisabeth's warning still

ringing in his ears. And yet a part of him disagreed. The sooner Shea knew the truth, the better things would be for everyone involved. The sooner she knew her destiny and her place in all of this, the safer the realm would be. Of that he was certain. And yet, if she knew the truth, everything he had built with her in the gardens of Oakhurst would vanish.

That was what he feared most of all.

Though there were still probably fifty guests surrounding them, it was as if Connor and Shea were the only ones in the garden. He smiled down at her and moved in close to speak softly to her. "There is something you must know, Shea. The reason you're here. Do you want to know?"

Shea looked up at him, her green eyes piercing the twilight between them. "Yes," she replied. "I want to know."

Connor's brain was addled by her simple beauty, and he paused. He was just about to forget all about it, to lean in and kiss her. Then none of it would matter. His station. Her station. None of it would matter. He leaned in, then hesitated.....a little too long.

"Hey, who's on trash duty?" GiGi called to the pair. Seeing what she'd inadvertently interrupted, her cheeks flushed. "Oooh, sorry." She paused, then, "Trash?"

"That would be me," Connor said, raising his hand. He never once took his eyes off of Shea.

Shea smiled and looked down. "I'll get the gates, as usual."

Connor reached down and took her hand. "Meet you afterward?"

"Of course."

CHAPTER 28

Connor set off on his quest for garbage, and Shea headed back up toward the Carriage House. The ladies in the gift shop and snack bar had already closed up for the evening, and Shea went around and shut the lights off on the ground floor locking the big carriage doors from the inside and then letting herself out the other door that led to the public loo. She chuckled at the fae doorway beside it, labeled as such for the wee folk. Queen Liliana would *not* be amused.

Looking up toward the second floor she saw the lights were still on in the gallery, and she headed around to the side of the Carriage House.

"Hello?" she called up the stairway. Hearing nothing, she headed up the stairs. She hadn't seen the exhibit yet, so she thought she would take a quick look before closing it down for the night. She ascended the narrow staircase and stepped up into the small makeshift gallery at the top.

The collection of relics and antiques was amazing, and Shea found herself immediately drawn in. Slowly, deliberately, she walked the perimeter of the room, stopping to look at the pieces from Elisabeth's era, marveling at how different things were now.

But it was the items featured in the center of the room that captured her attention.

One was the crystal egg guarded by the bronze dragon that she had seen down in Collections. Its hollow eyes stared up at her, and she wondered what tales it might tell if only the gems were there. *Would it be an even more fearful beast?* she wondered.

The second relic, though it seemed somewhat familiar to Shea, was new. Perhaps it was that the pair was similar in design and style, most likely crafted by the same artisan. It was a staff that stood nearly six feet tall with a matching dragon at the top. This dragon was wrapped in a circle around a large, fiery quartz that was the most brilliant combination of reds and orange and yellows that she had ever seen.

She stepped closer to get a better look at it. Suddenly, the headpiece began to glow brilliantly, and Shea was amazed to see it begin to glow brighter as she stepped closer. It was as if a flame burned inside of it. Curious, she took two steps backward and instantly the headpiece returned to normal.

Wanting to get a closer look, Shea stepped toward it again, and the stone began to blaze from within. She instinctively reached up to touch it, fingers mere inches from it, when she heard the board at the top of the stairs squeak. Startled, she turned about, stepping away from the staff, its fire instantly fading.

"Connor," she said, with some relief in her voice, though she was trembling. "Trash detail all done?"

"Task completed," he said. "What have you found?" He stepped away from the stairs and moved toward her staying between her and the stairs.

"I, uh…I hadn't seen the exhibit yet, and the lights were still on. I locked up downstairs, but the gallery was still open."

"Well, good," Connor replied. "Wouldn't want to leave this unlocked. Mr. Pendragon might get his knickers in a twist if anything came up missing, don't you think?"

"Have you had the chance to study these pieces much?" Shea asked. "They're amazing."

"Not really," Connor replied, scarcely able to take his eyes from her. She was beautiful, and he didn't know how long he would be able to keep the truth from her. "We moved them here, but Mr. Pendragon and a couple of other guys set it up." He stepped closer admiring the artistry of the relics. They were simple yet elegant in their presentation and complemented one another perfectly.

"The egg looks familiar," Connor noted, gazing into the empty eye sockets of the dragon. "Wonder what went in here?"

"Darius said jewels, probably," Shea replied, "but watch the staff. It does the strangest thing."

"What?"

"Watch."

Shea stood there for a moment staring at the staff. She looked to Connor, then stepped toward the staff. Slowly at first, it began to glow. The closer she got, the brighter it glowed.

Amazed, Connor chuckled as he looked from the staff to Shea and back to the staff again. "How did you do that?" he asked.

"I don't know," she answered, laughing softly as she took a step backward. The glow diminished as the distance between Shea and the staff increased, and she laughed.

"Now you try," she urged Connor, taking an extra step backward.

Connor moved closer to the staff until he was nearly standing on top of it, but nothing happened. Looking to Shea, he stepped away.

Stepping back up to the staff, Shea reached out toward it, and it glowed brilliantly. Her small hand was merely an inch or so from the smooth, round stone in the middle.

"*Miss* Remington," came a voice from the top of the stairs. Shea jumped, immediately withdrawing her hand, and both she and Connor turned on their heels to find Darius Pendragon standing at the top of the stairs.

"I'll thank you kindly not to touch the artifacts," he said in his rather proper manner.

"I'm sorry, I –"

"Aht!" Pendragon said sharply, raising his hand, "I don't want to hear it."

"But –"

"We just came up to turn off the lights," Connor said, in an attempt to defend her. It was not going well.

"These relics are centuries old," Pendragon scolded them. "We can't have them handled by just anyone. Do you understand?"

He walked slowly over to where they stood, eyeing Shea the whole time. It made her uncomfortable, and for the first time since her arrival she felt uneasy on the grounds of Oakhurst. She had originally thought it was just Pendragon, but the closer he moved to her, the more she felt that something was not right with him or the situation at hand.

Sensing her unease, Connor stepped toward her to both reassure her and ready himself to protect her. He was roughly the same size as Pendragon, though Darius seemed a little more solid compared to Connor's youthful frame. Connor hoped it would not come to that.

Pendragon's lips curled into a rather odd smile in a pitiful attempt to put the pair at ease. He stepped around them and reached out to lift the Dragon's Keep from its resting place. The eyeless dragon's empty gaze looked back at him.

"The relics have a story, did you know?" he asked them as he turned his gaze to the bronze dragon. "A sad one, really, filled with treachery and betrayal," he said, looking back at them, "and death."

Shea and Connor exchanged glances but said nothing.

"The staff had been lost for centuries. A powerful Dark Warrior possessed it and garnered great power as he wielded it throughout the land. But the people didn't understand, and they revolted. The Dark Warrior, unable to take his true form due to the lack of a third object, was lost in battle, and the staff became a spoil of war."

"What happened to him?" Shea asked, a little afraid of the answer.

"He fell into the sea," Pendragon replied. "His body was never recovered."

"What of the egg?" Connor asked. "What happened to it?"

"It was lost in a raid on the Palace of Erebos. In later years those whose kingdom had stolen it lost it the same way they obtained it. In a fierce battle it was liberated and hidden away. When it was recovered generations later, it was discovered that the eyes were missing from their settings. Lost forever, I'm afraid."

"It was later in the hands of a foolish king who was unaware of the power it possessed," Pendragon sneered. "He displayed it proudly as a family heirloom, a gift from his father-in-law."

Connor looked away, trying desperately to remember where he had heard that story before. Was it in the court at Ravensforge? Or perhaps merely a bedtime tale told to him by his mother. *If only he could remember...*

"Anybody up there?" came a sudden call from the bottom of the staircase.

Grateful for the intrusion, Shea and Connor stepped away from Pendragon, who quickly replaced the dragon egg artifact back on the display stand.

"Yes," Shea called out to the interloper. She glanced nervously at Connor then moved toward the stairs, and Connor followed suit.

"Oh, hey," Sam said, as he poked his head over the rail. "Connor, Shea," then looking beyond them, "Oh, hi, Darius. History lesson?"

"Of sorts," Pendragon said, in his stodgy, always-proper manner.

“Saw the light and thought I’d go ahead and close ‘er down for the night. You finished up here?”

“Yes,” Pendragon replied, looking at Connor and Shea.

Shea felt a chill though she couldn’t exactly be sure why. It was mid-July and typical Indiana summer weather, definitely not the conditions for any sort of chill.

“All done!” Shea said, perking up as she grabbed Connor’s arm. “Time to go!”

“Very good,” Sam said, watching Darius heading for the stairs as well.

“Thanks,” Shea whispered, as she passed Sam on the stairs. “I owe you one.”

Perplexed, Sam only smiled.

“Have a good evening,” he said.

ꙮ ꙮ

Shea and Connor walked back toward Oakhurst, the security lamps softly lighting the way.

“Are you alright?” Connor asked Shea.

“Yes,” she replied. “I’ve never seen Pendragon act like that. It was a little creepy.”

“True.” Connor said.

“All that faerie tale stuff he was talking about, it sounds like he should get with GiGi to write for FSL.”

Connor laughed, but inside he was still trying to put his finger on exactly where he’d heard that tale, where he’d seen that relic. And the empty eye sockets…

“Oh, you’ve got to be kidding,” Shea groaned, looking up at the window of the apartment.

"Almost forgot," Connor said absently. "Are you sure you didn't just leave the light on?"

"I don't ever leave them on. The light is so good in there I rarely turn them on during the day." Shea looked concerned but not fearful. Connor admired that in her. *If only she knew...*

"Do you want me to come up with you?" Connor asked. "It's a big house. We could check it out together if you want, then I'll go once you're comfortable with it."

"Do you mind?" Shea seemed relieved, and she took the key from her pocket and unlocked the back door. She reached inside and flipped on the lights.

Slowly the pair made their way through the first floor, checking every closet, cabinet and cranny, including the dumbwaiter. Shea went ahead and locked the basement door from her side so as not to have any surprises just in case.

Ascending the main staircase they headed up to the second floor, past the securely locked sleeping porch and the stained-glass man guarding the bathroom. A quick lighted check of each of the galleries showed nothing. Quietly they moved down the hallway to Shea's apartment.

The door was slightly ajar, and Connor raised a finger to his lips and cautiously entered the apartment. A heavy sigh on his part told her all she needed to know. She eased her way past him and looked around her home.

Every light was on and the place was an absolute wreck!

The bathroom cupboards had been emptied onto the floor. The bedroom looked as if it had literally been turned upside down. The contents of the chifforobe had been emptied onto the floor, and the mattress had been stripped and leaned against the window blocking the breeze through the screen.

Connor continued down the hallway toward the tiny kitchen and living room. Shea followed, somewhat fearful of what she would find.

The kitchen cupboards and refrigerator had been totally emptied with glasses and jars smashed on the floor. The cushions off the couch were scattered about the room, and the Center's television Sam thought Shea needed in case she got bored, was toppled over, the screen smashed beyond use.

Shea gasped. "Who would do such a thing?"

"What were they looking for?" Connor asked somewhat stupefied at the damage. "Do you have any idea what they were looking for?"

Shocked, Shea could only shake her head.

CHAPTER 29

Sam and two uniformed Muncie police officers arrived in short order, and Sam surveyed the damage as the officers interviewed both Shea and Connor in the gallery across the hall.

"Was anything stolen, ma'am?" one of them asked.

"Nothing I could tell," she replied quietly.

"This is not the first time someone has broken in here," Sam said, upon his return from the tiny apartment. "We had a break-in earlier this spring, but nothing like this. We had hoped that moving someone into Oakhurst might deter something like this from happening."

"Who might have done this?" Connor asked.

"We had hundreds of guests on the grounds," Sam reminded him. "It could have been anyone."

Connor watched Shea for any reaction beyond exhaustion. They were all tired from the day's events, but this was a bit much. She seemed fine, but he wanted to make sure.

"I'm sorry," Sam said after a good moment's pause, "but I'm afraid I have to go. I hate to leave you with such a mess, but my wife's aunt is taking the Red Eye in from California and we have to pick her up at the airport in a couple of hours. Otherwise I'd stick around and help you clean up. Maybe if you leave it until tomorrow, we can get a few folks down here to help."

Shea nodded in silence. Sam looked at Connor who spoke up.

"I'll keep an eye on her."

ꟈ ꟈ

After the police officers left, Shea sat down on the sofa in the apartment. Her hands had finally stopped trembling, and she began to pick up the mess. Silently, Connor stepped in and began to help.

"Connor, you don't have to stay," Shea said quietly. "It's been a long day, and I know you're tired. Tomorrow will be a long one, too. I'm only going to do a little bit here, just make a big enough space in the bedroom where I can lie down and just go to sleep. I'll clean the rest of it up after FSL."

"I don't mind staying," Connor replied, as he picked up broken glass off the kitchen floor. "Besides, it's not like I have anywhere I need to be."

Shea watched as he swept up the shards of glass into the dust pan and dumped the contents into the trash can. It had been quite a day, and between what had been going on in the human realm and the theft of the sacred relic of Nebosham in the fae realm, it had been an epically bad day all the way around.

He looked up catching her watching him. Dust pan midair, he stopped. "What?"

"Nothing," she sighed. "I just…thank you."

"You're welcome," Connor smiled at her. "What do you suppose they were looking for? It was obvious they were searching the place for something. The bad thing is that there were people in and out of the house all evening long, and anyone could've slipped in here without any trouble at all. And the worst of it is that no one would have been any the wiser."

Shea shook her head. "It's not like I have anything of worth," she sighed. "I don't have –"

She stopped suddenly, her hand coming to rest just above her heart. Hidden beneath her fae dress was the amulet. Could it be? She struggled with whether to tell him or not, whether to share with him that the amulet around her neck might possibly hold the key to all of the strange goings-on in the gardens. From the arrival of the relics, to the theft of the Sacred Relic of Nebosham to the appearance of Elisabeth Ball in the gardens of Oakhurst at just such a time, Shea began to wonder if it were more than mere happenstance.

"What?" Connor asked, looking a little perplexed.

"I don't know," Shea answered. "I don't know what to think anymore."

Finished with the kitchen, Connor moved into the living room. Feeling the need for a break, he cleared a space on the couch and sat down putting his feet up on the coffee table. He rested his head on the back of the couch and closed his weary eyes to rest them for a moment.

"Maybe they were after something of value, of worth, something that we might not fully understand," he said.

Shea's heart beat a little quicker realizing how close to the truth he was. In that moment she steeled her resolve. Stepping around the post from the kitchen into the living room, she made a rather dramatic revelation.

"Maybe they were after this," Shea said, as she pulled the amulet out from inside her dress top.

Her own tired eyes came to rest on Connor who was sound asleep on the sofa.

"Maybe we're all a little crazy," she sighed, tucking the amulet back down inside her dress.

Maybe indeed...

CHAPTER 30

The tables were set for high tea in the Formal Garden, and the guests had begun to arrive. Shea and the other staff and volunteers stood back and watched as mothers and daughters, all dressed in their finest, came down the path from the main gate and entered the garden through the arbor. Some even chose to wear hats. It was a moment from days gone by, and Shea smiled as she thought about Elisabeth and the many events her family had hosted here.

Though it was hot in the sunlight, a nice breeze came through the trees and kept things comfortable under the shade of the tent. The ladies, young and old, made their way to their seats and fussed over the spread before them. Fancy china cups and saucers, all different, were mixed and matched for the occasion, and decorated cookies and other assorted pastries were there for the sampling.

"Welcome to Oakhurst Gardens, and thank you for coming to Queen Liliana's High Tea," GiGi greeted them. "As you can see, the queen's table has been set as well at the head of the table. With any luck she will grace us with her presence today."

The queen's table sat upon a small box that was covered in a fine lace doily. A gold lamé tablecloth draped elegantly over the tiny table that was set with a beautiful silver tea set from one of Elisabeth's doll house collections. It was exquisite, a table surely fit for a queen.

Shea turned her head to conceal her smile. She wasn't quite sure if the queen would be amused or not. Liliana didn't strike Shea as one who had an easy sense of humor, but perhaps it was because she didn't know her well enough. Her guess was very few, fae or human, truly did.

While telling her guests about Elisabeth Ball and her childhood fascination with the faeries of Oakhurst, GiGi made a point of "serving" Queen Liliana first before the other guests. This, she explained, was befitting of faerie royalty and was only proper. Once the queen's table had been set, the guests were invited to help themselves, and the staff and volunteers brought a variety of teapots filled with tea. Mothers poured the warm tea for their daughters, then themselves, and chatted with those around them.

"You're probably wondering why none of the china matches," GiGi said, as she smiled at the guests. "Elisabeth Ball was a collector of art and children's books among other things. She had a vast collection of fine china, and although she had two full sets, the majority of the pieces she had collected over the years did not match."

Shea thought of Elisabeth as she busied herself with serving the guests. She tried to imagine her as a grown woman, even as an old lady but had trouble picturing her past the child who had become her closest friend. The sad part was no one would believe her if she told them.

ꙮ ꙮ

From a tree branch on the garden's edge Queen Liliana watched the humans and their tea. Though she sometimes had little patience for them, she remembered that not all were annoying.

"They mean no harm, Highness," Elisabeth said quietly, as she watched the occasion unfold. "The tea, after all, is in your honor."

"I know," the queen sighed, offering Elisabeth a half smile. "Perhaps I should put in an appearance."

ꙮ ꙮ

The tea party wound down, and the guests were about to depart when something unusual occurred: a doe appeared at the edge of the garden! Mothers and daughters alike were thrilled as all eyes turned to watch the beautiful deer. A moment later a tiny fawn poked its head out of the summer foliage.

"Look, Mommy! A deer!" one little girl squealed rather loudly.

"*Shhhhhh!*" her mother hushed, and they all watched as the two deer came out of the thicket and walked across the yard.

The women and little girls were thrilled that the afternoon had ended on a high note, but none more so than GiGi.

"Thank you all for coming, ladies! It's been a pleasure having you all here today, and – " Her words stopped short out of shock and surprise.

"Oh, my," was all she could manage.

Before her on the table where the queen's table sat was the remains of Queen Liliana's tea and a few crumbs where the cookies had previously been. GiGi always set the table for the queen, and usually managed to get an "appearance," but this was more than she had expected. She looked around, but the rest of the staff were otherwise occupied. Not sure what to say, she decided to play along.

"Well, girls," she said proudly, as she gestured to Queen Liliana's table, "it seems the queen has graced us with her presence!"

Chapter 31

The courtyard was beautiful as the late afternoon sun sparkled through the leaves, lending a sense of magic to the Formal Garden. White lights were strung among the branches and danced on the breeze.

Shea made her way through the arbor and watched as the string quartet began to set up for the evening, running sound checks with the technicians and making final preparations for the night ahead.

Though she rarely wore dresses, Shea felt comfortable in her gown, almost at home. The large wings strapped to her shoulders were noticeable, but by no means annoying. If she were a bit more than four and a half feet shorter, she'd fit into Queen Liliana's court just fine.

She stood mesmerized at the garden's edge, hesitant to go any further.

"Beautiful, isn't it?"

Startled, Shea turned to find Connor at her side. Dressed in a turn-of-the-twentieth century suit, he was dashing. Shea caught her breath and felt her face go flush, quickly turning away.

"Yes, it is," she agreed. "I never imagined I'd live somewhere so wonderful, so full of magic."

"You look as though you were born to dress this way," Connor told her.

"I wish I knew," Shea replied, a sudden sadness washing over her face.

Connor immediately regretted his words but knew she had to be told. Elisabeth had cautioned him about telling her, but at this point, what could it hurt? She was beginning to remember a few things, and he found her reaction to the relics most intriguing.

He was quite unsettled by the attention Darius paid her. Though he seemed nice enough, there was just something about him that didn't quite ring true. Perhaps it was that he seemed so damned nice all the time. The fact that he was good looking didn't hurt either – he had all the women there practically swooning when he entered a room, almost in a drunken stupor. But in all honesty, it was Shea's reaction to him, as if she were leery, or almost afraid of him that made Connor wonder.

He had seen it in the upper room the night before when they were looking at the dragon staff and egg relic. Things were fine, and he thought they might have even been on the verge of a breakthrough when Pendragon entered the gallery. He had an almost hypnotic effect on Shea, like a snake on a bird right before it ate it, and Connor knew he didn't like it one bit.

"Do you remember anything?" he asked her, pressing just a little. "You look a little sad."

"I…don't know," she replied, somewhat deep in thought. "It is difficult to tell what is real and what is my imagination. And after the Gutiku, well, you know how that all ended. Some days I wonder if I'm not just losing my mind."

Connor chuckled at the thought, and even more so at the aftermath of thinking Oakhurst had been destroyed but finding it untouched. Somewhat emboldened, he stepped in closer to her placing his hand upon her shoulder. This could go either way, and he was hoping for the best.

"What if I told you I know who you are?"

Somewhat shocked and not sure if she heard him right, Shea stepped back from him. "What?"

Uncertain if he should proceed, Connor took in a deep breath, then continued. "What if I told you I know who you are? Where you came from."

Confusion, shock and sheer ire all converged on Shea's face as her eyes flashed. Though controlled, she knew she wouldn't be able to keep it down for long.

"You *know* who I am?" Shea asked him, as a twinge of anger began to rise within her.

"You say you can't recall your past or where you came from. Have you remembered anything?"

"Not much," Shea admitted, a sharper tone to her voice. "Just flashes of things, really. Faces I don't recognize. Places I feel I should know but don't. It's become quite frustrating." Aggravation knotted in her gut. "Honestly, some days I wish the dreams would just go away, and I could just live out my days here in peace."

"Do you think you would be happy with that?" Connor asked quietly. "I would think that missing piece of your life would gnaw at you."

She snorted rather cynically. "Yeah, you're right. It would probably eat me alive."

"Well, we can't have that, now can we?"

Connor's tone intrigued her, and Shea shot him a look. "What are you saying?"

"Come with me," Connor said. "I have something to show you."

ꟻ ꟻ

He watched in silence as the princess left the palace. This was not her first tryst, her first meeting with the prince of Nebosham, nor would it be her last. And that piece of information would be most valuable when the time was right. For now her absence afforded him the opportunity he'd long awaited.

From the upper window of the palace he watched Verena disappear into the foliage of the garden. Silently he moved down the corridor toward the temple, once again employing the dark magic. The traveling cloak was no longer necessary and, wings folded close, he walked swiftly toward his objective.

Upon hearing the news that the Relic of Nebosham had been stolen, Queen Liliana had ordered the guard doubled around the palace and tripled around the temple. It was as much to protect the palace from the sprites as from thieves and dark magicians.

Queen Liliana was smart and took no chances, only allowing those who had been in her service for a long period of time to even come close to the temple. All others were kept at a safe distance, both for protection of the relic and the kingdom. Both kingdoms.

"At ease," said Minister Foley, as he breezed past the guards at the door. "I am on a mission from the queen herself. There have been sprites spotted near the front of the palace."

"As you wish, My Lord," answered one of the guards, "but most must remain, by order of the queen."

"Very well," he agreed. "But as the Minister's consultant on defense, I need all the guards I can get. The princess is in grave danger."

This got the captain of the guard's attention. "What has happened?"

"The Prince of Nebosham has kidnapped the princess! The queen is beside herself, sick with worry. In this time of uncertainty, we must take no chances."

Immediately the guard pointed to the three standing ready at the door. In an instant, they headed at a dead run down the corridor. The captain ordered the other two to stand guard just outside the temple doors and lock them fast behind them. If intruders did arrive, at least the temple would appear to be more heavily guarded than it was.

Feeling somewhat relieved, the captain of the guard called over his shoulder to the minister.

"Minister, is there anything else that you require?" he asked. Garnering no reply, he turned to find the minister gone.

And so was the Sacred Relic of Oakhurst.

ᘐ ᘏ

Verena's gossamer wings carried her lightly to the forest floor where she quickly hid herself under the groundcover. It was their usual meeting place, and she waited patiently for the prince.

"You know, you shouldn't be out here alone," Royce said quietly, as he appeared from inside a nearby hollow log.

Verena smiled as she greeted him with a kiss. She pulled away, and his expression told her this would be their last meeting, possibly for a very long time. "Things are not well with your father, I take it?"

"No," Royce said solemnly. "It is all I can stand to hear the things he says about your mother."

"I'd rather not know," Verena said.

"I'd rather not tell you," Royce agreed.

Royce moved in again ready to kiss her when a rustle in the weeds startled him. Verena gasped and stepped away slowly. Royce gingerly turned his head to the right finding the point of a sword pressing into the flesh of his cheek. He did not move at all for fear of making it worse.

"You will come with us," the guard said sternly. "Princess, are you alright?"

Verena sighed, knowing that no matter what she said it would not convince her mother's guard that she was in no danger. The day she had long dreaded had come to her at last.

She would have to tell her mother the truth.

ᘐ ᘏ

Though there were people around, the Carriage House was relatively quiet. The shopkeepers had been busy in the late afternoon with the onslaught of eager little faeries and wood sprites and their parents. The lull left the staff huddled behind the counter, talking and laughing.

Connor nodded to them as he led Shea past the makeshift shop and around to the stairway that led up to the exhibit on the second floor of the Carriage House. He had helped set it up the earlier in the week and managed to talk his way onto the crew expressly for this purpose.

"Where are we going?" Shea asked, on their way up the stairs. He was a few steps ahead of her, and Shea gawked at the treasures and artifacts on display that helped to tell the story of the lives of George, Francis and Elisabeth Ball. Children's books and artwork surrounded her as she wondered if Elisabeth might be about. She had been rather distracted the night before when Darius arrived and hadn't seen most of the other pieces.

"Here," Connor declared, as he stopped in front of a trio of rather large steamer trunks.

"Are you planning a trip?" Shea teased him with a gleam in her eye.

"Of sorts," he smiled, as his eyes scanned the room. Except for them, the room was empty.

Connor drew an old skeleton key from his pocket and unlocked the large trunk first. Sitting on end, he opened it like a door, and from where Shea stood she could see only part of what was inside. Stepping nearer she leaned around the open trunk lid and peered inside.

Hanging in the back half of the steamer trunk was a set of battle armor. Shea's eyes narrowed, and she moved in closer to examine it.

She reached out, hesitating for a moment, then lightly ran her fingers across the shoulders and down the breastplate to where a small jeweled raven rested mid-chest.

"I don't understand," Shea said, her brows knit together. Everything was strange to her yet it had a calming beauty that brought her a sense of comfort.

"Maybe this will help," Connor said, as he knelt to unlock the second trunk. He gently, almost reverently, opened the lid and reached inside. His back to her, he rose slowly and turned toward her, his arms outstretched.

Across his hands lay a beautiful sword. The blade was easily three inches across, and it gleamed under the makeshift gallery lighting. Again, a jeweled raven adorned the piece, wings outstretched to form the hilt.

"Mind the blade," Connor warned, as he held it out to her, "it's –"

"—sharp," she finished for him. "Incredibly sharp."

Shea ran her fingers down the length of the blade, lightly brushing the cool metal beneath them. She brought them to rest on the raven at the hilt, his jeweled eyes gazing back at her. Shea could only stare at the raven mesmerized as the torrent of memories came flooding back to her.

Slowly she laid her hands out in front of her to accept the weapon. It felt surprisingly light and was well balanced. Images came rushing at her at light speed, filling her mind at such a rate she could scarcely keep up. The palace, the faces of the royals, the guard, and the carnage of her last night with them came rushing back to her at a rate that knocked the wind out of her. She gasped at the sights as they flowed through her mind, nearly dropping the sword.

Blinking, trying desperately to hold back the tears, she continued to stare at the sword.

"What do you know?" she whispered intently, as Connor began to circle her slowly.

"I know where the contents of this trunk came from," he said softly. His tone was firm and even as he spoke. "I know who wore this armor. I know who wielded this sword and why."

She felt herself shudder involuntarily, wanting to know the truth but fearful it would change things.

"I know what happened that final night as Ravensforge burned." Connor paused behind her, and Shea could feel his breath brush her cheek as he spoke. "And I know who you are."

Shea could only stare ahead of her as tears spilled down her cheeks. Her mind was filled with more images than she could process, and Connor possessed the key to it all with the answer to the question that burned inside of her.

"Who am I?" she asked, the question barely audible as her eyes fought back the tears.

Connor leaned in close, the hushed tones of his lips next to her ear meant only for her to hear. "You," he whispered, "are Shea, Guardian of Ravensforge."

ꕤ ꕤ

The dark figure paced anxiously on the edge of the Gardens of Oakhurst. His contact was late, and if this was ever going to happen, it would have to be on this night. In truth, he had thought it would never come to pass, for the simple fact that humans were involved.

One thing he knew for certain: Humans could not be trusted to handle anything of import in the first place, and humans who had crossed from their own realm into the fae realm were even less trustworthy.

ꙮ ꙮ

The sword fit Shea's hand perfectly, not the slightest bit unwieldy. She moved it from one hand to the other examining the hilt and its craftsmanship.

"Magnificent, isn't it?" Connor asked, the admiration evident in his voice.

She looked up at him watching his eyes dance across the blade as he spoke.

"Crafted in the fires of Ravensforge and blessed by the king himself. There is none finer in all the land nor any more cherished and sought after than those crafted in Ravensforge."

Her brows knit together. "Did you know me? Do you know my family?"

Connor measured his words carefully before he spoke. "We met only once before. In the Great Hall of Ravensforge. Do you remember?"

"There were a lot of people there," Shea recalled.

"It was a state dinner – a meeting of the royals."

Shea spoke slowly and deliberately as she began to piece together her past. "The…King introduced you and your…entourage."

"Yes," Connor chuckled realizing she hadn't fully remembered their meeting.

"The king," she reiterated, "led you down the table. He greeted you warmly as if you were family. Someone stood between you and me."

"Their names were Nola and Sela."

"Were?"

Connor continued. "I only know what occurred while I was at Ravensforge. The rest is what I learned after the fact. Nola and Sela were the king's daughters. I was there to choose one of them to be my bride."

Confusion again veiled her face as Shea of Ravensforge began to fight her way to clarity.

"You greeted the king, met his daughters…then introduced them to –" Shea's words froze in her throat as the realization hit her square in the face.

"—your mother?" A quizzical scowl told Connor she got it. Or at least part of it. "Your *mother?!*"

Rattled, Shea nearly dropped the sword. She wrapped her small hand around the hilt as she began to pace. She ran her fingers through her freshly cropped hair muttering as she began to piece it all together.

"Your *mother*," she said rather pointedly, "is *Queen Liliana?*"

"Guilty as charged," Conner quipped, a grin spreading across his face.

"Your mother is Queen Liliana?" Shea repeated, in an attempt to sort it all out. "That would make you—"

"Connor, of the Seventh Line of Ashtan, Crown Prince of Oakhurst."

ꕤ ꕤ

Glancing around while taking great care not to move his head, Royce was suddenly aware of the number of fae guards surrounding them. He looked to Verena with such an expression of shock that had a sword not been pressed up against his cheek, it might almost be funny. Mustering his best indignation while trying to suppress the quiver in his voice, Royce finally opened his mouth.

"What is the meaning of this?" he demanded, while still not making any unnecessary movements.

"Silence," the guard replied. "We will ask the questions." Then turning to Verena, "Are you injured, Your Highness?"

A little in shock, Verena could only shake her head.

"Very well," the guard replied, turning his attention back to Royce. "You will return with us to Oakhurst at once."

Finally finding her voice, Verena used it. "By whose order are you here?" she asked.

"Mine," came a voice from within the mass of fae guards. Dressed in a traveling cloak, Minister Foley emerged from the detachment.

Verena sensed immediately that something was not right. "Then it is to you whom I owe my thanks," Verena managed, sounding almost confident enough to fool even herself.

Royce straightened taking care not to turn his head in the wrong directions. His eyes plainly showed his confusion and hurt, although Verena could not return the look. Not with all eyes on her.

"I owe you my gratitude, Minister," Verena replied with a slight nod, "and my life."

"It is my honor and sacred duty, Highness," the Minister returned her nod.

"May I?" she asked.

"By all means," the Minister answered, a smile curling his lips.

Turning to the guard holding the sword to Royce's cheek, Verena put on her most official sounding voice.

"Guard," she commanded, "take the prisoner to Oakhurst where you will lock him in the tower until further notice."

"On what grounds?" Royce demanded, rather indignantly. This was almost more than he could bear at this point. *What was wrong with her?*

Verena could almost enjoy this if it weren't so serious. "You, Prince Royce of Nebosham, have committed an act of war."

"A *what?!*" Royce asked, his blood pressure rising.

Verena shifted slightly hoping her mannerisms would not give her away. She didn't know how many of them were in legion with the Minister, and it was best to just get back to the palace and find her mother. She would know what to do. Raising her chin and setting her resolve, she spoke in a regal tone. "An act of war," she repeated, somewhat haughtily, "by kidnapping the princess."

Minister Foley moved in closer, his words intended only for Verena's ears.

"Princess, I must leave you now," Minister Foley said as he spoke quietly to the princess. "I am on a most important mission from the queen herself."

Verena nodded knowingly at the lie acting most impressed. "Very well, Minister. I shall escort the prisoner back to Oakhurst and report to her immediately. Is there a message you would like to send to her?'

"Only that it will all be over soon. Tell her that we must amass the troops and storm Nebosham." He turned, looking at the shell-shocked prince. "His head on a pike might not be a bad way to go," he said rather sharply, "but that may be a bit much."

ꝏ ꝏ

"Mother, he knew I would know he was lying! Something is not right here!"

Queen Liliana stood at the window of the throne room looking out over the beautiful garden below. She was still stuck on the first point of the argument. "Why were you in the forest with Royce? Really, Verena...*Royce?!"*

"Mother! There are bigger things going on than whom I choose to spend my time with!" Verena held her ground.

Liliana turned to survey her daughter's lovely face. "Yes, dear one," the queen responded softly, "I know. But if things are to play out to our advantage, we must exercise discretion and patience."

Verena was unsure of where her mother was going with this. Frustration veiled her face as she tried to understand.

"We are aware of the duplicitous nature of Minister Foley. We have been aware of his practicing dark magic for awhile now."

"But even I was caught unawares," Verena sounded incredulous. "How did you know?"

"Good intel is worth almost as much as a beautiful, distracted daughter with the gift of discernment," Liliana smiled. "The only difference is the good intel doesn't talk back. Or sneak off with the sprite prince."

Verena lowered her eyes and smiled as her mother stroked her cheek.

"Have you heard from your brother of late?" Liliana asked.

Verena's smile faded as quickly as it came.

"Mother, I think there's something you should know. Something your good intel probably *didn't* tell you."

Chapter 32

"Connor has *what?!"* Queen Liliana exclaimed, shocked to her core at Verena's words. Feeling lightheaded she sat down in the windowsill overlooking the garden.

"It is true, Mother," Verena said calmly, trying to soothe her after delivering the shocking blow. "Connor has taken human form."

"To what end? There is nothing for him there. Is this some lark of his? I know he's a bit on the adventurous side, but this is going just a little too far!"

"He did say he went to seek out the Royals of Ravensforge," Verena said, trying to reassure her mother. "You did say, did you not, that they used the portal to cross over?"

"Yes," Liliana agreed, "but it was destroyed. There was no way to use it to get to the human realm." She paused looking away, knowing in her heart that was only half true. There were other ways to cross over, but most meant there was a high price to pay that eroded one's very soul, and most, if not all of them, were permanent. She hoped that was not the case with her son. Surely she'd raised him better than that.

"What's done is done," Verena told her, knowing that would not be the end of it. "Let us hope he has found them."

ꕥ ꕥ

Arland gathered the captains of the guard for their audience with the queen. The discovery of Verena in the forest with Royce was only a minor incident compared to the theft of the Sacred Relic. After the theft of the Relic of Nebosham, the theft of its counterpart at Oakhurst was not to be unexpected. But it was the brazen theft – in broad daylight, no less – by one of the queen's most trusted advisors and truly a slap in the face.

Foley would pay for it; Arland would see to that.

The guard stood at the ready as Liliana swept into the room.

"Majesty," Arland announced formally, as the assembled guard snapped to.

"Commander," Queen Liliana addressed him. "What have you learned."

"Word has it that the Keeper of Time will be released shortly."

ꕥ ꕥ

Dumbfounded, Shea stood in the Carriage House at an utter loss for words. *How could this be?*

"But you're so...*BIG*...and she's so...so –"

"Careful," Connor warned.

Shea's mind raced back to her last encounter with the queen, whom she offended greatly by noting she was small.

"—not...big," Shea finished hesitantly, her eyes narrowing. "But how – has the queen been shrunken by some dark magic?" she asked. "Or is she here only in spirit like Elisabeth?"

"No."

"I don't recall feeling bigger than everyone else in the Great Hall at Ravensforge. Nor you. Surely I would know?"

"You were not. We were all of the same size. You were the Guardian of the king's daughters. We are – were – all of the faerie realm."

"You mean I was –" Shea gestured small in an attempt to grasp what Connor was saying. "But how'd I get so –" Again, hands gesturing up and down her torso, taking care with the sword still in her right hand. "And you?" she asked pointing the sword directly at him.

Flabbergasted, Shea sat down on the remaining steamer trunk and laid the sword down next to her. She covered her face for a moment, then ran her fingers through her hair.

"What of my family?" Shea asked, fearing the answer. "This sword was a gift...from my father on my sixteenth birthday." The memory brought her some comfort. She could see her father's face vaguely and sensed pride in his expression. In her.

"I do not know," Connor responded. His eyes were vacant,

somewhere far off. "We had already returned to Oakhurst when we received word that Ravensforge had been attacked. By the time we gathered our troops and returned to Ravensforge, it was all over. The palace lay in ruin and everyone was…gone."

"My first duty was to find the Royals. When I arrived, I discovered the portal to this realm had been destroyed. A troll recounted what had happened, where the king's family had gone. I discovered your sword and battle armor shortly after my arrival here."

"If the portal was destroyed, how did you get here?" Shea asked.

"There are…other ways," Connor replied.

"Other ways?" Shea echoed back. "By what manner did you come to Oakhurst?"

Footsteps on the staircase brought silence to the pair one of the staff members made their way into the gallery. Shea lowered the sword to her side and smiled as they carried flyers to the station at the window, then retreated down the stairs.

Shea glanced at the collection Pendragon had brought with him. Something was different. *Something was missing.*

"Connor?"

"What is it, Shea?"

"The Keeper of Time. It is gone!"

Chapter 33

"At last, you have accomplished what I have asked of you," the dark figure acknowledged as Minister Foley handed over the sack that contained the Sacred Relic of Oakhurst.

"As you requested, My Lord," Minister Foley replied. His wings fluttered slightly as he held his ground. He was uneasy about their meeting and tried his best to hide it. "There were…complications," he admitted. "However, I rather think they will work to our advantage."

"Oh?"

"Prince Royce has been apprehended for trying to kidnap Princess Verena," Minister Foley smiled. "The ramifications will be most distasteful."

"Indeed."

"And the best part is, they won't even see what's coming."

The dark figure smiled at the thought of the fall of the two kingdoms. It had been a long time coming, and his hard work would finally pay off.

"Their arrogance will be their undoing," he said. "And I will be the catalyst to unleash it all."

ꕤ ꕤ

Prince Royce of Nebosham sat on the floor of his cell surrounded by darkness as twilight came upon the kingdom. His father would be wondering where he was by now. He could only hope that his father did not believe the worst of him, that he had stolen the Relic. And he was not sure of what had just happened in the garden, but he knew enough to know he'd been had.

Verena would never hang him out to dry like that, but then again, she had been awfully convincing. Could she have really just been using him as nothing more than a pawn? A way to learn more about the goings on and secret dealings of Nebosham? His father had warned him about faeries and the magic they wove around sprites.

Yet he still believed that on some level she still cared for him. If only he could be certain. If only he were totally wrong about her. If only –

"Pssssst!" came a hiss from the darkened corridor in the hollow tree branch.

Royce rose from his corner seat and stepped closer to the heavy door. He peered through the small, barred window but saw nothing.

Turning to go back where he came from he heard it again.

"Pssssst!"

"Who is there?" Royce demanded, losing his patience. "Show yourself."

Slowly the figure appeared in the light coming through the tiny window of the door to reveal the soft face of Verena. His heart quickened, and he didn't know whether to be glad to see her or angry. Valor being the greater part of wisdom, he held his tongue instead, letting her speak first.

"Royce," she said, somewhat out of breath. "We must get you out of here. There is little time."

"Oh, so now you'll claim me," Royce shot at her, a little quicker than he'd anticipated. "Or was this all part of your plan, or your mother's plan, to conquer Nebosham and rule over us all?"

"Royce, you know me better than that," Verena snapped at him, her voice carrying just a little bit of regret in it. "I had no choice."

Royce scoffed and turning his back on her, walked over to the tiny knothole window that looked out onto the backside of Oakhurst. "Thought I did," he said quietly. "I should've known. My father warned me, you know, but I wouldn't listen."

"Your father was wrong about a few things," Verena said, immediately regretting how it came out. "What I mean is, fae and sprites were not meant to live separately. They are equally powerful in their own right. Each kingdom has its own heritage, its own traditions, and it is through these elements that we are able to honor this place the way we do."

"Your mother is not exactly an 'all-for-one' kinda girl," Royce retorted sharply.

"True," Verena agreed, "but I do believe that she has the best interest of all of Oakhurst at heart. I truly believe that your father and my mother have more in common than either cares to admit. And if they'd just open up to one another about what they know of the other Kingdoms, we'd all be a lot safer and a lot better off."

"It would seem," Rogan sighed, "that we have reached an impasse."

"Perhaps not," Verena countered. "There is one hope left."

ꟷ ꟷ

Connor led Shea out of the back of the Carriage House. They emerged just in time to see a tall man in period dress head down the path toward the Formal Garden.

"C'mon," Connor whispered, as he moved to follow him. Shea followed closely, not sure what they would find. At this point they had little to go on, so this direction was as good as any. She began to wish that she had brought along her sword from the collection.

Her sword.

She smiled at the thought, certain that she would be able to claim her belongings soon, though she still wasn't sure quite how that would come about.

The man was easily twenty paces ahead of them when he disappeared into the thicket, and Connor quickened his steps as he made ready to overtake him. But as they rounded the honeysuckle and entered the woods, the man was nowhere to be found.

Instead, lying on the ground in front of them was the relic. Only it looked different.

“The dragon is missing,” Shea noted softly, as she knelt and reached for the crystal egg. It didn’t look at all broken nor even cut upon, and it no longer glowed from within.

“Uhhh, no,” Connor stammered, gathering his wits about him, “no it’s not.”

Shea looked back up at him perplexed, seeing not a look of fear, but rather one of amazement and total, utter disbelief. She wasn’t sure if it was the feeling of eyes on the back of her neck, or the hot breath moving her hair, or even the slight snap of the twig behind her that told her they were in danger.

Shea turned her head following Connor’s gaze, straight into the eyes of the dragon.

Chapter 34

Slowly at first, the dragon stretched and unfolded itself until it stood a good ten feet above Shea and Connor. The fading sunlight played off the aqua-colored iridescent scales that covered the beast. Though still young, it was no less fierce than if it had been three hundred years old. It blinked its fire opal eyes as if awakening from a long nap, and it looked rather put out at being disturbed at all.

Connor and Shea exchanged glances, daring to take their eyes off the dragon only for a moment.

"Got any ideas?" Shea asked.

"Not at the moment. You?"

"Run?" Shea replied, more as a question than a solution.

With that, the pair turned and burst out of the bushes into the Formal Garden and sprinted headlong down Aunt Emma's path toward Oakhurst. Connor hung a sharp left as the pathway spilled out near the back door and squeezed his way between the information table and the craft tent, startling the volunteers stationed there. He muttered something to them as he quickly swung the wrought iron gate shut and latched it.

Shea stopped dead in her tracks, more dumbfounded than anything, as Connor ran along the fence and pulled the smaller gate directly in front of the house closed as well. He turned and rushed back at her.

"Really, Connor?" she asked sarcastically. "*Really?!* It's not a sheepdog, for cryin' out loud…" She suddenly lowered her tone realizing how loud she'd been speaking. "*It's a dragon!*" she hissed.

"Yes, it is," Connor replied as he moved past her, "but with any luck his wings haven't caught up with the rest of him yet."

Shea turned and followed Connor back the way they came. They could hear the dragon crashing through the trees as Connor grabbed her hand and dragged her through the gate into Queen Liliana's garden located directly behind Oakhurst. A quick hop over the tiny stream propelled them forward into the wood again.

The primitive picket fences made of sharpened sticks demarcating the property lines of the previous Ball neighbors were the only man-made obstacles as they fled deeper into the underbrush.

The gate behind them, of course, was no match for the young dragon. They could hear it snorting and growling, gnashing its teeth as it crashed down the path and through the trees after them. The pair barreled through the briars and weeds trying to put as many obstacles between them and the pursuing beast as possible.

Shea caught hold of the end of one of the fences and flung

herself around it as she careened through the underbrush. *Damn this dress!* Why she'd ever put it on was beyond her. She made a mental note to herself that if she made it through the day alive she'd never put on a dress again.

Connor nearly ran her over as he rounded the fence behind her. *"Keep moving!"* he ordered sharply.

Out of the corner of her eye she saw it. The dragon was gaining ground, snapping off saplings like they were toothpicks and totally crushing the fence they'd just come around like it was a mere inconvenience.

"Connor? This is not working!" Shea cried out, as she sped up again. Things were going to be hard enough to explain, and no one else had seen the dragon yet. They had to keep it away from the crowds or who knew what would happen. The gardens at Oakhurst were big, but not big enough to hide a dragon for very long. The crowds would be here soon enough, and to say the staff would have a fit was an understatement at best.

They emerged at the back gate of the property near the Colonnade Garden, surprising Mary, one of Minnetrista's sweet, seasoned volunteers.

"Oh, hello, Connor! Hello, Shea!" Mary greeted them warmly, but a look of confusion quickly replaced the grandmotherly look of love on her face as Connor began to pull the wrought iron gates closed.

"Connor?" Mary asked quizzically. "Dear, what is the meaning of this?"

"No worries, Mary. Evangeline's orders," Connor lied easily, looking over his shoulder hoping the dragon would stay elsewhere. "Missing child."

"Oh," Mary nodded.

"We'll be back to open it up soon," Shea added over her shoulder as they trotted toward the Discovery Cabin. "Let you know when we find him…her."

"Alright!" Mary called after them. "I'll keep my eye out for her."

Connor and Shea sprinted back toward the cabin. Hearing the dragon heading toward Mary's post, Connor stopped suddenly, and Shea had to pull up short to keep from plowing him over.

"Hey!" he shouted, as he waved his arms above his head. "Hey, over here!"

A sharp crack of a tree followed by a snort and silence told Connor he'd gotten the beast's attention. The trees, mere yards away, rustled as the dragon came their way.

"Better move," Shea urged him. "*Now!*"

They were off again, headed for the front gate. As the pathway split off, Shea headed right instead of toward the gate. Befuddled, Connor stopped suddenly.

"Where are you going?" he called after her. She was half way to the sunken garden by now.

"Lock the gate. I'll be with you shortly."

"I surely do hope so," Connor said under his breath, as he sprinted toward the main gate. Behind him he could hear the crashing followed by a pause. Through the trees he could see the young dragon. It was stopped where he and Shea had parted ways, and raised up on its hind quarters sniffing the air as if it were confused, unsure of where to go.

It turned down the path Shea had taken and started toward the sunken garden. It might not have been a bad thing had

Shea been expecting it, but at this point, Connor couldn't take that chance.

"Oh, bad, bad," he said to himself, then in a loud voice, *"Hey, over here!"* He waved his arms, making sure the beast saw him and jumped up and down for good measure.

The dragon snorted, and Connor could hear its toenails scraping on the brick pathway as it made a hard turn back his way. Raised up high, it scanned the woods until it saw Connor's flailing through the trees. It laid its head back and let out a horrible bellow that chilled Connor's blood just before the beast came scrambling through the thicket again after him.

"Oh, right, *brilliant* idea, Connor," he chastised himself as he raced toward the main gate.

ꕤ ꕤ

The magical door was ready for guests who had already formed a line that stretched well down the sidewalk. The staff who were at their posts and ready to admit the first guests of the evening paused when they saw Connor come tearing around the curve of the walkway.

"Not yet," he hollered, "not yet!"

GiGi, who had been giving last minute instructions to the gate staff on the inclement weather policy, straightened up suddenly, somewhat miffed at Connor's behavior.

"Connor, what is the meaning ooo*uuuu* –" she was stunned to see what was chasing him and for a moment stood frozen.

The volunteers and staff scattered, screaming as they went. Connor dashed around the magical door pulling GiGi along with him as he grabbed the gates and began to close them.

“Hey, buddy, what’re ya doin’?” a father holding his small daughter asked rather gruffly.

“Sorry, won’t be long,” Connor tried to cover before dashing off.

“Look, Daddy! A dragon!” the little girl squealed with delight.

Her father looked up just in time to see the dragon emerge from the woods. It stood up on its hind legs just behind the magical door and bellowed again, this time crashing down on all fours and letting out a belch of fire that reached a good fifteen feet in front of it, singeing the trees and totally incinerating the fence near the tool shed.

The crowd on the other side of the fence was delighted and applauded as the dragon lumbered on down the walkway toward the Formal Garden. Though they were only about ten feet from the dragon, it seemed to ignore them as it followed Connor’s scent.

“Mommy! Mommy! I want to pet the dragon. Can I? *Please?!*” one little boy dressed as a wood sprite begged.

His mother, quite unsure whether it was animatronics or real, hesitated. “We’ll see, sweetie,” she said, as she stared after the creature in utter disbelief.

By this time Connor was running out of options. His abrupt appearance in the Formal Garden caught the attention of the musicians who had set up for the dance. When they saw what was following him, they all scattered knocking over chairs and leaving Connor alone in the garden with the beast.

Connor dashed through the tent and swung back around, running for the arbor. Freshly rebuilt, it was a good replica of the original one from a hundred years ago. He hoped it was strong, but had his doubts. He was just about to call out to the dragon again when he heard something.

Clang! Clang! He'd heard the sound before, that night at Ravensforge as the Guard assembled in a ceremonial show of strength. *Clang! Clang! Clang!*

Connor looked across the garden to see Shea, Guardian of Ravensforge, dressed in her battle armor and beating her shield with her sword.

"Hey, you!" she called to the dragon as she glanced around her. "Yeah, I see you in my garden. Look at the mess you've made!"

Clang! Clang! again with the shield and sword. The dragon shook its head as if the sound caused it pain, and it paced seemingly unsure if it should attack or not. It took a couple of half-hearted swipes at Shea which she dodged quite easily.

Shea sucked in a deep breath, held it for a count then slowly released it. This was the last thing she had expected to have to deal with today.

ꕥ ꕥ

Queen Liliana stood secreted away in her treetop palace. The summer breeze rustled through the leaves and for a moment, all was right with her tiny corner of the world.

"Your Highness," Arland said quietly, interrupting her thoughts, "it is time."

"The troops are ready?" she inquired.

"Yes," he replied.

"Then let us move."

ꕥ ꕥ

From the arbor Connor watched the dragon pace nervously as Shea smacked the shield with her sword. The beast postured and snorted, not sure if it was planning to fight Shea or if it had a belly ache. He'd not had much experience with dragons but knew enough to know that you didn't want to get too close. He held onto the support beam of the arbor, ready to move, scarcely noticing that the crowd from the sidewalk had wound its way around the fence to watch the action in the garden.

"I believe she's got her hands full, chap," came a voice behind him. Connor felt something sharp against his back and straightened, recognizing the voice instantly. "And so do you."

ꕥ ꕥ

Looking just past the dragon Shea could see them coming. She stopped for a moment and was ready to shout a warning when she began to understand what was going on. Connor stepped out from under the arbor followed by Darius Pendragon with a staff at Connor's back.

"Mr. Pendragon?" Shea inquired, still not quite certain what was going on. The dragon, surprisingly docile for the moment, had now become the least of her worries.

"You have something I want, Shea of Ravensforge," he said to her. "Something that belongs to me."

Shea's brows knit together as she thought, suddenly remembering the amulet tucked down in her tunic.

"I don't know what you're talking about," she lied. *Protect it at all costs,* her gut told her, sounding an awful lot like a nameless voice from her past.

"Don't be coy, Shea," Darius growled, as he jabbed Connor's lower back with the business end of the staff. Connor tried not to wince but did a rather poor job of it.

Shea started toward them, but Pendragon pressed the staff again, making Connor shift. "You've seen the power of the dragon staff," Pendragon barked. "I'm certainly not above using it."

"Let Connor go," Shea demanded.

"Why would I do that?" Pendragon mocked her. "He's the second most valuable asset I've got."

Suddenly the night of Ravensforge's destruction came rushing back to Shea with such force she nearly fell to her knees. Lightheaded, she struggled to take it all in, to process it all. She closed her eyes and let the memories wash over her for a brief moment, and when she opened her eyes it was as if she had never forgotten the events of that night.

"You!" she seethed, as she moved toward Pendragon. "You were there!"

"So I was," Pendragon sneered, as he prodded Connor again moving them both closer to Shea and the uncharacteristically docile dragon.

Shea glanced up to find it just sitting there looking at her, which she found very odd until she discovered why. Just beyond the beast, tucked neatly in the edge of the flowerbed, stood Elisabeth, gently petting the dragon as she spoke to it quietly. Whatever she was doing, it was working. At this point, very little was making sense anyway.

Darius shoved Connor forward with the staff still at his back, and the pair made their way across the Formal Garden.

Behind them a throng of onlookers that had not yet been let through the gate seemed content to watch the drama unfold from the other side of the fence.

"You have something I want, Shea of Ravensforge," Pendragon repeated. "Something I need."

"What makes you think I'm going to give it to you?" Shea shouted back at him, knowing he had them all right where he wanted them.

"Shea," Elisabeth warned. She had moved to Shea's side now, and one glance told Shea that Elisabeth had no more idea how to solve this problem than she.

"I'm 'bout out of ideas," Shea whispered, "so if you've got something up that hundred year old sleeve of yours, we'd better see it pretty quick."

Suddenly, an unnatural hush fell over the gardens of Oakhurst. In spite of the nature of the battle at hand, it was as if an old-fashioned melodrama was being played out for the crowd at hand. Only problem was, the stakes were much higher than the audience realized.

"I – I don't know what you're talking about," Shea lied again, sounding even less convincing than the first time.

Pendragon laughed and lifted the staff off the ground, bringing it across his body. The headpiece began to glow as he drew it closer to Shea, and when he brought it to rest mere inches from her chest, the amulet beneath her tunic began to glow brilliantly.

"Pendragon, what are you doing?" Shea cried out. The skies above Oakhurst blackened as Pendragon raised the staff above his head. Seeing his chance, Connor rushed Pendragon, but was deflected effortlessly by the immense power of the staff. The bolt of energy from the headpiece threw Connor across the garden. He landed in a crumpled heap at the base of a tall oak tree.

"Connor!" Shea shouted, running to his side. Quickly feeling his chest for breath, she was relieved to find him still alive. "What have you done?!"

"Nothing I shouldn't have done centuries ago," Pendragon sneered. "They were ignorant of what they had, the power these relics possess. With them, we can take over the human realm, enslaving the mindless folk through fear, of course."

Shea stood and raised her sword. At this point she was unsure of what she would do, but with Connor down, she had no one to protect. It was much bigger than that now. The entire fae realm was at stake, and if she had to go down swinging, better to die trying than walk away.

"Don't you see, Shea of Ravensforge?" Pendragon lowered the staff and stepped toward her. The blade was only inches from his face but he didn't seem to mind nor fear her. "You hold the key to all of this. Power brought together by three relics."

"The Keeper, and the two relics from Oakhurst and Nebosham," Shea surmised.

"No, the relics of Oakhurst and Nebosham were merely part of the Keeper of Time. His eyes, which had been lost long ago. The relic became nothing more than a kitschy trinket in King Beltran's court, really. Without its eyes, the dragon was useless. When in place and with the proper coaxing, the dragon, as you witnessed earlier, can be most effective."

Shea looked around at the destruction. The dragon, which had run rampant earlier, was now docile, almost sleepy. It seemed content to lie in the remnants of the havoc it had wreaked at the center of the garden.

He stepped slowly around Shea, sizing her up as he looked toward Connor's motionless body. "He will see your demise as well."

"He doesn't care about me," Shea lied, doing her best to put on her game face.

"Oh, come now, child. Lies do not become you. Can't you see? It's as plain on his face as it is on your own!" Pendragon chuckled. "Well, it was. He looks peaceful, doesn't he? Almost…*dead*."

"What do you want?" she asked of him sharply. He was standing so close she could smell his foul breath, feeling it on her cheek. She tried hard not to wince, but it was difficult not to gag.

"The amulet. Give it to me."

"Why? What makes it so valuable to you?"

"Let's just say there are those who would pay dearly for the opportunity to rule the world, not just in one realm but in both. And after that, what's next?" He paused, waiting for a response. Finding none, he answered his own question. "Who cares?" he laughed maniacally.

Shea was finding it difficult to stand still any longer. Sword in hand she wanted nothing more than to draw it up and cut his head off. Still, she wasn't sure she could do it swiftly enough that he wouldn't have time to hurt Connor or anyone else that stood nearby. And then there was the matter of the dragon.

The dragon!

"Doesn't sound like you've thought it out to its logical

conclusion," Shea chided him, suddenly brash as she once had been.

"Oh?"

"Yeah. You forgot about the part where I kick your ass and feed what's left of you to the dragon."

"*Tsk-tsk-tsk,* such language…" Pendragon scolded, his voice dripping with sarcasm. "I see you've been spending way too much time with the humans."

"I dunno," Shea responded. "I kinda like the humans."

"Did you know," Pendragon asked slowly, "that your friend here, Crown Prince of Oakhurst, can no longer return home? His mother will be so disappointed." Pendragon stepped back over near where Connor lie on the ground.

Confusion masked Shea's bravado. "What do you mean?"

"The portal was destroyed when you came through. It sent you to a different place than where your royal charges ended up. Theirs was the correct destination. Yours skipped and brought you to Oakhurst." He shook his head, his voice dripping with sarcasm. "Such destruction," he said, looking back at her. "Everyone *gone*. The palace lay in ruin. And the Prince? Well, he was desperate to find the one he'd given his heart to."

"No betrothal had been made yet. It was a formal introduction, nothing more," Shea corrected him. "The Prince has two seasons before his birthday, at which time he is to choose a bride." She was surprised at how easily it all came back to her.

"Oh, he made a choice, all right," Pendragon laughed at her naiveté. "But if his mother knew, there'd be hell to pay."

"What? Why?"

Pendragon strode back over to her standing nearly on top of her. *What was it with this guy? No concept of personal space?*

"He chose you."

It was as if he'd kicked her square in the chest, knocking the wind out of her. Her brows knit together as she processed his words.

"Come on, child, do I have to spell it out for you?"

Duty and honor and station all came back into play – everything that she'd been taught growing up, everything she'd ever been steeped in all came crashing down around her. How could this be? Could it *ever* be? She didn't dare think of it. She couldn't afford the distraction at this point. She was a Guardian, after all, sworn to protect and defend the royals placed in her charge. She'd kind of taken this one on as a last minute project, but the training and conditioning and everything her father and brothers had ever taught her came back into play. All feelings aside, she would die before she would let anything happen to Connor.

"He practically sold his soul to get here. But he wasn't looking for the Princesses of Ravensforge. It was their Guardian he sought." He laughed. "Looks like he found her."

Shea had had about all she could take. "If you want the amulet, just take it." She reached up to her neckline and pulled the amulet up out of her tunic. It glistened and glowed as the fire within awakened. "I have no use for it."

She stopped, suddenly ashamed of herself. Taking pause, she froze, chain in hand halfway to taking it over her head. Her hands trembled as the king's words rang in her head: *"Guard it with your very life."*

Pendragon reached out for it, expecting her to simply hand it over but was stunned when she suddenly stopped.

"Well, what are you waiting for? Hand it over."

"No," Shea said, dropping it back onto her breastplate. It glowed brilliantly now, adding light to the ruby eyes of the raven on her chest. Pendragon stepped toward her, and both the staff and the amulet continued to glow brighter.

"Refuse," Pendragon threatened, "and I will kill the prince."

"What's stopping you?" she asked, her confidence returning. "He's of little use to you. Kind of hard to reign as a future king of the fae realm when you won't fit in the throne. And last I heard, humans play a different role."

"Give it to me!" he shouted as he came at her, stopping just short of taking it. The staff headpiece and the amulet were nearly white hot now, and the dragon stirred, looking directly toward them.

It was as if it had grown in the short time since they had discovered it. Nearly twice its original size, the dragon rose to its feet and towered over them, sniffing the air. It was searching for something. Shea hoped it wasn't dinner.

It lifted its head and snorted the air, unfolding its wings. Fully spread, they spanned a good twelve feet now, and both Shea and Pendragon could only stare as it lumbered around, turning toward them at last. It crouched down, its hot breath blowing in Shea's face, moving her hair as the beast looked her up and down.

Shea froze not quite sure what to do next. Sword in hand, she might be able to get in one clean strike but more than likely that would just piss the dragon off and he would eat her before she had a second swing. Instead, she stared down the dragon. There was something about its eyes…

She looked back at Pendragon, then back to the dragon. "You need to use this with the staff to control the beast," she said, clasping her hand over the amulet as she made a stark realization. "And you won't take it because you can't."

ഋ ൽ

In the woods just beyond the dollhouse Verena waited. She had not been able to convince her mother that Rogan had spoken the truth about the missing relic of Oakhurst but was hopeful that Royce had made some headway with his father in terms of calming him down. She did avoid telling her mother that she had liberated the Prince of Nebosham from the prison in the branch of Oakhurst. She only hoped that Royce's efforts had been more fruitful than her own. The last thing they needed was a war on their hands.

Hearing a rustle through the groundcover she hid, silently moving into a nearby hollow log, crouching low and hesitant to even breathe.

"Verena?" a voice called. "Verena! Are you there?"

"Here, Royce," she answered, stepping out from her hiding place. She embraced him, then stepped back. The look on his face told her he had been unsuccessful.

"Your father?" she asked.

"Unwilling to listen," Royce replied. "He is amassing his troops as we speak."

"So is Mother. What are we to do?"

Royce opened his mouth to speak, but hesitated as a rumble came from the ground beneath their feet. Low at first, it grew as the earth shook. A few feet from where they stood, the access hatch to the tunnels bulged and rattled under the pressure exerted beneath it.

Suddenly, all was still.

Royce and Verena exchanged glances, the fear apparent on the princess's face.

"What was that?" she asked, moving closer to Royce.

With a giant *BANG!* the hatch to the tunnel blew off its hinges, taking the warped remains of the locking mechanism with it as it flew twenty feet skyward. It came crashing down just slightly off center from where it had originated and managed to bring several substantial tree branches plummeting down with it.

Verena screamed, and Royce pulled her into the hollow log covering her head in an attempt to protect her from the debris raining down around them. The limbs hit the ground with tremendous force, shattering as they smashed into the garden floor. Some of the sticks were driven into the ground like fence posts, the remainder of which pointed skyward.

Both Prince and Princess peered out of the log horrified at what they saw next.

Suddenly, a blackness poured out of the hole in the ground so terrifying, so hideous, they could scarcely look at it, yet couldn't bear to tear their eyes from the sight.

Gutiku – *hundreds of them* – poured out of the tunnel. They were more than twice as tall as the tallest of any fae or sprite either Royce or Verena had seen. Black, craggy skin was stretched taut over their lanky, bony frames. Their eyes glowed an unearthly green, and the scratching and clawing sounds as they scrambled out of the tunnel frame were almost more than Verena could bear.

The beasts moved swiftly over the ground toward the Formal Garden, and an occasional screaming tussle occurred as they practically ran over one another coming into the world. They climbed the trees, stripping off bark as they went, tearing through the underbrush, leaving little in their wake.

"We must warn Father," Royce said quietly.

"My mother as well," Verena contested. The look on Royce's face told her the last place he wanted to be was in front of Queen Liliana.

"Trust me," she told him taking his hand, "it's the only chance we'll have."

Royce took Verena's hand and cautiously peered out of the log. Seeing it was clear the pair ran along through the ground cover. Overhead the Gutiku moved swiftly among the branches.

Verena knew from the moment she saw the fae warriors in the trees that they were too late. Her mother was already aware of the threat the Gutiku posed to the kingdoms, and the look on Verena's face told Royce that his father knew as well.

"Any other ideas?" Royce asked her.

"We must find Connor," she answered gravely. "He will know what to do."

ꕤ ꕤ

Shea saw the guests on the other side of the fence recoil before she knew there was something wrong. She turned slowly to find the trees and ground crawling with the same black terror she had experienced that night in Oakhurst. The tree branches rustled, and the groundcover shook as the creatures advanced through the wood.

Through the underbrush and treetops they moved, spreading swiftly as a dark storm through the sky; their growling served as their thunder, their every movement as the wind. The trees began to sway violently under the weight of their small, yet numerous, powerful bodies. Their bony frames looked like wingless, naked bats as they made their way through the woods.

From the Formal Garden Shea could her them coming behind her. Perplexed, she turned to Elisabeth, hoping for answers.

"Gutiku," Elisabeth whispered.

Shea could see them here and there, fae and sprite warriors fighting desperately to stop the advancing dark minions that would destroy their home, but it was to no avail. They were fighting a losing battle. All seemed lost.

"No!" Shea cried out, as she watched the advancing horror. It pained her to imagine what was left of Queen Liliana's palace in the trees. She turned back to Pendragon, who had a horrible grin on his face. "Make them stop. I'll do what you want."

Pendragon raised his hands, and the staff headpiece began to glow. *"Stop! I command it!"* he said in a booming voice.

Suddenly the advancing Gutiku stopped in mid battle as if frozen.

The fae and sprite warriors were somewhat perplexed when their enemy froze in mid-strike or mid-slash. They continued battle with their still foes until they realized that it was a good time to take a breather. Arland and Rogan silently motioned for their troops to regroup, and they disappeared into what was left of the foliage.

"Rogan was always such a coward," Pendragon grumbled. "Never was brave enough to get the job done."

He stepped over to Shea and held out his hand.

"Now give me the amulet."

CHAPTER 35

In a burst of insanity, Shea ran for the dragon, startling it. Thrown by her sudden brazenness the dragon recoiled, raising its head and shoulders a good ten feet above her. Rearing back on its hind legs, wings spread, it towered over her, and Shea ran beneath its chest as it came back down toward the earth, barely escaping the full weight of the beast. She scrambled over its hindquarters and climbed up onto its shoulders, settling in squarely between its wings.

Leaning over its neck, she held on for dear life as the beast thrashed about, trying desperately to throw her. Its claws reached backward over its shoulders, first on one side, then the other. Shea was just beginning to think she'd gotten the hang of it when the dragon caught hold of her. She felt its claws wrap around her leg, and she held onto the dragon's neck, but the strength in its small arms was too much for her. That and there was little to hold onto; the dragon's neck was too large to wrap her arms completely around.

She felt herself being dragged off the creature's back and knew it didn't look good. She could hear the collective gasp from the crowd on the other side of the fence as they watched the young woman being dragged to certain death, held up like a prized goldfish to be gobbled up by a frat boy.

Shea cried out as the dragon pulled her around to just in front of its face, snorting and sniffing her as it tried to decide whether to eat her or incinerate her. She reached for her sword pulling it from its sheath, but the dragon jostled her and she watched helplessly as the weapon tumbled toward the ground beneath her, landing point down well into the manicured lawn.

"Bloody hell," she grumbled, hanging upside down. Her mid-length hair stood on end, and the amulet slid out of her tunic again, barely managing to hang on by the back of her head. Seeing it, she reached up and grabbed it as she stared into the dragon's face, its eyes studying her. She wasn't sure if she could face the end this way, and she closed her eyes tight, bracing herself for the worst. She drew in what she thought would be her last breath and held it for what seemed like a lifetime.

Suddenly, the dragon noticed the amulet and stopped.

Not sure of what was going on, Shea opened her eyes, first the right one, then the left. Fascinated, she cocked her head, her hair following the opposite direction of whatever way her head turned. She took the amulet and waved it around in front of the dragon, back and forth and watched as it followed it, first with its eyes and then with its whole head.

"Oh, I see how it is," she said to the dragon in the most soothing voice she could muster in spite of her frazzled nerves. "You aren't interested unless I have something to offer, huh?"

The dragon continued to watch her and, more to the point, the amulet as she doubled the chain and placed it back around her neck. She turned and looked back to where Darius Pendragon stood dumbfounded on the grass below.

"You need this to be able to control the dragon!" she accused Pendragon. "It wasn't enough to have the eyes to summon it, or the staff to direct it. You need the amulet to control it!" Shea smiled as she turned back toward the dragon. "And I'll just bet I don't need your old stick to get her to do what I want, do I?"

The dragon stood up taller, and Shea could've sworn it smiled at her. She was tiring of hanging upside down and decided to try something totally off the wall.

"Put me down," she said softly, "please."

The dragon reached up and carefully cradled Shea with the other hand, righting her and placing her gently on the ground.

Angered by her show of power, Pendragon raised his arms high. "So be it," he snarled as he moved the staff in a wide circle above his head. The silence in the trees was replaced by the renewed screech of the Gutiku as they resumed the battle. Many of the fae and sprite warriors had sought refuge when the creatures froze in mid-battle, but that wouldn't last long.

Planting the staff back in the ground next to him, Pendragon smiled.

"Check-mate," he sneered.

ꕥ ꕥ

From his perch above, Arland could see Rogan clearly. He was in distress, and from the looks of things, it wasn't going to get much better. They had had their disagreements over the years, and he was protective of Liliana and her throne almost to a fault. But when it came down to brass tacks, Arland knew that what was good for Rogan was good for the garden.

Three Gutiku had surrounded the sprite king, and he fought valiantly holding them off in spite of their combined strength. They came at him with their bare claws tearing at his royal robe as he sliced at them with his sword.

Arland leapt to the ground, his wings slowing his descent until he was right where he needed to be then, *WHAM!* he propelled himself straight into two of the nasty beasts. They screeched with surprise as he bowled them to the ground, slicing each one of them soundly in half. They instantly turned to dust, making a *fwhoop* sound as they hit the ground. He turned just in time to see Rogan finish off the third one.

"Well," the king said slightly out of breath, "three down, two thousand to go."

"If you say so, Your Majesty," Arland said with a grin. "I'll take twelve hundred, you can get the other eight."

"Oh, I think not," Rogan protested in jest. "I'll take fifteen hundred; *you* can get the rest."

"Done," Arland smiled as he flew off to rejoin his ranks.

Rogan shook his head and chuckled as he ran back into the thick of things.

ꕥ ꕥ

Verena caught her breath at the sight before her, and even from across the Formal Garden she knew it was bad. Connor's body lay motionless beneath the big oak tree.

Royce had just caught up with her, but she knew there was little time to spare. With a glance over her shoulder she flew quickly across the garden and lit gently on the ground next to Connor's head.

"Connor?" she said softly, as she moved in closer.

Royce followed, breathing hard as he pulled up just short of her. "What happened?" he asked

"I do not know," she replied, as she scanned the events unfolding a short distance away, "but I'd say it does not look good."

Royce turned to see Shea before the dragon and Darius's raised staff. He was presently preoccupied with Shea, but he had the feeling it wouldn't last for long.

"We must hurry," he urged her. "There is little time left."

Verena moved in close to her brother's ear.

"Please, Connor, you must wake up," she pleaded.

Verena was not used to seeing her brother in human form and the size differential was staggering. Though younger than she, he had been taller than her since before she could remember, but this was something totally different.

She tried to gently nudge his head to no avail. It was so heavy, and she was caught off guard when it lolled back toward her at a surprising rate. Royce grabbed her arm and quickly pulled her clear.

A decent-sized cut on his forehead had allowed blood to trickle down the side of his face. She pushed against his cheek again, harder this time, trying desperately to wake him.

Her frustration rising to a crescendo, Verena moved in closer to his ear.

"Connor, wake *up!*" she shouted in a manner most unbecoming royalty, and was nearly ready to give him a swift kick out of sheer desperation when Connor began to stir.

"He's been knocked senseless," Royce observed. "C'mon old boy, wake up."

"Verena?" Connor whispered. "What happened?"

"I'll explain on the way," Verena told him, her voice filled with urgency. "We must move. *Now.*"

ꕥ ꕥ

The cry of a lone hawk overhead pierced the roiling thunder of the Gutiku horde as it raged against the fae and sprite warriors on the other side of the garden. Shea looked up to see the large, red-tailed hawk soar straight into the tangle of small bodies amongst the treetops. Only a moment later it was followed by dozens upon dozens of hawks. From her vantage point, Shea could just make out the faerie warriors on hawkback .

"The cavalry has arrived," Elisabeth told her. "Warriors from the Kingdom of Hawksgate."

ꕥ ꕥ

"Where is the box?" Connor asked, still somewhat lightheaded as he stumbled headlong through the woods back toward Oakhurst. It would be nothing short of a miracle if he managed to avoid taking a tumble, only to be reclaimed by the garden floor.

"We were not sure what to do with it," Verena said from just off his shoulder. She kept up effortlessly in spite of the circumstances, and he was proud of her. He knew their mother would be, too. Of course, he was not looking forward to that encounter, but he could not be concerned with that now.

"We put the lid back on," Royce offered, from his place in Connor's breast coat pocket. "We weren't sure what to do with it, so we hid it away."

Connor ran along Aunt Emma's path to the back yard of Oakhurst, sprinted through the gate and hurdled the stream stopping just short of the primitive picket fence.

The battle raged on in the treetops above them. Connor looked up to see fae warriors engaged in mortal combat with thousands upon thousands of Gutiku.

"This way," Verena said, moving closer to the ground. Connor rounded the fence and knelt to get a better look, taking care not to end up in the concrete pit.

His head swam but he was feeling a little better as he drew in to where Verena had disappeared into the groundcover. Royce clambered out of his pocket and followed Verena in under the vegetation.

"Here," Verena called to her brother.

Connor pulled back the tangle of vines to discover a beautiful magic box.

"Think this'll work?" he asked her hopefully.

"It better."

Connor's hands trembled as he picked up the box. It was skillfully made, but he had no time to admire its craftsmanship. He rose, steadied himself, and quickly untied the ribbon. It caught and he tried in vain to undo the knot he'd inadvertently created before simply sliding the whole loop off sideways. He let the ribbon fall to the ground, took a deep breath and lifted the lid off the box.

He had not expected what came next and looked at Verena and Royce stunned.

A silence fell upon the garden as the battle overhead stopped for but a brief moment, followed by the most horrific screeching and carrying on ever witnessed by human or fae. Verena lit upon her brother's shoulder and drew in close, bracing herself.

"Hold fast, Connor," she warned him, as she steadied her position. "They are coming."

From below Royce gathered up the ribbon and managed to untie the knot. Securing it soundly around his waist, he began to climb upward on Connor's trouser leg.

A black vapor began to swirl out of the magic box and made its way skyward. Reaching the lower level of the canopy above them, it radiated outward in every direction, darkening the sky as it went.

"Are you sure about this?" Connor shouted above the din. The screeching was different now, louder but more of a mournful howling lower in a tone that Connor could feel resounding in his chest.

"No," Verena shouted from her perch upon his shoulder. The wind had picked up, and she held fast to his collar. She looked over as Royce took his place beside her, ribbon in hand. He looked as uncertain as she was and moved in close.

ഇ ଓ

"At last, King Astor of Hawksgate shows himself!" Pendragon snarled as he raised the staff, pointing it toward the incoming battalion of hawks. It discharged an energy bolt skyward that crackled as loud as any thunder Shea had ever heard.

"I don't *think* so," Shea murmured as she raised her sword.

She barely had the chance to advance on Pendragon when the beast behind her took over. It charged at them both, knocking Shea out of the way with its head as it moved in to grab at her adversary. Startled, Pendragon dropped the staff as the dragon knocked him to the ground.

Shea picked herself up just in time to hear Pendragon scream. She could see the flames as the dragon roared in what she believed to be Pendragon's direction. Though she could not see him, she was able to see Elisabeth's reaction as the little girl quickly covered her eyes.

Seemingly satisfied after the screaming ceased, the dragon turned back around to Shea. It towered over her as smoke billowed from its nostrils, and when she picked up the staff off the ground, the beast appeared to bow down to her.

The crowd just beyond the wrought iron fence cheered as the dragon lay down at Shea's feet. Relief washed over her as she turned to Elisabeth.

The girl glanced over her shoulder toward Oakhurst. "I'm afraid it's not over yet."

ଌ ଓ

Connor looked up to see the fae warriors withdraw as the Gutiku began to be pulled downward by the black mist from the box in his hands. Even the hawks took refuge in the branches above them. The small, gangly beasts dropped from the treetops in a somewhat controlled descent, flailing wildly as they hurtled toward the trio on the ground at a most alarming rate.

"Here it comes," Connor said, as he braced himself for impact.

They swirled in from everywhere – behind him, above him, below him – as the Gutiku were pulled toward the magic box. He could feel the pull from the box and the weight inside it. It reminded him of his passage to Oakhurst as he had been sucked under the water before his rather unceremonious arrival that landed him smack in the middle of the White River.

He held the box at arm's length as the Gutiku were pulled violently into it. The black mist re-entered first, dragging its prey in with it. The mass of arms and legs and fanged, screaming maws flew at him at a frightening rate, and Connor could not tear his eyes away from the green, glowing eyes of the creatures as they plummeted toward the box. Never slowing down, they were spaghetti-ized as they were sucked into the tiny gold box.

The wind whipped and swirled around Connor, Verena and Royce as they watched the beasts disappear into the tiny portal. Light flashed and a strange thunder issued forth from the box as the creatures continued to be dispatched against their will. The current grew stronger as their number increased, and for one horrific moment, the air around them was black with Gutiku. The only light Connor could see was their horrible, green glowing eyes.

Connor was startled as something hit him squarely in the

middle of his back. Sharp claws dug into his flesh through his coat, and his body arched as he cried out. He knew he could not afford to attend to the creature on his back and held fast to the box and its task at hand.

Verena looked down her brother's back at the Gutiku that had firmly affixed itself to him in an attempt to avoid fate of the box. She was ready to take flight when a hand took a firm grip on her wrist.

"Stay here," Royce ordered, as he handed her the ribbon. "I'll go."

Worry was all over Verena's face, but she knew it had to be done. She took the ribbon, holding onto his hand for as long as she could. Tears welled up in her eyes as she watched him climb down her brother's back toward the nasty, snarling beast.

ꟷ ꟷ

Shea reached down and picked up the staff as it lay next to the smoldering patch of grass where she'd last seen Darius Pendragon, Esquire. The smell of singed flesh lingered in the air, making her stomach turn at the thought of what had happened to Darius. Lucy would be so disappointed things didn't work out with him. She'd had such high hopes for the exchange, as had Evangeline. Quickly dismissing the thought, she turned to Elisabeth.

"Where is Connor?" she asked, as she scanned the Formal Garden.

"I do not know," Elisabeth answered.

From the arbor they could see the swirling of the trees as the dark horde of Gutiku began their descent into the woods just behind Oakhurst. The pair exchanged glances, and Shea took off at a dead run down Aunt Emma's path toward Oakhurst. She reached the back gate and she saw Connor, Verena, and Royce at the center of the dark, swirling vortex. Connor held fast to the magic box as the air around him whipped at his clothes and hair, making it difficult to stand. Verena looped her arm through a buttonhole on his shirt collar and was struggling to hold on. Royce was halfway down Connor's back, desperately kicking at the head of a Gutiku that had a firm hold on Connor's jacket.

The gangly little monsters flew at the trio at such a rate it was a wonder they weren't all knocked senseless and sucked into the portal inside the tiny box. The Gutiku, sometimes two and three at a time, were stretched to nearly ten times their height and reduced to a third of the width of their former selves as they were pulled into the box.

The winds pulled at Shea and Elisabeth, and they dared not venture any closer. Shea felt powerless in spite of the fact that she possessed the two relics Pendragon was so certain held the key to power over the faerie and human realms. Horrified, they could only watch from the gate.

Fully engaged with the creature at hand, Royce held on for dear life as he fought to disentangle the claws of the beast from Connor's coat. First the hooky right hand, then the left, and the creature was left flailing about while holding on with the claws on its feet. Then Royce made his first mistake.

Royce moved down the middle of Connor's back, just inches from the feet of the tiny beastie. He got a firm hold of the fabric and soundly planted both feet on the shins of the creature, which brought a rather loud protest. Sensing some progress, Royce tried it again. This time the Gutiku caught him off guard as it reached up and grabbed the prince by his shirt and released the claws on his feet. The monster's actions sent the pair into a terrifying upward freefall toward the box.

"No!" Shea screamed as Royce and the creature were pulled toward the vortex. She and Elisabeth watched in absolute horror as the Prince of Nebosham was swept into the stream of Gutiku and sucked soundly into the box.

In a few moments it was all over. The last of the creatures flew into the box, and the lid landed atop it. Connor quickly secured it with the ribbon tying it with a double knot. Stunned, Verena could only stare at the box.

"Royce," she whispered as the tears flowed down her tiny cheeks.

He was gone.

Chapter 36

Grief hung heavy in the air as the fae and sprite warriors gathered from all parts of the garden, followed by nearly a hundred hawks with warriors mounted on their back. They gathered around Connor and the princess in silence as she wept.

King Rogan stepped out from under the groundcover and looked up at the Prince of Oakhurst in his human form. Immediately recognizing the king, Connor knelt down.

"My…son?" Rogan asked, his uncertainty reflected in his eyes.

Heartbroken, Verena could not meet his gaze as she sensed the depth of his pain mingling with her own.

"He fought valiantly," Connor told him. "His sacrifice will not be forgotten." Connor winced at his own words. They sounded so hollow, so meaningless. He felt helpless, just as he had when he saw Royce fly over his shoulder and into the box and could do nothing to stop it. He hadn't dared to look inside for fear it might be even worse than what he'd watched flow into it.

Elisabeth and Shea joined Connor as he spoke quietly with the king. Elisabeth looked around the garden noting a slight change.

"The queen is coming," she said softly.

Queen Liliana arrived momentarily with a full complement of guards as she nodded to Arland and his men on a job well done. She noted the humans among the warriors of all three kingdoms and looked up at Elisabeth.

The expression on Liliana's face changed instantly to one of bewilderment as she looked beyond Elisabeth seeing a familiar face in a most unusual form. "*Connor?*" she asked in amazement. "Connor, is that you?"

Connor moved in next to Elisabeth and leaned in toward the fae queen. "Hello, Mother," he said softly.

The queen was stunned for a moment fighting tears as she longed to hug her son. A flood of relief washed over her at finally seeing with her own eyes that he was well. "I thought you were lost! When Arland returned without you, I was devastated."

"How is Caeden?" Connor asked, suddenly remembering his cohort in their ruse of his escape. "Is he well?"

His mother raised an eyebrow at him. "Oh, he's fine. He was sure he'd lose his head for what you'd both done, but after he managed to regain my trust, we got along just fine." She paused for a moment, remembering the devastation at Ravensforge and the surrounding region.

"How did you get here? The portal was destroyed. You were with me when we found it."

"Let's just say I found someone who knew a thing or two about realm travel."

"Dark magic? Connor, I taught you better than that. Your *father* taught you better than that!"

"Yes, but –"

"We'll discuss this when we get home. Speaking of which, how do you cross back over?"

"Um… I – can't."

"I'm sorry, what did you say?"

"I don't believe I can return, Mother."

The queen staggered slightly, feeling faint. Arland stepped in taking her elbow to steady her.

"My Queen, are you all right?"

"Yes," Liliana said, steadying herself.

Stunned, she walked over to King Rogan who sat on a rock beneath a small shrub.

"Rogan, I am so sorry for your loss," she said. "Truly, I am. No parent should have to lose a child."

The king sighed heavily in agreement. "No, indeed."

CHAPTER 37

The staff and crew of Minnetrista gathered in the Formal Garden to survey the damage from the evening's chaos. Shea and Connor joined them and rounded up the dragon. In conjunction with the staff and the amulet, neither of which Shea understood nor controlled, the dragon submitted to their presence and was reduced in a moment of magic to a small bronze beast that wrapped itself jealously around the crystal egg before once again becoming frozen in time.

Securing the relic in a pouch she'd found nearby, Shea smiled up at Connor, and he kissed her. The cut on his forehead had stopped bleeding, and though his suit was rumpled and torn, he looked dashing nonetheless. Still in her battle armor, Shea held the sword at her side, grateful that it was all over.

"We've got a bit of a problem here," Shea pointed out. "In what universe is this going to work out?"

"In the one we have in this moment, right now," Connor said, and he kissed her again. From beyond the fence, the forgotten guests of Oakhurst cheered and clapped and whistled. The pair ignored them for a moment, but finally Connor gave them a wave.

"Well, this kind of puts a bit of a kink in our plans," GiGi said, as she came around from where she had watched most of the events unfold. "The gardens are a bit of a wreck. I don't know how we can make this happen."

Shea looked at Connor and smiled.

"Easy. We let the guests in and tell them the most amazing faerie tale they've ever heard!"

ꝏ ꝏ

For the next two hours, Shea sat in the Formal Garden and related the story of Ravensforge and how she got to Oakhurst, and how the kingdoms of Oakhurst, Nebosham, and Hawksgate worked together to defeat the dark forces of Erebos. Connor, on the other hand, was more than happy to take the guests on a tour of the grounds, showing them where the dragon had come to life and consequently destroyed the woodland in the process. He had taken Clair with him, one of the gardeners, who explained how the vegetation could be replaced and what would be involved in making the gardens look great again in no time.

By the end of the night with the Unlighting Parade at hand, the guests were exhausted and chattered happily among themselves as they headed back to their homes.

ꝏ ꝏ

The lights twinkled in the trees lending an even greater sense of enchantment to the evening than the truly magical events prior. Oakhurst's gardens were beautiful in spite of the mayhem earlier in the evening. Shea stood under the large oak tree near the pathway to the Formal Garden satisfied just to take it all in.

Oakhurst had become more than a place to lay her head – it was home. A place to be cared for and protected, she relished her role, and even though there were many unanswered questions in her mind, the parts of the truth she did know brought her a sense of peace.

"Isn't this where we started out?" came a voice over her shoulder. It was Connor, a little cleaner than he had been an hour ago and none the worse for wear thankfully.

"It would appear so," Shea agreed. "Are there any dragons about?"

Connor rolled his eyes, "I sure hope not."

"I don't think we have to worry about any of that for awhile." Shea smiled up at him in the twilight. He was quite handsome, and she felt comfortable with him after all they'd been through together in spite of her new-found knowledge of their respective stations in life.

"Would you care to dance?" he asked, as he offered her his hand.

Shea smiled shyly, took his hand and followed him to the lawn just outside the tent. He wrapped his arms around her small waist, and she her arms around his neck, and they began to dance.

ഇ ൽ

From across the lawn she saw them, and they looked perfect together. And the dance itself looked much like it had a hundred years before when the family Ball lived in the houses along the boulevard. The music was acoustic, a string quartet, and brightened up the dusk in the garden, much like the twinkle lights that danced amongst the branches of the trees overhead.

She smiled as she watched the spectacle before her and marveled at how people are so alike in spite of the generations that separate them. It had been a wonderful adventure this time around, but in her mind she knew it was time to move on.

Connor and Shea were in their own little moment, and she wouldn't take that from them, not after all they'd been through. She'd seen Shea grow in the short time she'd known her, and though she'd known Connor practically all his life, she'd seen him become a man before her very eyes. She was nearly ready to walk away when Shea caught her eye. She smiled, then turned and headed slowly up the path to Oakhurst.

ഇ ൽ

From the outer edge of the tent she saw her, and Shea nearly couldn't believe her eyes. She stopped cold, leaving Connor in a gentle lurch.

"Is something wrong?" he asked her, as he turned to follow her gaze.

"I – don't know," she said softly, breaking away from him and moving toward the pathway. She quickened her steps, trying to catch up with the woman before she disappeared. She'd been there just a moment ago, but was nowhere in sight along Aunt Emma's path. Shea began to trot and halted where the path emptied out onto the main walkway.

There in the garden just behind Oakhurst stood an old woman. Her white hair was done neatly in old lady fashion, and her simple dress, shoes and glasses looked as if she'd stepped straight out of one of the photos that graced the gallery walls inside.

Shea walked slowly through the gate toward the woman. The woman looked back at her and smiled, and Shea knew her in an instant.

"Elisabeth?" she asked quietly. "Is that you?"

"Yes, Shea, it is me." she answered.

"But – I…I don't understand," Shea stammered, as she tried to wrap her head around what she was seeing.

Standing before her was Elisabeth Ball as she had been in her old age. She was slightly stooped, but her eyes still twinkled under the glow of the security light, and the smile was the same though the face had aged.

"Why are you… *old?"*

"Well, you know us old souls," Elisabeth chuckled. "At some point we look like what we are."

"Yes, but –"

"Elisabeth?" Connor asked, dumbfounded, as he caught up to Shea.

"Hello, Connor," she smiled at him. "Did you get the chance to smooth things over with your mother?"

"Uh, yes. We spoke further a short time ago. Why?"

"I hated to keep such a big secret from her but had little

choice. From the very start you played an important role here without even realizing it. I've known you since you were this big," Elisabeth smiled, leaving only half an inch between her thumb and forefinger, "and I've always known you were destined for great things. I thank you for the role you've played in bringing Oakhurst its newest Guardian."

"I'm sorry?" Shea asked.

"You, Shea of Ravensforge," Elisabeth said proudly, "are the Guardian of Oakhurst."

"I am?"

Elisabeth laughed softly as she watched them both. "From the moment I met you I knew who you were, Shea. But I only suspected what you might be able to do, what kind of potential you had. Unfortunately, I had to keep this information from your mother, Connor. If the queen had known, she would have grilled Shea for information on Ravensforge that she was unready and unable to give her. That is why it was so important for you to wait until the right time to reveal to Shea her true identity. Remember when I told you not to tell her? It was for her benefit as well as yours."

"But what of Ravensforge? And the royals I was sworn to protect? Surely all were not lost." Shea was trying to keep up, but it was a lot to consider.

"That is yet to be seen," Elisabeth answered solemnly. "We can only hope that they were able to survive, that the Guard kept them safe long enough to get them away from the dark threat from Erebos. The princesses are in this realm, but I am not sure of the king and queen."

"And my family? My father and brothers were there. And – *Arn…*" Shea said as the fog began to clear in her mind. She wasn't sure she liked where it was leading her.

"That I do not know," Elisabeth told her. "We can only hope they are safe with the royals."

"Then I must find them," Shea said forcefully grasping the idea that they may be in need of assistance.

"That is a choice you must make. Regardless of what you choose to do, I will be moving on."

"But who will watch over Oakhurst and Nebosham? You can't just leave them to fend for themselves! The human realm is a strange and sometimes cruel place. Do you really think they can manage on their own?"

Elisabeth laughed. "Shea, they have been here much, much longer than the humans have, and are more than capable of taking care of themselves."

"Yeah," Connor chimed in. "You'd better not let my mother hear you talking like that."

She turned on him in an instant. "What about you, Connor? You said you can't go back. Why? What have you done that prevents you from returning to the fae realm? Surely your mother will not approve." Frustration tinged her tone as she spoke, partly out of concern for him but mostly because of his chiding.

"I don't know exactly," he answered back quickly. "And, no, my mother does not approve."

"Maybe she can help." At this point Shea was looking for some kind of answers.

"Perhaps, but I am not holding out hope." He smiled at Elisabeth. "Besides, it's not so bad being a human. And honestly, I think I can do more for Oakhurst on this side of the divide than as a faerie."

"But – your throne! What are you going to do about that? Aren't you next in line for the throne?"

"Yes," he said, "but what can be done?"

"There may be a way," Elisabeth said, "but you must discover the path back for yourself. I cannot be of help in this."

Elisabeth turned to go.

"Wait," Shea called to her. The old woman paused, turning back to them. "What if we need you?"

Elisabeth smiled, knowing full well they would manage just fine without her. "You are now the strength of Oakhurst, the Guardian that protects and cares for them. You do not need me now anymore than you did when you were Guardian of Ravensforge."

"Yes, but that was different," Shea told her. "That was a lifetime ago. Or at least it seems like it."

"I almost forgot – I have something for you," Elisabeth said softly, holding out her hand. Shea looked down to see a beautiful handmade box resting in Elisabeth's open palm.

"A magic box," she smiled. "But why do I need a magic box?"

"Because you will need a way to summon the faeries should you have occasion to converse with the queen," Elisabeth smiled.

Shea reached out and took the box examining it closely.

"But what if I don't want to be the Guardian of Oakhurst?"

"That is your choice," Elisabeth said. "Do you wish to return to the faerie realm?"

"I don't know," she said, glancing over at Connor. "I

haven't really had time to think about it. And truthfully, I'm not sure what exactly I would go back to anyway. Connor says Ravensforge is gone, and my family…" Shea's voice trailed off, and she looked away.

"This is all true," Elisabeth agreed, "but a return trip is not out of the question if you so desire. You may return on occasion as your station requires of you. That is an option I never had. Oh, how I would have loved to have been able to explore the fae realm, to see my friends as they truly appear!"

"We look different when we're there?" Shea asked.

"Sort of," Elisabeth grinned. "Everyone looks 'normal.'"

"Normal?"

"They don't have wings," Connor added out of the side of his mouth. "And, they're not, you know, *tiny*."

"Shhh! Don't let your mother hear you say that!" Shea teased, as she turned the magic box over in her hands. "Ok, so how does this work?"

"It's simple, really. You open it up, whisper a rhyme, and it summons the faeries."

"A rhyme?"

"A rhyme," Elisabeth nodded. She leaned in and whispered the rhyme in Shea's ear.

"That's it?"

"That's it."

Shea looked at Connor and Elisabeth, then slowly removed the lid from the box. She closed her eyes and whispered the rhyme Elisabeth told her a moment before as she turned around three times. A swirl of light wafted up from inside it like smoke as it went skyward a few feet, then headed into the woods. A mere moment later the trees above the garden were filled with tiny lights that danced on the breeze. Mystified, Shea could only watch and smile as the Queen of Oakhurst and her Guard arrived.

"Shea of Ravensforge, to what do I owe the pleasure?" Queen Liliana asked with a smile. "Hello, Elisabeth."

"Your Majesty," Elisabeth said with a nod. "I will be taking my leave of you."

"You will be sorely missed," Liliana sighed.

"And I will miss you," Elisabeth told her old friend. "But I leave you in the capable hands of Shea of Ravensforge, the newest Guardian of Oakhurst."

"Is this true?" the queen asked as she looked up at Shea.

Shea felt conflicted as she stood before the queen. Connor was at her side, but would it always be so? And though she longed to return home she knew there was nothing there for her. Her family, her friends, those whom she had guarded so faithfully were all – gone.

Elisabeth had made it look so easy, and yet Shea knew that the task at hand would be even more arduous now that it was known that she alone possessed the Dragon's Triad. Word would get around regardless of which realm she chose to dwell in, of that she was certain.

She looked at the faces around her, all expectantly awaiting her answer.

Shea bowed deeply to the queen. The amulet that hung from her neck glistened in the dimly lit courtyard.

"Your Majesty, I am ever at your service. I am honored to be the Guardian of Oakhurst."

The works of J. Wolf Scott

THE CHILDREN OF AUBERON SERIES

The Guardian of Oakhurst

The Embers of Ravensforge

Erebos Rising

The Secrets of Oakhurst

Midst the Dragon's Fire

Also by J. Wolf Scott

All are available on Amazon.com in paperback and for Kindle.

About the Author

J. Wolf Scott lives in the rural Midwest with her husband and two children, who indulge her habit of bringing her imaginary friends home with her. More of her work can be found at jwolfscott.com

Made in the USA
Lexington, KY
26 June 2017